KILLER CRULLERS

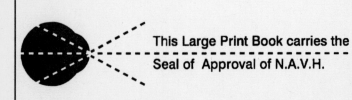

This Large Print Book carries the
Seal of Approval of N.A.V.H.

A DONUT SHOP MYSTERY

KILLER CRULLERS

JESSICA BECK

WHEELER PUBLISHING
A part of Gale, Cengage Learning

GALE
CENGAGE Learning

Detroit • New York • San Francisco • New Haven, Conn • Waterville, Maine • London

GALE
CENGAGE Learning®

LIBRARY OF CONGRESS CATALOGING-IN-PUBLICATION DATA

Beck, Jessica.
    Killer crullers : a donut shop mystery / by Jessica Beck. — Large print ed.
        p. cm. — (Wheeler Publishing large print cozy mystery)
    ISBN 978-1-4104-4878-1 (pbk.) — ISBN 1-4104-4878-9 (pbk.) 1. Coffee shops—Fiction. 2. Private investigators—Fiction. 3. Doughnuts—Fiction. 4. Large type books. I. Title.
PS3602.E2693K55 2012
813'.6—dc23   2012009202

Published in 2012 by arrangement with St. Martin's Press, LLC.

Printed in the United States of America
1 2 3 4 5   16 15 14 13 12

FD191

*To all the donut makers in the world,
both professional and amateur.
And to those of us who enjoy
the fruits of their labor!*

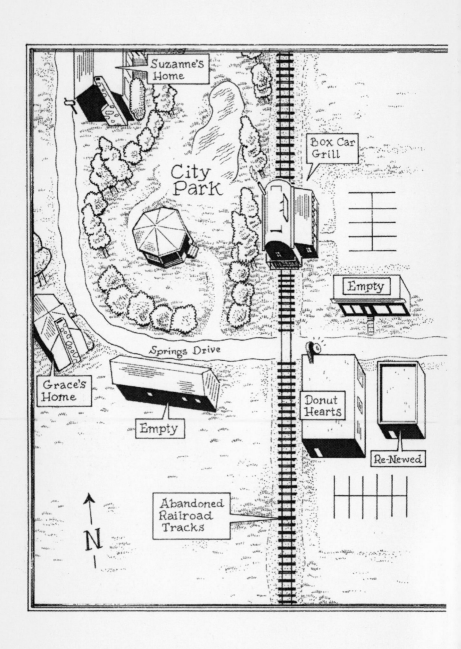

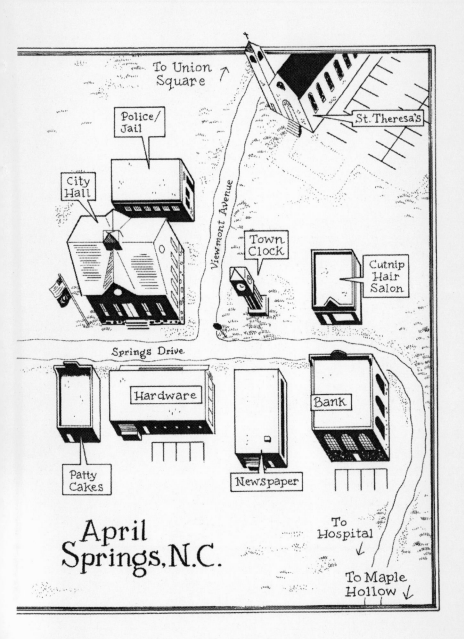

To Union Square

Police/Jail

City Hall

St. Theresa's

Viewmont Avenue

Town Clock

Cutnip Hair Salon

Springs Drive

Hardware

Bank

Patty Cakes

Newspaper

To Hospital

April Springs, N.C.

To Maple Hollow

"I owe it all to little chocolate donuts."

— John Belushi

CHAPTER 1

"Give me a dozen of whatever you still have on hand," a tall, dark-haired man in his thirties asked me curtly at my donut and coffee shop in April Springs, North Carolina. I'd aptly named the place Donut Hearts, since my name is Suzanne Hart, and I couldn't imagine being anywhere else than in my shop, a reclaimed train depot on the edge of our small downtown business district. He added with a frown, "I don't care what they are. Just make sure they're loaded with icing."

It was near closing time, and I wasn't sure what I could give him, since even my glazed donut stock had been depleted at that time of day, but as I studied the case, I realized that Simon Henson had neglected to pick up his special order for the second time in a month. Simon always made a big fuss over my crullers, and the first time he'd ordered a dozen nearly drowning in icing, he'd paid for them in advance. The next time, he "forgot" — both to pay for and collect his order — and when he didn't pick them up, I was stuck with his crullers and had to end up giving them away. I told Simon if it happened again, he was going to lose his ordering privileges, and he'd sworn that he'd remember the next time.

Only he hadn't.

"Are crullers okay?" I asked.

"Let me see one."

I held up an iced monstrosity and was afraid he'd back out of his offer, but instead, the man surprised me by saying, "Those are perfect." I boxed a dozen crullers and put them on the counter, and he shoved a twenty across the counter toward me.

As I handed him his change, I said, "I hope you enjoy them. The icing might be a little much for most folks, but the crullers themselves are really good."

"That doesn't really matter. I'm not going to eat them," he answered as he took the box and jammed his money into his front pocket.

That was certainly an odd response. "Do you mind if I ask you what you're going to do with them, then?"

"Sure, why not? I'm going to throw them at the woman next door," he said with a grim nod as he walked away.

That could only mean that he had a problem with Gabby Williams, and now I was going to be drawn into the middle of it, whether I liked it or not.

"Emma, cover the front," I yelled out to my assistant in back as I raced outside after him.

I didn't even wait to see if she'd heard me.

I hurried to Gabby's shop and found my customer doing exactly what he'd threatened, throwing those heavily iced crullers at the door, window, and brick façade.

"Stop that," I screamed as Gabby herself came barreling out of ReNEWed, her gently used clothing store that was beside Donut Hearts, barely missing getting pelted, as well.

"Not a chance until you admit what you did," the man said as he hurled another cruller.

Gabby snapped, "Knock it off, Desmond Ray, or I'll call the police."

"Go ahead. Call them," he said as he hit the door again. With the heavy icing, some of them hit, stuck for a moment, and then slid down the side of the building, while others seemed to explode on impact.

"Gabby, I had no idea what he was going

13

to do with those," I explained.

"I'll deal with you later," Gabby said as she glanced over at me for a bare second. When she turned back to the man, she said, "That's it; I've had enough. I'm calling the cops."

The threat didn't even faze him. "Fine, go ahead. Then you can tell them how you stole from my aunt."

That certainly got my attention. As a fellow shop owner, I knew how important our reputations were to us, and if this man was slandering Gabby, whether there was merit to his complaint or not, it could end up doing some real damage to her business.

Gabby put her cell phone back into her pocket and stepped between Desmond Ray and her shop. "I told you before; there wasn't any cash or jewelry in your aunt's coat when it arrived. I checked it thoroughly before I put it on sale."

Desmond's face reddened, and for a moment, the cruller missile pastry in his hand lowered slightly. "She told me she had ten thousand dollars stashed there, and don't forget the diamond brooch."

"Did she have the queen's tiara tucked somewhere in there, as well?" Gabby asked. "The woman's delusional, and we both know it."

"Aunt Jean was positive about where she left the cash and the brooch," Desmond replied.

"She might be, but she's still wrong," Gabby said.

"Are you calling her a liar?" The cruller rose again, and then left Desmond's hand a moment later, shattering against the glass door, chunks of it flying through the air after the ricochet.

I was amazed by how calm Gabby seemed to be, though I had to believe she was seething inside. "I'm telling you, there was no cash in that coat, and certainly no brooch. I let you check the jacket yourself fifteen minutes ago. You saw that the pockets were empty."

"After you cleaned them out," Desmond said angrily.

There were still three or four crullers in the box, and while the man was distracted with Gabby's replies, I grabbed it from him.

"Hey, those are mine," he shouted as he tried to get them back.

I pulled a ten out of my pocket and threw it at him. "I've changed my mind. They aren't for sale now. That should more than cover what's left."

Desmond gave me a look of icy evil, and then turned it toward Gabby. "I'm not go-

15

ing to forget this. You should know that I'm coming back. Both of you," he said, and then stormed off.

I hated confrontations, and I could feel my knees go a little weak after Desmond was gone. "Wow, that was bad," I said.

"It's not the first time someone has accused me of acting unjustly." She bent and began retrieving bits of crullers as she spoke. "Suzanne, please don't just stand there; help me clean this mess up. After all, it's as bad a reflection on you as it is on me."

Not quite, I almost replied, and then decided to keep that particular thought to myself. While it was true that shattered crullers on the sidewalk and even sticking to the door and window weren't the best advertisement for my business, having someone shout that Gabby was a thief was a thousand times worse for her.

As we worked at cleaning up the destroyed crullers, I said, "I didn't know Jean Ray had a nephew. That is the 'Jean' he meant, right?"

"None other," Gabby said. She made a face as she picked up a particularly mangled piece of cruller and dropped it into the box as though it were radioactive. "I knew she'd been slipping a little lately, but if you ask me, the old woman's gone completely off the bend."

That was odd. Jean came by my shop occasionally, and I'd never found her to be anything short of sharp and lucid, though she had to be approaching her eightieth birthday, if indeed it hadn't already come and gone. "She seemed fine to me the last time I saw her," I replied before my internal filter could stop me.

Gabby stopped what she was doing and looked hard at me. "Are you telling me that you actually believe that donut-throwing maniac?"

"No, ma'am," I answered quickly. "I know what it's like to be falsely accused. I'm on your side in all of this."

Gabby seemed to consider that a moment, and then, to my relief, she nodded her acceptance of my explanation. Gabby Williams was not a woman I wanted to be feuding with, especially since my innocent crullers had been dragged into the fray purely by the sin of proximity.

We had nearly finished our cleanup when a squad car pulled up in front of Gabby's shop, and our chief of police — and my mother's current beau — Philip Martin got out.

"What seems to be the problem, ladies?"

17

he asked.

I wasn't about to say anything, but I was beginning to wonder if Gabby was going to respond at all when she finally said, "Everything's fine here, Chief. There's no need for you to get involved."

I wasn't sure the threats we'd both received qualified as everything being okay, but this was Gabby's mess, and for once, I was thrilled that I wasn't in the middle of a public confrontation.

"That's not the way I heard it," Chief Martin said as he hitched up his pants. It appeared that the man's diet was still going strong. If he lost much more weight, the chief was going to have to get new uniforms instead of having his old ones taken in to fit his new, sleeker figure. I didn't know how he was able to do it with all the home-cooked meals my mother had prepared for him over the past few months, but more power to him. I'd probably lose weight myself, if I could only figure out how to quit sampling the donuts I offered for sale.

"Who exactly has been speaking with you about my business?" Gabby asked, and I knew that the chief was on thin ice. No one, not even the police department, wanted to go toe-to-toe with Gabby, and that included Chief Martin.

He wasn't thrilled by the conversation they were having, that much was clear, but the chief had a job to do, and I had to admire the way he took a deep breath, and then said, "Desmond Ray came by my office a few minutes ago. He claims you stole something from his aunt, so I need to hear all about it."

"I'll tell you the same thing I told him," Gabby said. "Those coat pockets were empty, and Jean Ray is either lying or mistaken. Either situation is not my problem. Then again, she could be insane, and if that's the case, it clearly runs in the family. I explained all of that to Desmond when he came by, and I thought it was resolved until the maniac returned and began throwing donuts at my shop."

"Actually, they're crullers," I piped up.

Both Gabby and Chief Martin looked at me at the same time, as though I'd lost my mind by clarifying the distinction.

"Well, they're not the same thing," I explained.

The police chief shook his head, and then turned to Gabby. "Just to make Desmond happy, will you let me search your shop?"

"I didn't do anything wrong," Gabby said. "Why should I allow you to paw through my things?"

"I can't make you, at least without a warrant," the chief said with a sigh, "but don't you think it might look better to everyone if you cooperated with the investigation?"

Gabby frowned, and then looked at me. "Suzanne, what do you think I should do?"

I didn't even hesitate. "If you don't have anything to hide, you should let him look around. That's what I would do."

I saw the chief smile, but it started to fade when I added, "Don't worry about your things getting mussed. We're going to witness the search ourselves."

Gabby nodded and turned back to him. "That's the deal, then, take it or leave it. You may search my business, but Suzanne and I get to watch you do it."

The police chief looked at me and frowned. "What's the matter, Suzanne, don't you trust me?"

"Chief, it's not a matter of trust. I just want Gabby to be protected."

He shrugged. "Suit yourself. You're both free to watch."

As Chief Martin reached for the radio on his belt, I asked, "Who are you calling?"

"We need to get this over with quickly, so I'm calling in for backup." He hit the transmit button, and then called out,

"Grant, I need you at ReNEWed, right now."

I heard the officer reply in the affirmative, and I was glad the chief had called him. He was my favorite cop on the force, and often stopped in for donuts, both when on duty, and off.

When Officer Grant arrived two minutes later, he flashed me a quick grin, and then turned to his boss. "What can I do, Chief?"

"You can help me search this shop," he said.

Grant nodded, and then asked, "Anything in particular we're looking for?"

The chief nodded. "Ten grand in cash and a diamond brooch."

"A what?" Officer Grant asked.

"It's a pin," Gabby explained curtly, "and don't bother looking too hard; you're not going to find it."

Officer Grant clearly didn't know how to respond to that.

After we all walked inside, the first thing the police chief asked to see was the safe.

"What makes you think I have one?" Gabby asked.

"I know you," Chief Martin said. "You're careful with your money, so you're not about to leave it lying around. You're too sensible for that."

Gabby nodded. "I like to think so."

As we all headed for the back, the police chief said, "Gabby, before we even open it, don't try to tell me you've got ten thousand dollars on hand in your safe."

She shook her head. "I wouldn't dream of it. You should know, though, that I keep five thousand dollars in small bills on the premises at all times, and any jewelry I might take in to resell." Before the police could ask any questions, Gabby continued, "There are a few rings, a necklace, and a small emerald pin there at the moment, but no diamond brooches."

He'd whistled softly when he'd heard the amount of cash. "That's a lot of money on hand for such a small shop, isn't it?"

She explained, "Chief, I deal in a strictly cash business. I am constantly buying and selling items, so I need that size of reserve, but I won't keep more than five thousand here on hand at any time."

"You don't mind if I confirm that myself, do you?" the chief asked.

"Be my guest," Gabby said as she opened the safe, being careful so that none of us saw the combination. I envied her having a safe, not because of the steel, but because she actually needed one. The proceeds from a day selling donuts would fit into a shoe

22

box, nothing nearly substantial enough to require a safe to store until I could make my deposit.

The chief looked inside, counted the money, inspected the jewelry, and then nodded. "Thanks. You can lock it back up."

Officer Grant asked, "Does that mean we're finished here?"

"Not a chance. We're just getting started." He turned to Gabby and said, "I'm sorry about this, but it's going to take a while, and you're going to have to close while we conduct our search."

"If it will help clear my name, I'm more than willing to cooperate. Suzanne, would you help me with my sign up front?"

Why on earth did she need my assistance to lock the front door and hang a sign in the window? I wasn't about to question her, though, so I followed her to the front. Was it my imagination, or did the chief continue to watch us as we made our way to the door?

"Thank you, Suzanne," she said as she lightly touched my hand at the door.

"For what?"

She looked at me as though I were a little slow. "For being here so I don't have to face this alone. I know folks around town have an image of a tough old broad when they think of me, but this is quite unnerving."

"I'm glad I can help," I said. "Do you need my sign? I have one that says BACK IN AN HOUR that I'd be glad to loan you."

"I'm hoping they won't be here that long," she said, "but if they are, I'll just set the hands on my BACK AT clock."

She set the sign for 1:30, and then locked the door. As she did, I saw Emma hurrying up the street toward us.

"I need a second," I told Gabby. "Would you mind letting me out?"

"Suzanne, you're not deserting me, are you?" The look in her eyes was enough to tell me that she truly was unsettled by what was happening to her. Gabby was ordinarily the queen of her domain, and having the police rummage through her wares was bound to shake her up.

"I just need to tell Emma what's going on," I explained.

"You're going to tell her the whole humiliating story, aren't you?" Gabby asked.

"No, but I need to tell her why I just took off like that," I said.

Gabby nodded, and then unlocked the door.

I opened it a crack as Emma stood on the other side.

"What's going on, Suzanne? Why did you just disappear?"

"I'll explain later, but do you mind closing up the shop for the day?"

She frowned. "I already did. It's after twelve, after all. That's okay, isn't it?"

"It's fine," I said. "After you finish the dishes, don't worry about sweeping the front or doing the deposit. I'll take care of them myself later."

"The floor's already been swept, and the cash register report is on your desk," she said. "I hope you don't mind, but I wasn't exactly sure when you were coming back."

"You did perfect," I said.

"Suzanne," Gabby said beside me, "we need to get back."

I nodded, and then turned back to my assistant. "Thanks, Emma. I've got to go."

"Sure thing," she said, as Gabby shut the door and locked it soundly. I could see the look of confusion on my assistant's face, but I'd have to clarify it later. Right now, I had to help Gabby.

We were walking to the back of the store when I heard the police chief say aloud, "What's this?"

Had he found something that he shouldn't have? I couldn't imagine what it might be, but I hoped that it wasn't ten grand in cash, or worse yet, the diamond brooch the police were looking for.

EGGNOG DONUTS

We were having fun in the kitchen just before Christmas one year, and on a lark, I added whole eggnog instead of milk to the recipe. Wow, what a nice result. These are easily one of our favorite donuts to make these days when eggnog's available in the store.

Ingredients

Mixed
- 1 egg, beaten
- 1/2 cup sugar, white granulated
- 1/2 cup eggnog (whole milk can be substituted)
- 2 tablespoons butter, melted

- 1 teaspoon vanilla extract (omit unless using milk instead of eggnog)

Sifted

- 1 1/2 cups all-purpose flour
- 2 teaspoons baking powder
- 1/4 teaspoon nutmeg
- Pinch of salt

Directions

This one's easy! Mix the beaten egg, sugar, eggnog, and melted butter in one bowl, and in another bowl, sift together the flour, baking powder, nutmeg, and salt. Slowly add the sifted ingredients to the wet mix just until it's combined. Drop bits of dough using a small-sized cookie scoop (the size of your thumb, approximately). Fry in hot canola oil (360 to 370 degrees F) 1 1/2 to 2 minutes, turning halfway through.

Yield: 12–16 donuts

CHAPTER 2

"What is it? Let me see what you've found," Gabby commanded as we hurried to the back room.

Chief Martin held a receipt up in the air. "It's an itemized purchase slip dated yesterday and made out in the name of Jean Ray."

"Do you see a brooch, or cash, listed there?" Gabby asked a little crankily. Honestly, I was amazed how well she was holding it all in, but I could tell from the tone in her voice that she wasn't far from losing it.

"No, but it proves you bought a coat, a hat, and two sweaters from her," the police chief said.

"I never denied it," Gabby said, her voice growing louder with each syllable.

Chief Martin shrugged. "Where are the items listed here?"

Gabby walked past him to the rack closest to her back door. I knew that was where she sometimes stored the gently used clothing and accessories she took in, and it was a handy place for her to go through the inventory before she sent it all out to be dry-cleaned and gussied up a little before anything hit her sales floor. She pulled the items in question from the rack and put them down on the counter by the door. "Be my guest. Explore away."

The chief did a thorough search, and after he was finished, he turned to her. "There's nothing in any of the pockets, or even the hat band, for that matter."

"That's exactly what I told you that you'd find," Gabby said. "As I said before, the Rays are both mistaken accusing me of anything."

The police chief just shrugged, and then he went back to his search. I noticed that Officer Grant was still out on the sales floor, so while Gabby watched the chief, I decided to watch his employee. Okay, it might have been an excuse to get away from the pair of them, especially knowing how volatile the situation was, but I'd promised Gabby my help, and I was going to do the best that I could for her.

Officer Grant looked at me as I came out from the back. "What was the commotion about?"

"The chief just searched the items Gabby

bought from Jean."

"He came up empty, of course," Grant said as he continued his search.

"Of course he did. Does that mean you trust Gabby?" I asked, being careful to keep my voice low as I did.

Grant smiled slightly. "Not exactly. I just know that if Gabby Williams were ever inclined to steal something from a customer, she wouldn't be dumb enough to leave it just lying around after she took it. If that cash or that brooch were ever here, they're long gone by now."

"Not exactly a vote of confidence, is it?" I asked.

"Hey, you asked, I answered," he said, "and if you quote me on any of it, I'll tell my boss you imagined it." Officer Grant added the last bit with a grin, and I couldn't help smiling slighty myself.

As he continued his search, I found a stool where Gabby sometimes perched, and watched his progress. He didn't seem to mind one bit having an audience.

Twenty minutes later, the police chief joined us up front, with Gabby close on his heels.

I couldn't help myself as I asked, "Did you have any luck?"

"Of course he didn't," Gabby answered

for him.

Chief Martin appeared to ignore the jibe as he looked questioningly at his only reinforcement. When Officer Grant shook his head, the chief nodded, and then moved to the other side of the store.

In forty-five minutes, the officers finished their search at nearly the same time.

"There's nothing here, Chief," Officer Grant said.

In reply, the police chief said, "Go back to the station," and Grant did as he was told. I let him out, and then turned to the chief. "Can I go ahead and leave this unlocked? After all, Gabby has a business to run."

He wanted to say no, I could tell by his rigid stance and the frown on his face, but he glanced at Gabby and must have known that he didn't want to have that particular fight on his hands. "Go ahead."

I took the sign out of the window, then I unlocked the door. The chief started to leave, but before he did, he turned to Gabby and said, "Thank you for your cooperation."

Gabby smiled broadly at him, and then said, "It was my pleasure to be of assistance."

After he was gone, Gabby slumped against the counter where she'd been standing.

"I'm glad that's over," I said.

Gabby just shook her head. "I only wish it were, but Desmond isn't about to give up that easily. He's coming back, that you can be certain of."

So much for my celebration. As I started to go, I said, "Gabby, if you need me, I'm just a phone call away."

"Thank you, Suzanne. I might just take you up on that."

After I left her, I popped back into the donut shop to make sure everything was in order. It wasn't that I didn't trust Emma. In fact, when I took one of my rare days off, she ran the shop for me, with the help of her mother. I just knew that I wouldn't be happy until I'd gone over everything again myself. My life, not to mention my entire savings, were invested in Donut Hearts, and I wanted to be sure that everything there was in perfect order.

I was still going over the books when there was a tapping at the front door.

What was that all about?

I walked out front, and to my happy surprise, I found Jake standing there smiling at me.

I hurried to the door and opened it for him. "What are you doing here?" I asked breathlessly as I hugged him. Jake wasn't as fond of public displays of affection as I was, but I was slowly breaking down his resistance.

My boyfriend, a state police investigator, managed to break free from me, and then grinned. "I'm happy to see you, too, Suzanne."

"I thought you were going to be in Asheville all week," I said. A friend of Jake's, another investigator who'd retired to take a teaching position at the University of North Carolina-Asheville, had asked him to guest lecture for a week in his criminal justice classes, and before Jake could answer, he was told by his supervisor that it was important that Jake do it, so he'd reluctantly accepted the assignment. It wasn't that Jake didn't want to help his friend, but he had a real dislike for public speaking of any kind, and he'd once told me that he'd rather face an armed criminal than an audience.

"I'm headed to Asheville right now," he said. "I really wasn't in any position to turn Grayson down. I'm not sure what he has on my boss, but whatever it is, I wish he'd share it with me. I could use a little blackmail information myself."

I glanced at my watch. "I thought you were supposed to get started today."

"Hey, you're supposed to be glad to see me, no matter the circumstances."

"You know I am," I said as I hugged him again. "I just don't want you to be late on your first day because of me."

"Nothing to worry about. My first inquisition isn't until four, so there's still plenty of time to get there. Is there any chance you've changed your mind about taking a few days off and going with me? Asheville's beautiful this time of year."

"It's beautiful every time of year," I said, "but I can't. I have donuts to make."

He nodded. "And crullers to create before you sleep."

I must have looked oddly at him when he mentioned crullers, because he asked, "Was it something I said?"

"No, it's just that I had a bad experience with crullers today."

That didn't clear things up for him. "Did they burn, or were they raw inside?"

I shook my head. "They were fine when they left the shop, but I wasn't all that crazy about what one of my customers did with them after they were gone."

"Nobody died, did they?" Jake asked, suddenly very serious. My donuts had been used for evil in the past, and I shuddered whenever I thought about it.

"No, it was more like a case of assault."

Jake laughed at that. "How do you assault

someone with a donut?"

I said, "Some crazy man bought a dozen crullers from me and headed over to Gabby Williams's shop. By the time I got there, he'd thrown over half a dozen against the glass door and front windows of the place. Needless to say, Gabby was not amused."

"I can't imagine that she would be," Jake said. "Why the pastry barrage, anyway?"

"He claimed that Gabby stole cash and a valuable brooch from his aunt's coat when she brought it in for resale."

"How much cash are we talking about?" Jake asked, and I could see his gaze go into full-tilt police-investigation mode.

"Ten thousand dollars, and who knows how much the jewelry was worth."

Jake frowned. "That's a felony."

"*If* it's true," I said, "but I don't believe it for one second. Gabby is many things, and everyone knows that I'm not her biggest fan, but I refuse to accept the idea that she is a thief."

Jake held his hands up as though he were defending himself. "Hey, take it easy. I'm on your side, remember?"

"Sorry, I guess I'm just a little sensitive about the plight of the small business owner. It's hard enough to get by without having folks accuse you of wrongdoing.

Gabby's really bothered by this, and I am, too." I neglected to tell Jake that Desmond had threatened me, too. After all, it had been in the heat of the moment, and I was certain that he'd already forgotten about me. Gabby, I was sure, was another story entirely.

"That's one of the many reasons I care so much about you," Jake said as he gave me a kiss. Though we were in a deep, committed relationship, Jake couldn't bring himself to tell me that he loved me. I understood why, and promised myself that I'd be patient with him. He'd told me early in our relationship that he'd only been able to tell one woman in his life that he loved her, and that had been his late wife. I tried to tell myself that I didn't mind not hearing those three words from him, and usually I was able to let it go, but it would have been nice, just once, to hear him tell me that he loved me.

"Suzanne, if you're sure you haven't changed your mind, I've got to scoot."

"Sorry, I'd really love to, but I can't. I'll see you this weekend, right?"

"Barring a major catastrophe," he said with a grin.

"So then, it's a fifty-fifty proposition?"

"That sounds about right," Jake said, and then he left.

I was on my way to the bank when I heard a car horn behind me. I looked up in annoyance, but it quickly turned into a smile when I saw that it was Grace Gauge, my best friend. I was nearly at the bank, so I waited to respond until I could pull into the parking lot. Grace joined me, getting out of her fancy company car and heading for my Jeep.

"Are you done for the day already?" I asked her as we met in front of my car.

"Why not? You are."

"Sure, but I start a lot earlier than you do."

Grace smiled at me. "Hey, it's not my fault if you're the early bird. I've got things under control in my territory, and everyone under me is finally working hard, so I don't have to crack any whips or knock heads."

"How are you keeping them so dedicated to the company?"

Grace smiled. "What can I say? My people love me. Well, they fear me a little, too, but that's not necessarily a bad thing. If someone starts to slack off, I just let them know that there's a pile of résumés from people eager to take their places; it's amazing how motivating that can be." She looked me over from head to foot, and then added, "I've got say, Suzanne, I don't see any evidence."

"Of what?" I asked, honestly confused.

"The Great Donut Massacre," Grace said.

"It was more like a cruller skirmish," I admitted. "How did you hear about it?"

"How do you think? In the same convoluted way any rumor gets spread around April Springs," she said. "I'm sure it wasn't as spectacular as I heard. In that version, there were iced donuts hanging from you and Gabby Williams like you'd both just been decorated for Christmas."

"It was a handful of crullers, and they all hit her building. We both escaped relatively unscathed."

"Care to tell me about it?" Grace asked.

"How about over lunch?" I suggested. "After I make this deposit, I'm free."

"Lunch it is," Grace said. "I've got a few calls to make, so I'll meet you out here when you're finished."

I went into the bank, deposited my day's receipts, and on my way out, Desmond Ray walked in.

"I saw that ugly Jeep of yours out front, so I knew I'd find you here," he said, blocking my way out of the building. "You need to butt out of this, Suzanne. It's between Gabby and me."

"I wouldn't be involved at all if you hadn't used my crullers to assault her."

He shook his head. "I never hit her, just her precious shop, and don't flatter yourself. You were just within easy reach of her place with ammunition for sale. She deserved worse than that."

I couldn't let him get away with talking like that about Gabby. "I believe her. Your aunt must be mistaken."

Desmond raised his voice, and I saw some of the folks in the bank looking our way. So much for keeping a low profile around town. "You're as bad as she is. What happened, did she give you half the money she stole from my family so you'd keep your mouth shut? When I'm done with her, I'll settle my score with you, donut girl."

"You're as crazy as a bag full of rabid bats," I said, something my uncle Ned had been fond of saying when confronted with someone else's insanity.

Bennett Jenkins, the aging security guard for the bank, walked over to us. "Is there a problem here, folks?"

"No, we're fine," I said as I brushed past Desmond and left.

I half expected Desmond to follow me, but when he didn't, I told Grace, "Let's go."

"I'm fine with that, but where are we headed?" She must have noticed my expression. "Suzanne, is something wrong?"

"We'll talk about it later. I'll meet you at the Boxcar Grille."

As I drove to the Boxcar, I had to wonder if Desmond was focusing on me, now. If he was, I didn't like it. Maybe the next time something like that happened, if it ever did, I'd keep my nose out of it.

Fat chance that could ever happen, I admitted to myself.

I waited by my Jeep in the diner parking lot, but Grace apparently decided not to follow me. I gave her four minutes, and then dialed her phone number.

"You didn't get lost, did you?" I asked as I reached her.

"No, I think I can find the Boxcar on my own. Sorry, but one of my underlings just called. It turns out that all the wheels aren't turning as smoothly as I'd thought."

"Did you wave those applications under her nose?" I asked.

"I was just kidding before. Suzanne, I hate being managed with fear, and I won't do it to the people under me, no matter how tempting it might be sometimes."

"Does that mean you have to cancel lunch?"

I heard her laugh as I saw her drive up. "Not a chance. Erica is just going to have

40

to get herself out of this jam herself."

She hung up, and joined me by the Jeep. Before we went in, I said, "Grace, I really don't mind if you need to go."

"Not a chance," she said as she steered me toward the Boxcar. "We're going to have a long and leisurely lunch, and then I'll deal with Erica."

"If you say so," I answered. I had no desire to change her mind. Hanging out with Grace was one of my favorite things to do, and in a way, it made up for the fact that Jake was so far away most of the time. If I had the chance, I planned to surprise him in Asheville while he was there, but for the moment, I had enough on my hands to keep me busy. I yawned, and realized that it may have just been after one P.M., but my internal timepiece constantly reminded me that I'd been up since one-thirty that morning.

"Let's go in, I'm starving," she said as we walked into the converted train car that was now one of my favorite places to eat. Trish met us at the front counter with a grin so broad I thought her face was going to explode.

"Why are you so happy?" I asked as she led us to a free table. "Did you win the lottery or something?"

"It's even better than that," she answered with a smile.

"Did you get a new man in your life?" Grace asked with a twinkle in her eye.

"Hardly," she replied with a shrug. Trish had a notoriously difficult time finding a boyfriend. Perhaps it had something to do with the fact that she was so picky. She'd once claimed that the man for her hadn't been built yet, and I'd realized that might be what it would take to satisfy her high standards. I knew Jake had his flaws, but I loved being in a relationship with him. I wasn't sorry for my friends; both Trish and Grace were wonderful young women, fun to be around, and funny in their own ways. None of us needed a man to complete us, or to even make life more interesting, but there were times when they did come in awfully handy.

"So, what's the good news?" I asked.

She looked carefully around us, and then leaned forward. "Allison turned in her notice today. She's gone."

I knew that Trish had hired Allison Jackson as a favor to her mother, Lilly, or more likely, because of an implied threat. Lilly was much feared, and little loved, in our small town. I sometimes thought it odd that of the folks who had been killed around town, Lilly had never made the list as either suspect, or even more likely, victim. It just showed that fate could be a cruel and capricious woman, indeed.

"Allison actually quit?" I asked. A thought suddenly occurred to me. "Oh, no. You don't think she's going to apply at the donut shop next, do you?" I wouldn't hire her, and Lilly couldn't make me, but that still didn't mean that I wanted to get on her bad side. It was hard enough dancing that fine line with Gabby.

Trish took my hands in hers. "Don't worry, you're safe. She's getting married."

Grace looked amazed by the declaration. "Someone actually proposed to her? The girl is so dense she'd have trouble pouring water out of a boot."

"From what I heard today, none of that matters. Kevin Kraus is in love, and his little Alley Cat isn't about to work another day of her life."

I grinned. "He actually called her his Alley Cat?"

"I heard it myself," Trish said. "It's dreadful, isn't it? But who cares? She's out of my hair, that's all that matters. What can I get you ladies?"

"We were going to just order cheeseburgers," Grace said, "but this is reason enough to celebrate." She pretended to study the menu, and then declared, "We'll still have the cheeseburgers and Cokes, but bring us pie after we're finished."

Trish nodded, and then leaned forward. She nearly whispered as she said, "Tell you what. You two saw me through my troubling times with that nincompoop. The pie's on the house."

"That sounds good," Grace said before I had a chance to comment.

"We shouldn't take advantage of her," I said to Grace after Trish left.

"Are you kidding? You heard her. We're helping her celebrate. How rude would it be if we didn't join in?"

"Okay, but I'm going to bring her donuts sometime soon to make up for it."

"You have a good heart, Suzanne."

After Trish delivered the sodas, Grace said, "Now, tell me what happened out in front of Gabby's shop today."

"It's really nothing," I said, trying to keep my voice low. The last thing I needed was for all of April Springs to hear yet another version of the day's events, no matter how deeply my story was rooted in reality.

"Come on, give."

Grace wasn't going to fold. "I was innocent enough this time, if you can believe it. A man came in and ordered a dozen donuts, so I sold him iced crullers I had on hand."

Grace nodded. "Did Simon Henson stick you with another order without paying?"

"For the last time," I agreed. "Anyway, I told him to enjoy them, and he said they weren't for eating. I followed him outside to Gabby's, and when he dropped his guard, I bought them back from him." I grinned, and then admitted, "Okay, I stole them, but I flipped him a ten, so we were more than even. He actually threatened me, too, can you believe it?" I didn't tell her what had happened at the bank.

"Why was he pelting her place with crullers in the first place?" she asked.

"That's where it gets tricky," I said. "It was Desmond Ray, and he claimed that his aunt Jean left ten grand and a diamond brooch in the coat she sold to Gabby."

Grace shook her head and asked, "If she bought the coat, doesn't that mean that she owns what's in the pockets, too?"

I hadn't thought of it that way. "It doesn't matter, because Gabby swears that the pockets were all empty."

Before I could explain my point further, Grace said, "I bet it matters to Jean and Desmond."

"Gabby claimed that there wasn't anything in the pockets except lint, but Desmond didn't believe her. They had quite a row on the street, and my crullers were in the middle of the action."

Grace shook her head. "You just can't seem to keep trouble from following you around, can you?"

"It's a curse," I agreed as our food arrived.

The burgers were perfect, and after we finished, I looked at Grace and said, "I'm not at all sure I could eat a piece of pie, can you?"

"If it's on the house? You bet I can. I'll find some way to choke it down."

I had to laugh. "I'm sure that's what the pie maker had in mind when she created that pie."

"Hey, it is what it is."

Trish came back with three pieces of pie, not the promised two.

"I thought I'd join you," she said as she slid onto the bench seat in the booth beside me. "If you two don't mind, that is."

"You don't even have to ask; you're always welcome," I said.

She took a bite of apple pie, and then smiled broadly. "That is good, if I say so myself."

"Did you make it?" Grace asked as she

46

tasted a bit herself.

"No, I leave the pie making to the experts. I can appreciate a work of art as much as the next gal, though. Now, what were you talking about? I want in."

I wasn't about to say anything when Grace volunteered, "Desmond threatened Suzanne and Gabby after some really nasty pastry fighting."

Trish asked with a frown, "Are we talking about Desmond Ray?"

"Yes, but the most intimidating thing he did today was pelt Gabby's shop with my crullers." That wasn't true by any stretch of the imagination, but I didn't want to admit everything that had happened to my friends. They would just worry about me, and I already had a mother who was constantly concerned with my well-being.

Trish played with her fork a second before saying, "He's got a temper, Suzanne. I wouldn't take him too lightly. Tell me exactly what he said to you, and don't sugarcoat it."

I didn't have much choice. I might avoid telling my friends something alarming, but I wouldn't lie to them outright. "He said he'd be coming back for me, and that he'd settle with me next."

"That sounds like a real threat to me,"

Trish said as she pushed her pie away.

"I'm not going to change anything about my behavior to avoid him," I said. "If I do that, he wins."

Grace and I were finished with our slices of pie, so we paid our tab, and walked back out into the warming sunshine. It was in the low fifties outside, but with the sun, I almost didn't need the light jacket I was wearing.

"What should we do next?" I asked Grace.

She glanced at her watch, and then said, "Honestly, I'd better go check on Erica. It's hard to tell what trouble that girl's gotten herself into by now."

"What happened to letting her deal with it herself?"

Grace smiled. "What can I say? My heart's just a little too big sometimes. See you later," she said. After she got in her car and left, I decided to head home. It might be nice to take a shower, and then grab a quick nap on the couch before dinner. Momma had told me that she was making something special tonight, and that I shouldn't miss it.

For once, there was no possible reason that I should.

At least as far as I knew at that point.

CHAPTER 3

My cell phone woke me, and I nearly fell off the couch as I reached for it. It was barely three in the afternoon, so I'd only slept for ninety minutes, but that was a longer nap than I usually got.

"Hello?" I said as I sat up and brushed my hair out from my eyes.

"You were sleeping, weren't you?" I heard Momma ask. "Suzanne, I'm sorry. I didn't mean to wake you. We can talk later. Go back to sleep."

"No, that's fine," I said as I sat up. "I needed to get up anyway. What's going on?"

"I may be a little late coming home tonight, so you're on your own for dinner."

As I stretched, I asked, "Do you have another big date with the chief? You two are getting to be real regulars, aren't you?"

"We're going out quite a bit, I admit, but it's rarely more than three times a week."

I suddenly remembered her earlier promise of a special meal. "What happened to the feast you were making tonight?"

"I'm sorry about that, but you know better than most. Plans change," she said simply.

"No way you're getting away with that explanation," I said. "You're not the most flexible person I've ever met. Once you plan for a meal, it takes an act of Congress to get you to change."

She laughed at my comment, proving that she was in a good mood. "I admit that I might have been a little rigid in the past, but perhaps I'm capable of changing, after all."

"Not without motivation," I replied. "What's the scoop? Come on, Momma, you can tell me."

"I honestly would if I could, but Phillip was quite mysterious about the urgency to change our plans this evening. Will you be all right on your own?"

"Don't worry about me. Are you coming home to change before your mysterious date, or will I see you tonight?"

"It's going to be later, I'm afraid. Have a lovely evening, Suzanne."

"You do the same yourself," I said.

After I hung up the phone, I realized that I had no plans for the rest of the day.

Normally that wouldn't bother me, but for some reason, I wasn't all that crazy about being alone at the moment. On a whim, I dialed Jake's cell phone number.

He picked up on the third ring. "Do you miss me already, Suzanne?" he asked when he picked up. "I was just there."

"What can I say, I have a bad craving for some Jake time." On a lark, I suggested, "If you don't have dinner plans, why don't I drive to Asheville and take you out to eat? I love Cheddar's, or maybe we could go to Mellow Mushroom."

"Sorry, I'd love to, but there's some kind of faculty mixer tonight, and I'm being dragged to it against my will. I can try to get out of it, if it's really that important to you."

I didn't want him to change his plans on my account, particularly when it wasn't all that important to me in the first place. "Nonsense, you go and have fun."

"What happened to your mother's big dinner?" he asked.

"It appears she got a better offer," I said with a smile. "Don't worry about me, I'll give Grace a call. I'm sure she's up for anything."

"That's what I'm afraid of. Well, if the two of you get in trouble, remember, I keep bail money on hand just in case, and I happen to have some connections with the local law enforcement."

"We won't get that rowdy," I said with a laugh, "but it's good to know that you're prepared, just in case. Call me tomorrow if you get a chance."

"Since I won't be free until long after your bedtime tonight, I hope you have sweet dreams."

"Right back at you."

I hung up, missing my boyfriend even more. I'd had the chance to go to Asheville with him, but my loyalty to my donut shop hadn't allowed it. Donuts were great, but they weren't much fun cuddling up with on the front porch swing, and they couldn't touch one of Jake's good-night kisses. Maybe next time he offered to take me someplace with him, I'd surprise us both and say yes.

I called Grace's number, and she laughed the second she knew that it was me. "I was just thinking about giving you a call," she said.

"Great minds think alike. Momma canceled our dinner. Is there any chance you're free tonight?"

Grace hesitated, and then said, "Sure, why not? I can do that."

I knew my friend well enough to realize that she was holding something back from me. "Grace, what's going on?" I had a sudden thought. "You don't have a date, do you?"

"I wouldn't exactly call it a date," she admitted. "It's a fix-up I've been putting off for weeks, so it's no big deal if I push it back another night. Let me call him first, and then I'll be over in ten minutes."

"Don't you dare. You are not changing your plans on my account. How can you live with the thought of crushing some poor guy's spirit by bailing out on him like that?"

Grace laughed. "If he's lived without me this long, I'm sure he'll be able to make it a little longer."

"I don't want to be the cause of somebody else's disappointment. We'll do something tomorrow night. I promise."

Grace paused, and then said, "Hey, I've got a crazy idea. Why don't you call Jake and ask him out? He'll flip out if you drive all the way to Asheville just to take him out to dinner."

I didn't have the heart to tell her that I'd already tried that plan, and that it had failed completely. "I might just do it. Have fun, and call me tomorrow. I can't wait to hear the details of what happens."

"Trust me, I can recap everything that's going to occur right now. We'll have an average dinner filled with bland and mundane conversation, and then he'll take me home, where we'll share an awkward good-bye before he leaves my life forever."

I had to laugh at her prediction. "Wow, with that kind of buildup, how can you not have a good time?"

"Trust me, it's like I can see the future. I'll call you tomorrow."

"I'll talk to you then," I said. "And Grace? Give the guy a chance. He might just surprise you."

"If he shows up without his mother and a way to pay for at least his half of the meal, I'll be absolutely flabbergasted."

As we hung up, I realized that I'd just explored my last viable option. It appeared that I was going to be on my own tonight, whether I liked it or not. Sure, I could have called Max — my ex-husband and the Great Pretender — and I was certain he would have come by gladly, but I wasn't that desperate for company tonight, and I hoped I never would be again.

For the moment, I was a single woman on my own with the whole world at my feet.

When the doorbell rang a little after six, I

opened it with my wallet ready. I'd already changed into my sweats and an old T-shirt, so I wasn't exactly fit for company, but I figured the pizza guy had seen worse than me, and that was just tonight.

"How much do I owe you?" I asked as I took the pizza from the college-aged young man making the delivery.

"That will be twelve dollars, plus tip," he said.

"It's just a small pepperoni pizza," I protested. "How can it be that much?"

The kid shrugged. "We have a twelve-dollar minimum order; didn't they tell you that on the phone? They're supposed to."

"I'm in the wrong business," I said as I handed him a ten and four ones. It was a lot to pay for one pizza, but I wasn't exactly dressed to go out to dinner.

"Tell me about it." He put the two dollars in a separate pocket, and smiled at me. "Thanks for the tip. Enjoy."

I went back inside, and had a slice as I hit the play button on the DVD player. At least the pizza was still warm, something that wasn't always guaranteed.

After the movie, it was close to my bedtime. Some folks might have wondered about the way I'd chosen to use my time alone, but I'd enjoyed it, so what did it matter what anyone else thought? Sometimes it was good being by myself, though I knew that I'd grow weary of it pretty quickly if I lived my entire life that way. For the most part, I enjoyed being around people, which was a good thing, given my chosen line of work. Selling donuts was as much about being good with people as it was with the pastry treats we made at the shop.

I was about ready to call it a night at seven-fifteen when the house phone rang. I rarely got calls there anymore, and I nearly let it go to voice mail when it rang. After the conversation, I would wonder why I hadn't listened to that impulse.

I recognized her voice the second she spoke. "Gabby, how are you?"

"I'm concerned," she said. "Has Desmond spoken with you?"

"Tonight?" I asked. "No, I haven't seen him since I ran into him at the bank this afternoon."

"What did he say?" Gabby asked. There was clear anxiety in her voice, and I realized that she sounded frightened, something unusual to hear coming from her.

"He threatened me again," I admitted. "The man is convinced that he's right." Before Gabby could proclaim her innocence again, I quickly added, "I told him he was wrong about you, but he wasn't buying it. Why do you ask? Has something happened?"

"He spent three hours this afternoon on the bench across the street from my front door, just staring at my shop as though he were willing it to burn to the ground."

"You should tell the police," I said. I was no stranger to threatening behavior, and I knew how it could wear you down if you gave in to it, ducking behind every tree and flinching at the sound of a car door slamming.

"What could I tell them that they don't already know? Chief Martin wasn't all that pleasant with us when we spoke with him today, so why should I expect him to be any different now? After all, I suppose that Desmond hasn't done anything illegal. It was just unnerving seeing him over there every time I looked out my window."

"He's trying to rattle you," I said.

"If that's his goal, then he's getting spectacular results," Gabby said.

I knew I'd regret it, but I couldn't take the helplessness I heard in her voice. "You could always come over here if it would make you feel better." The last thing I wanted to do was entertain Gabby when it was time for me to sleep, but I didn't really feel as though I had much choice.

"What? No, don't be silly. I was just calling to see if *you* were all right."

Clearly her moment of weakness had disappeared as quickly as it had first appeared. "No worries about me; I'm fine," I said.

"Then I'll say good night," Gabby said, and hung up before I could even reply in kind.

How odd. Desmond had done something I wasn't exactly certain was even possible; he'd gotten under Gabby's skin and put a few cracks in her overwhelming armor of confidence.

I wondered what I could do to ease her mind, but every scenario involved me changing out of my grubby clothes and being rebuffed if I dared approach her in person, so I did my best to forget about it. I was tired, and it was late — at least for me — so I did one of the most rational things I could come up with.

I went to bed.

I woke up just past ten that night, not sure what had brought me out of my deep sleep. I had to get up at one-thirty, and I rarely awoke until then once I managed to nod off. I had been having some serious second thoughts about our hours lately. We were at the donut shop too early, and stayed too late, and I had been thinking about doing something about it. I sat up in bed, looked around in the darkness, but could see no reason why I had awoken. Usually when that happened I had an easy time getting back to sleep, but not now. I tossed and turned, counted sheep, and then began to list the donuts we'd made over the years, starting with plain glazed. By the time I hit variety forty-two, I knew it wasn't going to work. This was miserable. After suffering through the rest of the night, I finally gave up and just got out of bed a full twenty minutes before I had to, threw on my clothes, and grabbed a power bar on my way out the door.

Driving to the shop, I noticed the flashing lights of a patrol car ahead, and then another, and another. What had happened? As I got closer, I saw that it was near my donut shop! Had we had a break-in? I wasn't sure why anyone would bother with us given our bottom line, but I felt myself go cold inside as I neared the scene.

The odd thing was, though, they weren't in front of my shop, or Gabby's place, either.

Instead, the cars were all pulled up in front of the narrow grass strip of land between them.

■ ■ ■ ■

I got out and found Chief Martin standing near his patrol car. He was on the phone, but I didn't care.

"What's going on?" I asked as I tried to see what was happening.

He held up a hand, a clear sign that he wanted me to be quiet. There was no way that was happening, and we both knew it. I started to go around him when he shook his head, and then hung the phone up.

"Suzanne, what are you doing here this early?"

"I always open this time of morning," I said. I refused to call it nighttime, since it was after midnight. Besides, it made me feel better, more normal somehow, if I thought of my hours as closer being in synch with the rest of the world.

He glanced at his watch. "You aren't due for another fifteen minutes."

That surprised me. "You know my schedule?"

He said softly, "Take it easy. Whoever is on night patrol can set his watch by you. We all know your hours. I'll ask you again, why are you so early?"

"Something woke me up around ten, and

I couldn't get back to sleep," I admitted. "Why does that matter?"

"Was it a gunshot, perhaps?" he asked intently.

"I hope not, but I honestly couldn't say." I tried again to look around him. "Are you going to tell me what's going on?"

"Somebody was shot back there, and from what we know so far, it most likely happened right around ten last night."

"Was it Gabby? Is she okay?" I started again to go around him, but this time he put an arm out to keep me from looking. Gabby Williams could be a real pain in my life sometimes, but I considered her a friend, albeit a conditional one most days. Nevertheless, I hated the thought of her lifeless body lying back there crumpled up on the ground.

"Gabby's fine, as far as we know," he said.

At least that was something. "If it wasn't Gabby, who was it?"

He shook his head. "I'm not ready to say just yet. Why don't you go into your shop and get started, and I'll come by later." He must have seen my reluctance to leave, because he added, "Suzanne, it's the only way you're going to get anything out of me, so you might as well do as I'm asking you."

I knew he was right. If I cooperated, I

actually stood a chance to learn what had happened without waiting for the town grapevine to supply the answers.

"Okay," I agreed. "I still have to move my Jeep, though."

He shook his head. "I'll have one of my people move it for you," Chief Martin said as he held out his hand for my keys.

I pulled the Jeep key off the chain, and handed it to him. "Be careful with it. It's a real classic."

He didn't even smile. "We will."

I started to walk next door to my shop when I noticed that he was in step just behind me.

"I don't need a police escort to Donut Hearts," I said, pointing to the building a few feet away.

"Sorry, you're going to get one, anyway."

I thought about that for a second, and then said, "You want to make sure no one's hiding inside, don't you?"

He nodded. "Grant went to get Gabby. Don't worry; she's getting the same treatment you are." He looked at the lock on my shop door, and then said, "Go on, open it. It doesn't seem to have been tampered with."

I unlocked it, flipped on the switch near the door, and the chief drew his service revolver as he stepped ahead of me. "Stay right here," he said softly. I was amazed by how competent he sounded as he said it. I knew I didn't give our chief of police much credit most days, especially since he'd started dating my mother, but at that moment, I was glad to have him with me.

He did a quick but thorough search of the front, and then went back into the kitchen where I couldn't see him. I waited and waited, holding my breath as I expected to hear gunfire at any second, but two minutes later he came back out, his weapon now holstered.

"You're good to go. It's all clear," he said.

"Thanks. Do me a favor and knock on the front door when you're ready to tell me something," I said.

"Will do."

Chief Martin waited outside until I locked the front door again, and then he disappeared back into the night.

I stood there for a few seconds trying to figure out who might be dead, but that wasn't getting me anywhere, and I had donuts to make. I glanced at the clock in the kitchen and saw that despite my early arrival, I was going to get a late start. It was closer to three than I ever wanted to start making donuts, but that would make it a perfect dry run. If Emma and I could manage today, we were officially changing our hours. Three A.M. to eleven might be a brutal schedule for some folks, but it would be a great deal better than one-thirty to noon. If I could swing it, who knew, I might even be able to start having a life. If we opened at six, that would give folks five hours to buy donuts, and if they couldn't make it by then, I wasn't going to worry about it.

Emma came in ten minutes after her usual starting time, unwrapping her scarf as she walked into the kitchen. "Sorry I'm late, but did you see what was going on next door?"

"It's hard to miss, what with the squad cars everywhere and their lights flashing," I said as I measured out ingredients for our cake donuts. "Someone's been shot."

Emma looked at me in disbelief. "Seriously? Who was it?"

"Chief Martin wouldn't tell me, but he said he'd let me know as soon as he could. It's not Gabby; that's all I know."

"Why would someone kill Gabby?" she asked. Emma suddenly frowned. "You don't mean that crazy cruller guy, do you?"

"Why not? He threatened both of us," I

said. "Who knows who else he might have threatened? Anyway, we don't have to worry about him at the moment. The chief checked the place out, and we're safe here." I looked at my lone employee and said, "Coming in late has clarified something for me. I've made an executive decision, Emma."

She looked worried. "Suzanne, I honestly couldn't get through the police cars so I could park. You're not going to fire me for being a little late, are you?"

"Don't be silly," I said. "You know that I would never fire you."

The relief in her face was obvious. She asked with a grin, "Never? Not even for burning the coffee or dropping a tray of donuts on a customer's head?"

"I guess that would depend on the customer," I said, answering her grin. "Emma, think about it. Why would I fire you? If I did that, I'd have no way of giving you a hard time about what you'd done if you pulled anything like that." Getting serious, I said, "I hate to be the one to break it to you, but as long as you want to work here, you've got a job with me."

"That's a relief," she said. "If that's not it then, what's your big executive decision?"

"We're changing our hours, as of right

now," I said.

She groaned, and I asked her, "What's wrong?"

Emma was obviously upset as she explained, "I swear, I love working here — you know that I do — but I'm not sure I can work any more time every day than I already do."

I laughed. "Would you mind working fewer hours, then?"

"Are you kidding? If I could sleep another hour every morning, I'd be in heaven." She paused, and then frowned as she asked, "Hang on a second. That means less pay, too, doesn't it?"

I hadn't even thought about that ramification of my decision for her, financially. On a rash impulse, I asked, "How about if I split the difference with you between what you make now and the hours you work? You'll take a smaller cut, and in exchange, you'll get more free time."

Emma looked at me shrewdly, and then asked, "Do I get a new title with my raise?"

"Who said you were getting a raise?" I asked as I continued mixing the batter for our basic cake donuts.

"I'm making more per hour than I did, according to your plan," she said with a grin. "That sounds like a raise to me. If I had a new title to go with it, Dad might get off my back about quitting and going to school."

I knew Emma's father wasn't all that pleased with his daughter working for me in the donut shop, but I hadn't realized he'd been putting pressure on her to quit. "Is it that bad?"

"Not really," she said evasively. "Forget I said anything."

"Okay, how does 'Assistant Manager' sound to you?" I asked.

"You don't have to give me a title, seriously," she answered.

"Why not? You are, you know. You're second in command around here."

Emma laughed. "I'm also the lowest one on the totem pole," she replied, "but who knows? It might just make him happy."

I had a sudden thought. "I know how to make him happier."

"How?"

"Tell him about the shooting," I said. "He can write it up for the paper, and I have a hunch he won't mind your crazy hours so much if you can feed him a story every now and then."

"That's brilliant," Emma said as she grabbed her phone. She made a hurried call, and then beamed at me. "He actually thanked me, can you believe it?"

"Does he still pay for phone tips?" I asked. "You should collect from him."

"Even I'm not willing to push my luck that much," she said. "He's on his way. I wonder if he'll be able get anything out of the chief."

I shrugged, and as I prepared to drop the first batter into the hot oil, there was a loud knocking up front.

I put the dropper down and said, "Unless I miss my guess, we're about to find out what happened."

APPLE CIDER DONUTS

These donuts are very good, with a hint of cider in every bite. I tried substituting apple juice once when I didn't have any cider on hand, but it was bland, and I won't do them again unless I have real cider available.

Ingredients

Mixed
- 2 eggs, beaten
- 1 cup fresh apple cider
- 1/4 cup brown sugar, light
- 1/4 cup sugar, white granulated

Sifted
- 4 cups all-purpose flour, unbleached
- 1/2 teaspoon baking soda
- 1/2 teaspoon baking powder
- 1/2 teaspoon cinnamon
- 1/2 teaspoon nutmeg
- Pinch of salt

Added
- 2 tablespoons butter, melted

Directions
In one bowl, beat the eggs thoroughly, then add the cider. In a different bowl, combine the brown sugar and granulated sugar together, and then add that to the mix. After that's incorporated, take another bowl and sift together the flour, baking soda, baking powder, cinnamon, nutmeg, and salt. Add the melted butter last. If the dough is still sticky, add flour until it can be worked easily. Roll the dough out to 1/2 to 1/4 inch thick, then cut out donuts using a donut cutter (round with a hole in the center), a Bismarck cutter (log-type donut), or use your imagination! Fry in hot canola oil (360 to 370 degrees F) 3 to 4 minutes, turning halfway through. Dry on paper towels, and then serve dusted with confectioner's sugar or glaze.

Yield: Depending on shapes, from 6–16 do-nuts

CHAPTER 4

"Stay here," I said to Emma.

"Hey, that's not fair. I want to hear, too," she protested.

I didn't have time for open mutiny. "He's more likely to talk to me if it's just one-on-one. Don't worry; I'll leave the door propped open. You won't miss a thing."

"Fine," she said. "But be sure to keep your voice loud enough for me to hear."

I pointed to the dropper. "In the meantime, you can get started on those, Assistant Manager."

"I knew that title was going to end up biting me sooner or later," she said with a grin.

The chief was waiting patiently for me as I walked up front and opened the door.

"Can I get you a cup of coffee, on the house?" I asked him.

"That would be great," he said as he took a seat at the bar. I poured him some in a to-go cup, and then asked, "How many of your people are still here?"

"There are three left," he said.

I got more cups and started to fill them.

"You don't have to do that," the chief said.

As I put the lids on and placed them into a cardboard carrier, I said, "It's no trouble, honestly."

"They'll appreciate it, I'm sure." He took a long sip of his coffee, and then added, "I just spoke with the victim's next of kin, so I can tell you who was shot, but I have a question for you first."

"Fire away," I said, then immediately realized that it hadn't been the best choice of words, given what had just happened.

"Were you with Grace tonight, by any chance? Your mother was with me when it happened, so that rules her out. Jake's in Asheville, right?"

Apparently the police chief and my mother had been talking about me on their date. I thought about making a crack about them not having anything better to discuss than my life, but I decided to keep it to myself. "He is, and as for Grace, she had a blind date, so I was alone," I said.

"And you didn't speak with anyone, or see someone all evening?"

"The pizza guy came by, but he was gone by six." I finally understood why he was questioning me. "Chief, are you asking me for an alibi?"

He shrugged. "I don't like calling it that, but okay. Is there any chance you can help me out here?"

"Sorry, but I was alone. Who exactly was killed that you'd need an alibi from me?"

"It was Desmond Ray," he said simply, and I suddenly knew why he was asking me.

As I refilled his coffee mug, I explained, "I wasn't exactly thrilled about him using my donuts to attack Gabby's shop, but that didn't mean I wanted to see him dead."

Chief Martin looked older just then, as if the weight of his job was pushing him down. I didn't envy him the questions he had to ask sometimes, but that didn't mean I was okay with being on his suspect list, either. "To tell you the truth, you're not the main one I'm worried about," he admitted.

I didn't need ESP to realize who he was talking about. "I forgot to tell you. Gabby called me at home last night."

That got a flash of anger from him. "Suzanne, don't get yourself in trouble by lying to protect your friend."

"I'm telling the truth. You can check our phone records. She called the house around seven," I said.

"That hardly alibis her for ten o'clock,"

the chief said. As he drew out his notebook and jotted the information down, he asked me, "Just out of curiosity, what did you two talk about?"

I suddenly realized that I'd probably just done Gabby more harm than good. "It's not important," I said, lying through my teeth.

"Suzanne," he prodded, "you might as well tell me. I'll find out eventually."

I had no choice, and I knew it. "She was worried about Desmond stalking her," I said, feeling like a traitor as I spoke.

"Go on," the chief said.

I recounted what Gabby had told me, and then added, "That doesn't mean she shot him."

"It doesn't exactly clear her of suspicion, either. She's next on my list." He took another sip, and then put his cup down. "Thanks again for the coffee."

"Don't forget these," I said as I handed him the other cups.

"I won't," he said. "Sorry about everything tonight."

"I'm not blaming you. You're just doing your job," I said as I let him out.

When I got back in the kitchen, Emma had taken care of nearly all of the cake donuts, and she was just finishing up the small run of the new Orange Crush donuts I was trying out, using the sweet soda instead of milk in the batter. So far it was an epic failure, but if I didn't continue to experiment, how was I going to keep my customers coming in for new treats? I'd get it sooner or later, I was sure of it.

"Did you get all that?" I asked as I tasted a hot donut, and then spat it out again. It wasn't even close to being edible yet. "Those are awful."

"They're even worse than the last batch," Emma agreed with a smile.

"You don't have to sound so happy about it," I said as I threw them all away.

"Are you kidding? Now you can try adding more milk and less soda. At least you'll be heading in the right direction."

"I suppose so," I said. "You never answered me. Did you hear my conversation with the police chief?"

"I did better than that," Emma said with a mischievous smile. "I called Dad, and he heard everything, too."

I wasn't at all pleased with her using her telephone to eavesdrop on my conversation. "Emma, you just crossed the line. You shouldn't have done that."

She looked upset. "I'm sorry. I didn't see

the harm in it," she said.

Emma looked as though she were about to cry, but I couldn't let that get to me. I had an important point to make. "I have to have Chief Martin's trust if he's ever going to tell me anything," I said. "I'm not sure I can patch this up when he finds out what you did."

Emma reached for her telephone. "Don't worry. I know just how to fix it."

I put a hand on hers, stopping her. "Calling your dad is just going to make things worse. What's done is done. Just don't ever do it again, do you understand?"

"I won't," she said. Sometimes I forgot just how young Emma really was. She had a puppylike quality of being eager to please sometimes that made things hard for me, but I'd meant what I'd said before. I couldn't imagine the circumstances where I'd actually fire her. That didn't mean she was going to get away with this free and clear.

By the time we opened, there was a line of folks waiting to get into the donut shop. I had to wonder if it was more about what had just happened nearby than my offerings, but I couldn't be choosy, especially since I was about to start working new hours. I'd change the sign on the door at noon to give people warning about what I was doing, and I knew that I'd get a few grumbles from my regulars, but my mind was made up. If they fussed too much, I might even start closing the shop one day a week. Okay, that was probably an idle threat, but it was a nice thought, imagining what I could do with a day off every week.

George Morris was the first in line, and after I got him coffee and a donut, I waited on everyone else before we had a chance to really talk about what had happened. Once the line was gone, I grabbed a coffee for myself and joined him on the end of the bar so we could have a little privacy as we spoke.

I took a deep breath, and then said with a grim smile, "Before you say a word, I didn't have anything to do with what happened next door last night."

George looked surprised by my comment. "Suzanne, I never dreamed you did, but you're in the middle of it anyway, aren't you?"

It didn't surprise me that my friend knew all about what was going on in April Springs. "What makes you say that? What have you heard?"

George took a sip of his coffee, and then said, "I understand the murder victim used your donuts in a way you'd never intended when you made them."

"They were crullers, not donuts," I said.

George smiled slightly. "Point taken. We are getting involved, aren't we?" George Morris was a retired police officer who took part in my informal investigations. Along with Grace, and even Jake most recently, we tried to find stones that had been unturned by Chief Martin and his staff. It wasn't that our chief of police wasn't fully qualified to do what he did, but some folks would tell a donut shop owner something they wouldn't dream of saying to the cops.

"I'm not sure we should get involved," I said. "It reflects on Gabby, not me. My crullers were just collateral damage, as far as I'm concerned."

"Gabby's another story entirely, though, isn't she?" George asked.

I felt my skin go cold. "They didn't arrest her, did they?"

He shook his head as he explained, "No, but she was at the station for two hours this morning. The chief let her go, but she isn't supposed to leave town. She's in a real mess, Suzanne."

"I'm sorry for that, truly I am, but it still doesn't involve me."

"I'm not sure I agree with you. Have you

discussed it with Jake yet?" George asked. He was a big fan of my boyfriend, and they'd even worked together in the past to give me a hand in my investigations.

"He's lecturing," I said as I glanced at my watch. "I expect to hear from him later today, though."

"I'd be curious to hear what he has to say," George said. "I imagine he won't be any more inclined to let this drop than I am."

I grabbed a pot and refilled his mug. "I don't think so. I've got a feeling he'd rather I didn't get involved with these cases all the time."

"Just let me know if you change your mind." As George pushed his mug away and starred reading the paper, I started cleaning the counter, putting his mug and plate in the bin to be washed.

"Hey, can I buy a donut, lady?" a young man with long sideburns asked at the front.

"Sorry, I got a little distracted," I said as I joined him there. "What can I get for you?"

"Do you have any of those cursed crullers left?" he asked. "I hear they're killers."

I bit my lip a second, and then said, "I don't know what you're talking about. My crullers aren't cursed."

"Come on. A dude bought a dozen yesterday, and now he's dead. How is that not cursed? Don't get me wrong, I'm not complaining. I just want to taste something worth dying for."

"Sorry, but we're all out," I said, though we still had three in the case.

"What about those?" he asked as he pointed to them.

"They've already been sold. The owner's just waiting to pick them up."

He looked at me as though I were crazy, but I held his stare. "I'd be glad to sell you something else, though."

"No, that's okay. The crullers were all I wanted." He left the shop, and it was all I could do not to laugh out loud while he was there.

One of my regulars, Barry Vance, must have been eavesdropping. "You really are holding them for somebody?"

I grabbed a white bag and shoved the last crullers into it. "It's your lucky day, Barry. They're yours, free of charge."

When I tried to hand him the bag, I swore he started to back away. "Thanks anyway, Suzanne, but I'm full."

"They aren't really cursed," I said, but Barry wasn't buying it.

I cleared my throat, and then asked loudly,

"Does anyone want three crullers on the house?"

George saved me from standing up in silence when no one responded. "I'll take 'em," he said.

"You don't have to," I said softly as he approached.

"I don't have to. I want to. Now, am I going to get those, or not?"

"They're all yours," I said as I handed him the bag.

George looked around the dining area, and in particular at Barry, and then reached into the bag, withdrew a cruller, and took a healthy bite. "Man, that's the best thing I've tasted in a long time, Suzanne."

Barry just shook his head, made a mumbled excuse, and then left Donut Hearts. That seemed to break the tension in the air, and most of the folks in the shop went back to their breakfasts.

Emma came up front a little later and handed me a note.

"What's this?" I asked as I unfolded it.

"You had a call, but you were busy, so I took a message."

I looked at the scratches on the paper, and couldn't decipher what she'd written. "What does it say?"

She took the note from me, and as she pointed to different scratches, she said, "It says the book club is canceling their meeting today."

I couldn't believe it. Could Hazel, Jennifer, and Elizabeth honestly believe that I'd had something to do with Desmond's death? I never dreamed my friends would just ditch me like that. "Did they say why?" I asked.

Emma nodded, and pointed back to the note. "It's all there."

I handed it back to her. "Humor me," I said. "You read it."

She took it back, and then read aloud, "Elizabeth's dad is in the hospital, and Jennifer and Hazel are with her for moral support."

"What happened to him?" I asked. "Did he have a heart attack?"

"They didn't say," Emma acknowledged. "Should I have asked?"

"No, it's fine. I should send flowers, though."

"Do you know her dad's name, or even where he is?" Emma asked.

"No. I just assumed it was in April Springs," I admitted.

"Good luck with that," she said as she glanced at the clock. "It's almost eleven. Shouldn't you start shooing people out?"

"Our new hours don't start until tomorrow," I said as I looked around the dining area. We still had seven customers, and I was beginning to wonder if I was making a rash decision. After all, I wasn't in any position to turn away income, no matter how much I needed a break.

Emma must have been able to read my mind. "Don't let this fool you. At least some of the folks are here because of what happened last night," she said softly.

"I don't want to believe it," I said. My customers may have been there showing their loyalty and support, but I didn't think for one second that any of them were there for more ghoulish reasons.

"Want to check that with a show of hands?" Emma asked.

"No, if I'm deluded, I'd rather keep it to myself." I smiled as I swatted her lightly with a towel. "Now, back into the kitchen. We have another hour left."

"Yes, ma'am," she said with a smile. "But not tomorrow."

I didn't think noon would ever come around, but it made me happy that it was the last working one we'd see. As I shooed our last customer out, Emma popped in, boxed the last few donuts, and took the trays in back with her to wash. "Just out of curiosity, how many did we sell during the last hour?"

I did a quick count in my head, and then said, "Four donuts, one coffee, and one chocolate milk."

Emma nodded. "Excellent."

"Why would that make you happy?" I asked, honestly curious about her reaction.

"Hey, if we'd sold four dozen, you might have changed your mind."

"Not a chance," I said. "I called the painter, and he'll be here in the morning to change our sign to reflect 'six to eleven' as our new hours. Until then, this will have to do."

I held up the crude sign I'd made during a lull.

As of today, our hours at Donut Hearts are now six A.M. to eleven A.M. We plan to continue to operate seven days a week, so no worries, and thanks for your understanding!

"What do you think?" I asked.

She took the sign from me, and grabbed the black Magic Marker I'd used to create it. Without a word, she struck through the

84

second line, and added, "The Manage-
ment."

"Shouldn't we reassure our customers that
we aren't going anywhere?" I asked.

"No, let's present them with the facts and
leave the editorializing to people like my
dad."

I frowned at the sign and thought about
what she said. I must have taken longer than
Emma was comfortable with, because she
added, "I've crossed the line again, haven't
I?"

"Not at all," I said as I threw my original
sign away. I wrote another, this one to Emma's suggestion, and then studied it for a
second. "I like it."

"Then let's hang it up and make it official," she said as she handed me our tape.

I hesitated a moment, thinking about the
income we'd lose, but then I realized that it
just wasn't worth the time it cost us both.
Working seven days a week was bad enough,
but the hours I'd been keeping had been
wearing me out. It probably didn't sound
like much of a break to most folks, but I
was actually excited about the extra time I
was buying with the money I was sacrific-
ing.

I taped the sign in place, and then said,

"Let's get cleaned up so we can get out of here."

As I spoke, the donut shop's telephone rang.

"Donut Hearts," I said.

The woman's voice on the other end was hoarse from crying, it seemed to me. "Suzanne, could you come next door? I need you."

It was Gabby, sounding as contrite and frightened as I'd ever heard her in my life.

"I'll be right there."

Before I could hang up, Gabby added, "Suzanne, come in the back way."

"Why should I do that?" I asked.

She paused, and then admitted, "You don't want to run into the reporters, do you?"

"There are reporters at your front door?" I asked, incredulous that the murder had brought attention to our small town.

"I had to close the shop," she said, the worry clear in her voice. "They're from Charlotte, Asheville, and Hickory, and of course Ray Blake is out there, too. Emma's dad appears to be enjoying himself."

"Be by the back door, I'll be there in two minutes," I said.

I was tempted to walk outside to see the reporters stalking the shop next door, but fought the impulse and walked into the kitchen instead. "Emma, you can lock up after you finish the dishes. I'm going next door."

"That was Gabby on the phone?" she asked.

I nodded. "She needs me over there, and she sounded desperate. She even asked me to come in the back way." I didn't want to tell Emma about the press in front, especially her own father. The two of them had had their share of clashes in the past, and I didn't want to do anything to add to them.

"Go. I'll take care of things here."

I grabbed my jacket and headed out the back door, relocking it once I was outside. I glanced down the grass strip between our businesses, and found it still hard to believe that someone had been murdered there the night before, despite the police tape still in place and the trampled grass all around where the body had been found. What had Desmond been doing there, and why had the killer chosen that spot to strike? An unintended, or perhaps fully planned, result of the location was that suspicion had been cast both on Gabby and me. I was no stranger to police investigations from both sides, but I realized that it was new to Gabby, and no matter how brave a front she put on, I fully understood how devastating an accusation could be, whether it was voiced or just unspoken.

Someone must have spotted me as I lingered, because I heard a shout, but before they could do anything, I hurried to the back of ReNEWed.

I knocked on the door where Gabby sometimes took deliveries, and then had to knock again before it finally opened.

"Sorry," she said, dabbing at her eyes with a tissue. It was obvious that she'd been crying for some time, and I felt real sympathy for the woman, despite her general attitude and the grief she'd given me over the years. Normally a stylish fashion plate, Gabby looked haggard in rumpled clothing and her hair in disarray; for the first time since I'd known her, every moment of her real age showed on her face and the stoop of her posture. "Thanks for coming, Suzanne."

"Of course. Gabby, I'll do whatever I can to help," I said as I came inside. The door to the shop was closed, and we were in the storeroom.

"Let's go into my office so we can talk," she said, and I followed her in. While I'd had room for just a small office space in my donut shop/restored train depot, Gabby hadn't been constrained by square footage, and had put in a lavish desk, bright wallpaper, and three chairs in hers. She sat comfortably behind her big desk, and I settled into one of the chairs opposite her.

"How are you holding up?" I asked, desperate for something, anything, to say.

"It was awful. I was at the police station most of the night, and when they let me out, I came here instead of going home. That's what I should have done, but I wasn't thinking straight."

"Would you like me to take you home now? You could leave your car here, and I'll bring you back to get it later. My Jeep's just across the street."

I started to get up, and Gabby's commanding voice broke through, for just a moment. "I appreciate the offer, but before we do that, we need to talk," she insisted, and I settled back into the chair.

"I'm listening," I said.

"First, let me get this off my chest. I didn't steal from Jean Ray, and I didn't kill Desmond, either." The words came out in a rush, as though she'd repeated them over and over in her mind before she trusted herself to say them out loud.

"I never thought that you did," I said. At that moment, I believed it, no matter how many doubts I'd entertained in the past.

Gabby was many things, several of them quite unlikable, but I didn't see her as a thief or a killer.

"You're in the minority, then," she said as she dabbed at another tear. "Chief Martin is acting as though I'm some kind of menace to society. I was amazed when he let me go, but I have a feeling that it's just a matter of time before he finds a reason to throw me in jail. That's where you come in."

I still wasn't sure what she had in mind. "What can I do?"

"Find out who killed Desmond Ray for me," she said. "You can do it, Suzanne. I've seen the way you've worked in the past on other cases. You've even enlisted my help on occasion, and now I'm asking you to return the favor."

"Gabby, I wouldn't know where to begin."

She frowned at me. "That should be obvious. You need to speak with Jean Ray. I have a feeling she holds the key to what really happened."

"You don't think Jean murdered her own nephew, do you?" I asked. Jean didn't have a malicious bone in her body, at least as far as I'd ever seen. I knew that no one could tell what a murderer looked like, but Jean was as far from the stereotype as one woman could be.

"I don't know what to think," Gabby admitted. "It's difficult to imagine, but then again, I never thought of her as a liar before, either. If she didn't do it, I'm willing to bet that she has a good idea who might have killed her nephew. The two of them were really close."

Gabby was right about that. If I were going to investigate, it would be the perfect place to start. But I still wasn't convinced it was something I should be doing at all, despite her urging and George's expectation that I would dig into Desmond Ray's murder.

I had one last very real concern that I had to voice. "Why would Jean talk to me? I was there when you and Desmond fought yesterday. He threatened me, too, remember?"

"Don't you see? That gives you a perfect excuse. Tell Jean that you feel bad about the way you and Desmond spoke yesterday, and you want to find out who killed him to make amends. If you make yourself her ally instead of her adversary, she'll tell you anything."

"Even if her finger points straight at you as the murderer?" I asked.

"I would expect nothing less, given the circumstances," Gabby said, "but you have to push her until she tells you something more." Gabby opened a drawer, pulled out a long envelope, and then pushed it toward me. "I don't expect you to do this for free, Suzanne. I'm willing to pay you for your help."

I was tempted to peek inside to see how much she thought my aid was worth, but I knew better. I shoved the envelope back and said, "I don't charge to help my friends, Gabby."

She looked startled by my admission. "Then you consider us friends, as well? There have been times in the past when I haven't been sure."

Gabby had a point, and there was no use denying it. "We have our disagreements from time to time, but you said it yourself. There aren't many women who own small businesses in April Springs, and those of us that do need to stick together."

Gabby frowned, and after a moment, she said, "That wasn't exactly a declaration of fealty, was it?"

"We're friends, okay?" I said, probably just a little too tartly, but Gabby had a tendency to bring that out in me.

Instead of being offended by my tone of voice, she actually looked pleased. "Good. That's better. You are not to use kid gloves with me, Suzanne. Is that clear?"

"Be careful. I'm willing to bet you're not going to be happy with my questions for you," I said.

"I'm a tough old broad, as we both know," she said with a slight smile. "Ask away."

I took a deep breath and plunged in, realizing just how inflammatory what I was about to ask would be.

"Gabby, have you ever stolen anything from any of your clients in the past?"

CHAPTER 5

"What possible relevance does that have to your investigation?" Gabby asked coldly. Her good nature had plummeted to a frigid stare in an instant, but I couldn't let that stop me.

"It's something I need to know," I said. "I don't want to tell Jean you've never done it before if it's not true."

Gabby appeared to think about that, and then shrugged. "I suppose it's relevant. You need to define your idea of stealing."

Was she *trying* to be difficult? "Taking something that's not yours. It's pretty much everyone's definition, isn't it?"

Gabby seemed to consider that, and then finally said, "Suzanne, who is to say what true ownership means? If I buy a box full of books at a yard sale and find a hundred-dollar bill inside one being used as a bookmark, don't I own it, though it wasn't specifically being offered for sale?"

"Are you saying that there actually *was* ten thousand bucks and a diamond brooch in Jean's jacket?" I couldn't believe she was confessing the theft to me.

"Of course not," Gabby said, a little too quickly for my taste, as though she'd been prepared to make the denial as soon as I'd asked the original question. "But from time to time, I discover small, forgotten things. Is it my obligation to always return them?"

I wasn't quite sure how to answer it. "I'd have to think about it before I could give you an answer one way or the other," I said.

"I've wrestled with my stance countless times since I've been in business," she admitted. "Would you like to hear the standard I've set for myself?"

It was an intriguing conversation about an issue that I'd never have to deal with in my donut and coffee shop business. I had to wonder exactly where I would have drawn the line myself. "Please enlighten me," I said.

She nodded. "First, if its value is equal to or less than that hundred-dollar bookmark we discussed earlier, second, if I don't know beyond a doubt exactly who the original owner was, and third, if I can possess it in clear conscience, then I usually keep whatever I find as a sort of salvage fee."

"And if its value is greater?"

"I do everything in my power to track down the original owner and return it. Believe me, that's not always easy, considering the estate sales and blind buys I make throughout the year. Things have a way of getting jumbled, and for all I know, I unknowingly pass along objects of even greater value myself without even realizing it."

I doubted Gabby let anything go out onto her sales floor without a thorough inspection first, but I wasn't about to challenge her on that. "I can use that, I guess."

"You'll have to. Is there anything else you'd like to know?"

I leaned back in my chair. "Make yourself comfortable. We're just getting started."

She was clearly surprised by the instruction, but she nodded her agreement. "Go on, then. I'm at your disposal."

I took a deep breath, and then plunged in. "When was the last time you saw Desmond Ray, to the minute, if you can remember?"

Gabby just huffed instead of answering.

"If you want my help, you're going to have to tell me," I said. "I'm not being nosy. I don't have access to police interviews, so we have to start fresh."

"I understand," she said. "The last time I

saw him was when I was with you."

"In front of your shop when he was throwing crullers," I clarified.

"Yes, of course." Her eyes narrowed for a moment, and she added, "But you saw him later than that, didn't you?"

"Like I told you, we ran into each other at the bank," I admitted again. Had Gabby already forgotten her telephone call to me when she'd admitted seeing him staked out in front of her place all afternoon the day before? "You didn't see him again by yourself? I thought you told me that he was in front of your shop yesterday."

Gabby looked at me a little petulantly. "I assumed you meant when I actually spoke to him face-to-face. We spoke briefly on the telephone, and he camped outside my shop, but when he was there, we didn't share a single word. I've already gone over my telephone conversation with the man with you. Surely you still remember what I said."

It was another jab, but I didn't mind. Maybe Gabby was getting some of her spirit back, and if she was going to fight this, she was going to need every ounce of spunk she could muster. "I remember," I admitted.

"And when was the last time you spoke to Jean?" I asked, an innocent question that was voiced more out of curiosity than anything else.

"At the police station this morning," Gabby admitted.

"What did she have to say?" I asked. This was certainly new information.

Gabby looked uncomfortable recounting it, but when she started to protest, she must have noticed how intent I was on getting an answer. "She asked me why I killed Desmond," Gabby reluctantly admitted. "I told her I was innocent, but she didn't believe me. Neither did anyone else at the station, as far as that's concerned. I could see the accusations in their gazes as I walked past them."

"Nobody said this was going to be easy," I said. "You may have to endure worse than that before we can prove you didn't do it."

"Do you have any more questions?" she asked.

"Let me get my Jeep," I said as I stood. I'd probably gotten all I was going to out of her at the moment, but at least the dam had been broken and she knew our ground rules. "I'll run you home."

"I appreciate the offer, but you've got work to do, don't you?"

"The donut shop's closed for the day," I said. Being up all night must have skewed Gabby's sense of the time of day, and I noticed she wasn't wearing a watch. Her office was without a window, so it could have been any time of day or night as far as we were concerned.

"I'm talking about your investigation," Gabby said.

"Right, I get that. But how are you getting home?"

"Don't worry about that. I'll call Muriel. She owes me a few dozen favors, so I'm going to collect one right now." I knew Gabby had done a great deal for Muriel Stevens in the past, even driving her to West Virginia to stay with family so she could escape a killer on the loose in April Springs who was intent on doing her in. This was a small thing to ask in return, and I imagined Muriel would be happy to oblige.

I stood, and headed for the front door without realizing it.

"You can't go out there, Suzanne," Gabby said as she took hold of my shoulder.

"No, of course. I wasn't thinking."

When she opened the back door, I stood in the shop for a moment before I stepped out. "I can't make any promises, Gabby, but I'll do my best."

To my great shock, Gabby leaned forward and hugged me. "I know you will. Thank you, Suzanne."

"I just hope something turns up," I said as I stepped outside.

As Gabby started to close the door, she said, "You can do it. I have faith in you."

As the dead bolt slid closed, I thought, *At least one of us does.*

Whether I liked it or not, I had been dragged into the middle of another crime. I hadn't been able to tell Gabby no, and I was just hoping that I'd be able to help her. I understood that the chief of police wouldn't be thrilled with my meddling, but at least Jake had started to come around when it came to what I could contribute to a murder investigation. I would have loved to have him help me now, since Asheville wasn't that far away, and if he had any breaks, I was going to do my best to convince him that his assistance would be welcome.

In the meantime, I would go see my partner in crime, or crime solving, at any rate. I just hoped Grace had the opportunity, and more important, the inclination, to help me this time. Gabby and I had a seesaw relationship, but between her and Grace, it was all negative. There was something about the two women's personalities that tended to generate sparks, but I hoped my best friend could see past all of that and realize what really mattered, keeping someone innocent from being punished for a crime they didn't commit.

If I could only persuade Grace that Gabby was innocent and deserved our help.

"Hey, stranger," Grace said when I showed up on her doorstep. "Where have you been? I was expecting you here right after you closed the shop for the day."

"Why? We didn't have plans, did we?" I asked as Grace took my coat.

"No, but I phoned the shop and spoke with Emma. She told me you were at Gabby's, and I figured it wouldn't be long before you came here. Want some coffee?"

"Sure, why not?" I said.

As I followed her into the kitchen, Grace said, "Suzanne, we're digging into Desmond Ray's murder, aren't we?"

I had to laugh, despite the seriousness of the subject. "I should know better than to try and do anything under the radar in April Springs."

"Honestly, I imagine that there's a lot more anonymity in a big city than a small town," Grace said as she handed me a cup. "And in answer to your unspoken question, I accept. I've got a light schedule for the next week, so I'm ready to help in any way

I can. I'm dying to hear what Gabby had to say."

I recounted her denials as we sat in the kitchen drinking coffee, and after I finished, I handed her my empty mug.

"That was great," I said. "It's nice to be waited on for a change."

"Glad to be of service," she said as she rinsed our mugs and then put them in the sink.

"To tell you the truth, I still can't believe Gabby came to me for help," I said.

Grace nodded in agreement. "It must have been surreal hearing her ask you. Are you telling me she wasn't the least bit snippy with you when you spoke?"

I remembered a few times in our conversation when Gabby had allowed echoes of her acerbic attitude out. "I wouldn't go that far, but she's clearly afraid, there was no hiding it."

"Who can blame her? I'm not the woman's biggest fan, but her being accused of murder makes me sympathetic toward her." She paused, and then asked, "This may be a silly question, but we don't think there's any chance she actually did it, do we?"

"Let's just say I'm inclined to believe her," I said after hesitating for a moment. "But you should know that if we uncover any evidence to the contrary, we're handing it over to Chief Martin. Agreed?"

"You won't have a problem convincing me of that," she said. "So, where should we get started?"

"I haven't had lunch yet, have you? I'm starving, and I'm not at all sure how much investigating I feel like doing on an empty stomach. Have you eaten yet?"

She glanced at her watch. "I had breakfast four hours ago, so sure, I could eat. Should we go to the Boxcar?"

"Why not?" I asked. "I'm always in the mood for something from Trish's place."

Grace nodded as we walked out into the hallway. "Then it's settled. Lunch first, and crime fighting after."

"That sounds like a plan," I said.

We were heading into the Boxcar Grille as my ex-husband, Max, was coming out. There was a quite pretty young and leggy brunette with him, and though she looked a little familiar, I knew that I'd probably never seen her before. Was this the Great Impersonator's latest in a long line of conquests?

I was about to make a snippy remark when the woman did the oddest thing. She threw her arms around me in an embrace that nearly knocked me off my feet.

"Excuse me," I said, trying to untangle

myself from her. Was she on some kind of medication, acting like that?

"Suzanne, don't you recognize me?" the young lady asked as she allowed me to finally break free.

I took a step back, and then it hit me. This pretty young lady was indeed someone I knew. "Ashley, is that you?"

She twirled around, her coat spinning out from her body for just a moment. "In the flesh. How have you been? I've missed you so much."

Ashley was Max's little niece, though she wasn't so little anymore. "What's it been, five years?" I asked.

"Closer to six," she said. Ashley turned to Max and slugged his arm, not at all playfully, but with force behind the blow. From the way he winced, I could tell that she hadn't held anything back. "This guy is an idiot for what he did to you, and don't think I haven't told him that a thousand times. I voted to throw him out of the family and keep you when you two divorced, but I was outnumbered." She looked hard at Max, and then added, "Not that the vote wasn't close."

"Hey, I've apologized countless times," Max said.

"Not enough yet, as far as I'm concerned,"

Ashley said.

I couldn't believe how lovely she'd turned out to be. "Ashley, what are you doing here? How long are you going to be in town? Maybe we could have lunch."

She frowned as she explained, "I'm headed off to school, and I thought I'd stop by and see my uncle, the scoundrel."

"Hey, some of your other uncles are worse than me," Max protested.

"Don't even try to convince me of that," Ashley said.

"Where are you going to school?" I asked her.

"I'm at UNC-Asheville, and I just love it."

She must have seen something in my face. "What's wrong, Aunt Suzanne? Did I say something wrong?"

It was odd being called aunt, since I was an only child, and I figured the statute of limitations had run out on my being related to her, but I didn't correct her, since I kind of liked the way it sounded, coming from her. "No, but my boyfriend's teaching there."

"He's a professor? What's his name? What does he teach?" she asked the questions in a rapid-fire staccato.

"I thought he was still with the state

police?" Max asked.

"Keeping tabs on him, are you?" Grace asked.

"No. You know how it is, though. April Springs isn't all that big. Word gets around."

Grace nodded, her expression showing clearly that she didn't believe him for an instant. "Sure it does, Max. Keep saying that, and somebody might believe it someday."

"Forget about him," Ashley said dismissively. "What's the scoop on your boyfriend?"

I explained, "He's not a professor, at least not full-time. Jake is lecturing for a friend in the criminal justice department."

"Maybe I'll audit one of his classes," Ashley said, grinning to show her dimples.

I nodded, and smiled as I added, "You should do to him what you just did to me. Walk up to him out of the blue and give him a big hug, then call him Uncle Jake. Let me know what he says when you do."

She had a spark in her eyes as she answered, "You know, I might just do it." Ashley glanced at her watch, and then added, "It's been fun catching up, but I've got to run. I'm going to be late as it is." She turned back to Max, who took a step back as she moved toward him. Instead of another slug, though, she wrapped him up in her embrace. "Stay out of trouble, Uncle Max."

"Right back at you," Max said affectionately.

I wasn't sure what I mourned more about the death of my marriage, losing a husband, or the wonderful family that came with him. I'd tried to keep in touch with some of them, but it had been awkward, so after a while, I'd stopped. Seeing Ashley made me regret it, but there wasn't much I could do about it now.

After she was gone, Max turned back to Grace and me. "I'd offer to take you ladies out to lunch, but I've already eaten."

"Thanks anyway," I said.

Both Max and Grace looked surprised by my mild tone, but seeing Ashley had made me a little mellower in dealing with my cheating ex-husband.

Grace and I stopped up front and decided to order club sandwiches as a change of pace since we were in a bit of a hurry, and then we made our way to one of the tables in back.

Once we were seated, Grace asked, "The girl got to you, didn't she?"

"What makes you say that?" I asked.

"Come on, you were actually gracious with Max just then. Ashley is quite the fireball, isn't she?"

I laughed. "She always was. I just wish I could see Jake's face when she gives him one of her hugs."

"Was that the best idea?" Grace asked softly.

I had no idea what she was talking about. "What do you mean?"

Grace shook her head. "I don't think I'd point that beauty at any man of mine. She might still be your once-upon-a-time niece, but she's turned into a gorgeous young lady."

"I trust Jake. Besides, he prefers his women a little more mature," I said.

"But not that mature," she answered, and we both laughed.

"Did I miss something?" Trish said as she brought us our clubs and two sweet teas.

"Just a pair of fools laughing," I said.

"But not old fools," Grace added.

"No, I'd say we're just the right age," I said with a smile.

Trish had no way of knowing what we'd just been joking about, but she was still game enough to smile at our banter. "Then let's make it three of a kind," she said, adding her own laugh to the mix.

After we ate, Grace and I paid for our lunches and then made our way outside. I buttoned my jacket to ward off the sudden cold breeze, and I noticed my friend do the same. It wouldn't be long until our nights were short, and our days cold, but I was ready for a change. Late autumn was one of my favorite times of year, a little past the glorious display of leaves but before hard freezes set in. "Where to?" Grace asked.

I didn't even have to think about our next destination.

"It's time to speak with Jean Ray and see what we can learn about her nephew Desmond, but first we need to go by the donut shop."

"Why?" Grace asked. "You're long past closing time."

"I left a few loose ends when I went to see Gabby, and I'm hoping Emma boxed up the donuts that were left over so we can take them as an icebreaker."

Grace laughed. "You're not above using your donuts to wedge your way into tight places, are you?"

"Why not? It's a rare person who can turn down a dozen free donuts. I'm glad you decided to finally give my decadences a try."

She'd loved the donut, and had immediately asked for another.

"What can I say? You convinced me that not everything I eat has to be healthy. One donut a month isn't going to kill me."

"Wow, can I use that phrase in my next ad campaign? You really have a way with words."

She grinned at me. "What can I say? It's a gift."

Grace pulled up in front of the donut shop, and as I got out, I said, "You don't have to come in, if you don't want. I shouldn't be more than ten minutes."

"Take your time. I have a few phone calls to make anyway."

I left her in the car and walked into the shop. It was always a little bit like coming home when I came back in, even if I'd only been gone a few hours. The plum faux finish of the walls and floor were soothing to the eye, and the comfy couches and chairs made it feel more like a living room than a donut shop. Only the display cases and the long counter with stools made it look like a place where someone could buy donuts. The old train depot purchase had been a whim born out of desperation, despair from a recently failed marriage, but it had become so much a part of me that I couldn't ever imagine doing anything else with my life.

I expected to see dirty floors and a display area in need of cleaning, but to my happy surprise, the front of the shop was spotless, and to my further delight, two dozen donuts were boxed and ready for me. Emma had cleaned up after me, and I felt a twinge of regret that she'd been forced to do it, but happy that my sole employee, coworker really, and now assistant manager, had stepped up in my absence. It was great having Emma as part of my team, and I'd have to find some special way to thank her. I couldn't exactly afford a real raise, or any bonus for that matter, but I could give her a few extra hours of sleep sometime in the next few days. I knew that meant as much to her as a little extra money in her college fund.

The kitchen was clean, as well. I had to call Emma and tell her how impressed I was with her work ethic, so I went into my tiny office, and as I picked up the telephone, I saw a note from her on top of a large envelope. Putting the note aside for the moment, I peeked into the envelope and saw the cash register report and the day's deposit slip all ready to go.

When I looked at the note, I had to laugh.

Hey, Suzanne,

I knew you'd be busy with Gabby, so I took the liberty of closing the shop. I'm beat, so I'm heading home. Hope you survived the ordeal.

Don't worry about the overtime; I'll swap you an hour of sleep tomorrow for what I took care of today. If that arrangement's okay with you, there's no need to call. If not, let me know and I'll be there bright and early tomorrow.

Emma

Tidbit Balls

These are fairly easy, quick, and can often be made with items you've already got. A good place to start if you're nervous about dipping a toe into the donut-making water!

Ingredients

Mixed
- 1 egg, beaten
- 3/4 cup whole milk
- 1/4 cup butter, melted

Sifted
- 1 1/2 cups [sifted] all-purpose flour
- 1/4 cup sugar, white granulated
- 1 tablespoon baking powder
- 1 teaspoon nutmeg
- 1/2 teaspoon cinnamon
- A pinch of salt

Directions

In a bowl, beat the egg, and then add the milk and melted butter, mixing until smooth. In a separate bowl, sift together the flour, sugar, baking powder, nutmeg, cinnamon, and salt. Slowly add the dry to the wet, and mix thoroughly. Drop dough into oil from a small cookie scoop or a teaspoon. Fry in hot canola oil (360 to 370 degrees F) 1 to 2 minutes, turning halfway through, or until golden brown. Confectioner's sugar is good topping for these after they've drained on a paper towel.

Yield: 6–8 balls

CHAPTER 6

I picked up the phone and dialed Emma's cell phone number. "It's Suzanne. Thanks for taking care of things here today."

There was a touch of disappointment in her voice when she asked, "Does that mean I don't get to sleep in tomorrow?"

"Actually, you read my mind. There's just one problem, though."

"The books balanced; I checked them twice," Emma said quickly.

"Everything here is perfect. That's why I want you to take two hours to sleep in instead of the one you offered."

She squealed in delight, and then said, "Suzanne, you are the best boss ever."

"I try," I said. "See you tomorrow."

"It's going to be like taking a minivacation," she said.

"I don't see how," I said with a laugh.

"Trust me, you should try it sometime."

"When pigs bark at the moon, and men

want to talk about their feelings," I said.

"In other words, never," she said, giggling, and then hung up.

That wasn't entirely fair, not about the pigs, but the crack about men. I'd had my share of strong, silent types, but the two men I'd been most attracted to in my life — Max and Jake — had both learned to open up to me, given enough time and nudges in the right direction. Max had sealed his own fate sleeping with another woman, but I had high hopes for Jake, even though we were taking things glacially slow. His spirit had nearly been crushed when his wife and child had died in a car accident, and I was thrilled that he was trying so hard to move on with me. If I could hear him say he loved me just once, I wouldn't ever ask him to say it again, but for now, I promised myself to be content with what I had, a man who cared deeply about me, and one I could feel the same way about.

I tucked the note from Emma into my top desk drawer, and then grabbed the donuts and the envelope with the deposit in it.

Grace was deep in conversation when I got back to her car, so I waited just outside of it until she finished. As I looked at the old abandoned railroad tracks, I saw the oddest thing. A big, burly man with unruly black hair and dressed in a pair of faded overalls was studying the nearly buried track as though it were the most fascinating thing in the world.

I couldn't help myself; my curiosity was too strong. I put the donuts on a bench near Grace's car and walked over to him.

He was so focused on what he was looking at that he must not have noticed me approach. "What's so fascinating?" I asked him.

I thought he was going to jump out of his skin when he looked at me. "You startled me," he said.

"Clearly," I replied. "My name's Suzanne Hart." I looked down at the twin iron rails. "You know, I've seen those tracks all of my life, but I've never been as interested in them as you are right now."

"I'm James Settle. They're a bit of history, aren't they?" he asked.

"I like them," I said. "I just didn't realize anyone else cared about them."

"Are you kidding? Do you have any idea what I can do with the metal?"

I had no idea what he was talking about, but suddenly I wasn't all that thrilled with his presence. "Mr. Settle, I'm sure they're worth something on the open market, but they belong to the town."

He shook his head. "Actually, that's not true. They were the railroad's property all along, and since the line is now defunct, they're in the public domain. I can make a thousand bookends out of these."

"Is that true?" I asked, horrified by the idea that anyone could step in and take a part of our history.

He nodded. "I'm on my way to city hall to file for a permit to remove them, and then I'm all set."

I didn't say a word as he walked off, but I did grab my cell phone.

I happened to know the older man who ran the permit office for April Springs. He'd just gotten the job, and he liked me and my donuts.

"Henry? It's Suzanne Hart," I said.

"Suzanne, how are you?"

"I'm good. Listen, I need a favor. A guy's about to come in to get a permit to tear up our railroad tracks. Is there any way to stop him?"

Henry whistled. "I don't know about that. It's a tall order."

I said quickly, "I'm not asking you to do anything illegal, or something that might get you fired. I just want to slow him down long enough to find out if he's legit."

Henry paused a few moments, and then I

118

heard a shredder operate in the background. Had he forgotten all about me? I was about to hang up when he came back on the line. "Sorry about that, I had to take care of something."

"I know you're busy. I'm sorry to bother you."

I was about to hang up when he said, "Hold on a second. Now, what were you asking me about?"

"I wanted to know if you could slow the permit process for a man who wants to tear out the railroad tracks." Henry had retired after working thirty years with a large industrial company and had moved to April Springs soon after. I knew the man was in his mid-seventies, at least. Could he be losing it a little?

"Goodness, I'm afraid he's not going to be able to do anything. I just accidently shredded the last of our permits, and I can't issue any until I get the next shipment from Raleigh."

The old fox had known the exact thing he could do to slow the process. "When exactly will that be?"

"At least a week," he admitted. "Does that give you enough time?"

I couldn't help but smile. "That would be great. Next time you come by the shop, the donuts are on the house."

"I can't take anything that might be construed as a bribe," he answered, "but thanks for the offer."

I'd find a way to slip him some free donuts somehow, but for now, the problem was on hold until I could come up with a way to keep James Settle from destroying part of our history.

When I got back to Grace's car, she was off the telephone and staring at me. I retrieved the donuts on the bench and joined her in her car.

She didn't start it, though. "What was that all about?"

"What?" I asked.

"Don't play coy with me, Suzanne. I saw you talking to that man."

I nodded. "He was going to tear up the tracks, can you believe it?"

Grace shook her head. "It's not right. Did you stop him?"

"I did the next best thing," I admitted without going into any more detail.

"You're not telling me the rest of it, are you?"

"I don't want to violate a trust," I said.

Grace knew that I wouldn't budge when it came to my word, so she started the car. "Are we going straight to Jean's?"

"After we swing by the bank, we can head over there."

"Sounds good."

After the bank deposit, we drove to Jean's house in Grace's company car. Something occurred to me, so I looked over at her and asked, "By the way, I forgot to ask you earlier. How was your date last night?"

She glanced at me for a second, and then said, "It was okay."

"Just okay? Come on, you can do better than that. I want details."

Grace slowed her car down a little, but I wasn't at all certain that it was intentional. "Why do you ask? Did someone say something to you about it?"

She was being pretty defensive about the whole thing. "Grace, no one said a word to me. Why are you acting so oddly all of a sudden?"

"No reason," she said. "Jean lives on Claremont Avenue, right?"

"Her house number is 42," I said. "Stop being so evasive. Was it so bad that you don't even want to talk about it?"

"Just the opposite," Grace admitted. "I don't want to jinx it by talking about it with you."

I'd never heard her say anything like that before. "Hey, that's not fair. You get to meddle in my life all the time. Give me something, anyway."

Grace seemed to think about it, and then said, "You're right. I'm being silly. It's just been a while since I've felt something had potential."

"That's wonderful," I said, "but maybe you're right. If something happens to ruin it, I don't want you to think that telling me had anything to do with it."

She seemed to think about that, and then said, "Tell you what I'll do. If we're still seeing each other after three dates, I'll tell you all about him."

"Why three dates?" I asked as we pulled up in front of number 42.

"If he lasts that long, he might just be a keeper. Thanks for understanding," she said.

We stopped in front of Jean Ray's place, and I couldn't help wondering what the rambling old place had looked like when it had been newly built. In my mind, I replaced the faded and chipped paint with fresh, gleaming coats of forest green and cream, and then saw the lawn landscaped instead of being filled with overgrown weeds and clutters of leaves everywhere. If Jean had money, as that ten grand and diamond brooch implied, she clearly hadn't spent any of it keeping up the exterior of her place. I could only imagine what the inside looked like.

We rang the doorbell, and Jean opened it. She was a heavyset woman with hair frosted so deeply it was tough to even guess what her original color had been. I'd always admired her broad smile and ready, infectious laugh, but for the first time since I'd known her, she looked immeasurably sad.

"We're so sorry for your loss," I said.

"Thank you, Suzanne," she replied, and then turned to Grace. "And you are?"

"Grace Gauge," she said as she extended a hand.

Jean didn't look all that pleased by Grace's presence, but I'd had no way of knowing that's how she would react. If I'd known, I would have had Grace wait in the car.

There was an awkward silence, and I was beginning to wonder if she was going to let us in. There was just one more thing I could do.

I thrust the boxes of donuts forward and said, "These are for you."

Jean nodded, smiled ever so slightly, and then sighed as she took them from me. "Won't you come in?"

"Thanks," I said, and Grace walked in behind me. She shot one eyebrow skyward as she did, but I just shrugged. It was amazing how many ideas we could convey with a shake or a nod.

Inside, I was expecting more of what we'd seen outside, imagining shabby furniture and dead plants crowding the corners. Instead, the place looked as though it had been plucked from a recent catalogue shoot. Fine furniture with crisp upholstery, oriental rugs bright with color, and beautifully polished hardwood floors greeted us. Grace, usually the more tactful one of us, said, "It looks so different in here."

Jean stared at her. "Different from what?"

Grace started to stammer so I knew that I had to save her. "The exterior doesn't prepare you for the loveliness of the interior, does it?" It was as diplomatic a way as I could come up with to explain our reactions.

Jean nodded, and that slight smile returned. "I rarely go outside, so why bother keeping it up? Here is where I live, not out there." She paused, and then added, "Besides, burglars would never guess what I have in here based on what they see outside."

She had a point. "Have you ever *had* a problem with burglars?"

"Of course not. Don't you see? That means it's working."

It was a skewed sense of logic, but I'd heard worse over the years. As the three of us entered her formal living room, Jean said, "I'd offer you coffee, but I'm afraid I'm all out. I find I don't have the heart to shop."

"Would it help if I got some for you?" Grace volunteered, surprising me.

"That would be delightful. If I may, could I impose on you to pick up a few other things? It was Desmond's shopping day today. I don't know what I'll do without him." She looked as though she were on the verge of crying, but she managed to hold it back at the last second.

"Make a list, and I'll take care of it," Grace said.

"Wonderful. I'll be back in flash," Jean said.

As soon as she was gone, I turned to Grace. "What's going on?"

"She knows you, Suzanne, but I'm a stranger to her. Surely you saw how disappointed she was when I showed up, too, didn't you? I've got a hunch that Jean will speak a great deal more freely if I'm not here. Besides, it wouldn't kill me to help her out. She seems so lost."

"She is," I said. I leaned over and hugged my friend.

"What was that for?" Grace asked.

125

"For being such a good friend," I said, "to me, and anyone else who needs one."

"You're all very welcome," Grace said.

Two minutes later Jean reappeared with a list, and a single hundred-dollar bill. "That should cover it, and as I always told Desmond, you may keep the change."

I glanced at what she'd written over Grace's shoulder and realized that it would be some tip, more than the cost of the items listed.

"That's not necessary," Grace said.

Jean frowned, and then snatched the hundred back. I was amazed by how quickly she'd moved. "It's the only way I'll hear of it," she said.

Grace knew it would be crazy to fight it. "As you wish."

Jean nodded and began to hand her back the bill, but Grace wouldn't take it.

Jean looked perplexed. "What's wrong?"

"I need to know that it's okay with you if I donate what's left to the April Springs Humane Society. I was talking to Patty Lee yesterday, and she told me they were low on just about everything and needed donations."

Jean nodded. "One moment." She returned a few seconds later with another, matching hundred in her hand. "Please pass this along, as well."

"I wasn't fishing for donations," Grace said.

"Then be glad you caught one, anyway," Jean said. "I love animals. In many ways, they're the only ones we can really trust, aren't they?"

I didn't know about that, but I wasn't going to counter her argument. If I tried, Grace would never get out of there.

"Back soon," Grace said, and then walked out the door.

"She's quite kind, isn't she?" Jean asked once my best friend was gone.

"Grace has a big heart, a quick wit, and a wicked sense of humor," I admitted.

"Desmond would have liked her," Jean said, tearing up a little. I didn't think there was a prayer that the two of them would have gotten along, but I wasn't about to tell her that.

I was about to say something else when Jean added, "I was so happy when he finally broke up with that awful Katie Wilkes."

"Had they been dating long?" I asked. She might be a perfect suspect. There was nothing like a romantic interest scorned, whether man or woman, to bring out the "crazy" in folks who ordinarily were quite sound of mind.

"For nearly two years. Katie was under the impression that they were engaged, and when Desmond told her three days ago that it wasn't the case, she screamed at him in front of me. It was awful to witness; I've got to tell you it nearly broke my heart to hear the things that she said."

"Desmond meant the world to you, didn't he?"

She nodded, and then sighed deeply before going on. "I don't know how I'm going to function without him. I suppose Jenny will do, as little as I like the girl. Goodness knows she's hinted enough times that she would be thrilled to live with me here if I ever needed her."

That name was new to me. "May I ask who Jenny is?"

Jean motioned toward a picture frame, and I saw a plain-looking woman with mousy brown hair and a pointy chin staring back at me. "She's Desmond's cousin. Jenny Ray is a bit cloying for my taste, always too eager to please. Desmond was never afraid to speak his mind, and we had some spirited discussions after he moved in here with me, but it made me feel alive. Jenny, I'm afraid, has the spine of her mother, and my late dear sister was many things, but she never possessed a backbone in her life. I have health issues, though, so I suppose it's necessary for her to move in." Another tear tracked down her cheek. "I don't know how I'm going to face cleaning out Desmond's room. The police were here until late last night, and they told me they were finished with it, but what do I do now?"

"Grace and I can take care of it for you, if you'd like," I blurted out. I knew my friend wouldn't mind me volunteering her services for the duty with me. We'd learned early on that there was no better way to get to know someone than to pack away their things.

"I could never ask you to do that," Jean said. She looked shocked by the idea, but I couldn't let this opportunity pass us by, especially since the police were finished with their examination.

"You aren't asking, I'm volunteering," I said. "You shouldn't have to face this, and you just said you need Jenny here." I looked around the room, surprised she hadn't already staked her claim on her aunt. "Where is she, by the way?"

"She's in Tampa visiting friends," Jean admitted. "I was honestly surprised she had anyone that close to her. I just got in touch with her this morning, but she promised to be here by tonight."

"Then there's no time to waste," I said.

"As soon as Grace gets back, we'll get started."

"I can pay you," Jean offered.

"Tell you what. Your earlier donation to the Humane Society will cover our fees."

"I'll double it," Jean said, "and not another word about it. I'm afraid I won't be able to help you at all. It's not just my health. My soul couldn't bear it."

I had no problem believing that. "How about if we keep a box of personal items for you and we can donate or toss the rest."

"It sounds as though you were heaven-sent."

I didn't have the heart to tell her that I had ulterior motives making the offer. After all, why should I? We were indeed doing her a service by taking care of Desmond's things, and if we happened to stumble upon a clue or two while we were doing it, so much the better.

"While we're waiting for Grace, may I ask you something else?" I asked.

"Certainly," Jean answered.

"Had Desmond been fighting with anyone besides Katie recently?"

Jean frowned. "Do you mean besides that awful Gabby Williams?"

I didn't know how to reply to that, and Jean must have seen something in my gaze.

"Suzanne, I don't hold your friendship with her against you. It says more about your kind heart than it does her wicked ways. I don't believe for one moment that the cruller incident was your fault."

I was glad she could see that, but even though I knew I was endangering our investigation, I couldn't let the slam on Gabby go without commenting on it. "Jean, I can't imagine her stealing from you," I said.

As predicted, her face clouded over. "If she didn't take the money and the brooch, then where could they be? I distinctly remember giving Desmond the jacket, thinking that I had forgotten something important about it, but handing it over just the same. It wasn't until he returned that I remembered the cash and the brooch. She *had* to have taken it."

I could think of another possibility, that Desmond had checked the pockets himself before turning the coat over to Gabby and kept the swag for himself, but I couldn't bring myself to taint his image in her eyes without more solid proof than idle speculation.

It was time to get back on track. "Besides Gabby," I asked, "who else might make the list?"

131

She frowned, and then said, "Don't think I haven't been considering that very question myself since early this morning. I could come up with only two names."

I must have moved up to the edge of my seat as I asked, "Would you mind sharing them with me?"

"Why are you so suddenly curious about Desmond?" she asked.

I wasn't going to admit that I was investigating his murder on Gabby's behalf. I thought about what I could say, but then she answered for me. "You feel as though your crullers may have played a part in his murder. Is that it? No, I know. You saw him yesterday, and the two of you had words. He told me all about what happened, and I assured him that he was wrong in his assessment of you. In fact, he was planning to stop by Donut Hearts and issue you a formal apology today. I'm just sorry he never had the opportunity to do it."

"It's not necessary," I said. "I would like to find out what happened to him. Now, about those two names?"

She nodded. "After Desmond left you and Gabby, he ran into an old childhood friend of his, a man he'd had a falling-out with over the past few years. His name is Allen Davis."

"Do you know why they fought?"

"Over that tart, Katie," she said. Jean had a deep level of disdain when she spoke the name, and I wondered how Katie had managed to get so thoroughly on her bad side. "It's amazing to me how one bad woman can get between two good men."

"Or vice versa," I said, remembering an instance in the past where two good women had fought over one bad man.

Jean nodded. "Yes, I know that's true. You wanted the other name, correct?"

"Yes, ma'am," I replied, hoping she'd tell me before Grace returned from the store.

"Against my advice, Desmond did some business in Hudson Creek with a man named Bill Rodgers. I'm not exactly certain what it involved, but the man came to my doorstep three days ago demanding that I pay full restitution for the money he'd lost in the venture with Desmond."

"What did you do?"

"I showed him the door," Jean said. "Desmond was quite unhappy when I told him what had happened, and he promised me that I'd never have to deal with the Rodgers man again."

"Any idea what the business was?" I asked.

"I haven't a clue. I just know I wasn't about to pay him fifty thousand dollars for an obligation I hadn't taken on."

I was about to press her further when there was a knock at the door. Jean looked troubled as it continued. "People have been knocking all day, but I can't bear to see anyone."

"Would you like me to take care of it?" I asked.

"That would be wonderful," she said as she settled back on the couch.

I walked to the front door and opened it, prepared to rebuff any and all visitors.

Then I saw that it was Grace.

"Can I give you a hand?" I asked as I held the door open for her.

"There's a tray of coffees in the car. Would you mind grabbing them for me?"

"Not at all."

As I retrieved the coffee, I found Grace waiting on the porch for me. "I was beginning to wonder if you were ever going to answer the door, Suzanne. What took you so long?" she asked in a muted voice.

"I was sleuthing," I admitted. "Do me a favor and go along with whatever I say, okay?"

Grace's eyes lit up. "You've got it." I knew she was always up for a chance to stretch her acting skills. I didn't have the heart to tell her it was her cleaning abilities I'd be using instead.

Grace carried the grocery bags in, and I handed Jean a cup of coffee.

"Bless you, Suzanne," she said as she took it from me.

"Don't bless me; Grace is the one who brought them."

Jean smiled again, but then it died just as suddenly, as though she'd forgotten, for just an instant, the murder. "Then bless you both."

"Should I put these away for you?" Grace asked.

"I'll do it myself," Jean replied.

"I don't mind, really I don't," Grace replied.

"Dear, then how will I ever find anything? Besides, you and Suzanne have enough to do as it is."

Even though I'd warned her that something was coming, she looked slightly confused. "We do?"

"You'd better have a chat about it while I take care of these groceries," Jean said as she went into the kitchen and began putting things away.

I turned to Grace and said, "We're going to clean Desmond's room so his cousin can move in tonight. Do you have a few hours to spare?"

Grace looked at her watch. "That would be fine. I just have to be home by six."

"Are you going out again tonight?" I asked. She hadn't said a word about that to me on the drive over to Jean's house.

"I can cancel it if I need to," she said, though it was clear that she'd be reluctant to do so.

"Nonsense, we'll have plenty of time. It's just one room." I went to the kitchen and asked Jean, "That's right, isn't it?"

"Yes, it shouldn't take long. Would you mind getting started? I want to have fresh linens on the bed when Jenny arrives."

"Who's Jenny?" Grace asked.

"I'll tell you as we clean," I said. "Jean, do you happen to have any boxes around here?"

"Check the pantry," she said as she pointed to a door directly off the kitchen.

I opened it, and was stunned to find a stocked storage area that was nearly as large as Jean's kitchen. I wasn't sure what major disaster she'd been preparing for, but I was certain she'd be able to handle it, including flood or famine. Sure enough, there were a few large empty boxes stored under one of the shelving units.

"Thanks," I said as I retrieved them. "Grace, we should get started."

I turned to Jean, who was openly crying

now. As much as I wanted to snoop around in Desmond's room, I didn't want to cause this woman any more pain than I had to. "Are you sure about this?"

She nodded. "It's like a bandage, isn't it? It's best to rip it off in one motion and allow yourself to start healing."

"Let's go, Grace," I said, and then turned back to Jean. "Where exactly is his room?"

"It's just down the hall, the second door on the right. You can't miss it. It's the only door in the house that's ever shut. I just can't tolerate a closed door."

I wasn't sure how much we'd be able to talk if Jean was so close by, but I had to respect her wishes. I was about to say as much when she added, "I know it might feel a bit claustrophobic, but would you mind keeping it closed as you work? I don't want to know what you're doing."

"We'll be glad to oblige," I said.

Before we started down the hall, Jean said, "I can't thank you enough for doing this, both of you."

"We're just glad we can help," I said.

We were still outside the door when Grace hesitated. "Is there anything in particular we're looking for?"

"Anything that might explain why Desmond was murdered last night," I said.

CHAPTER 7

"Are you sure a man lived here?" Grace asked as we walked into Desmond's room.

"What do you mean?" I asked as I took in the neatly made bed, the carefully organized closet, and the immaculate floor.

"There's no mess," she said. "In all the time you were married, was Max ever this neat?"

I remembered my ex-husband's house keeping skills, or lack of them, and realized that she had a point. "I've heard there are neat men out there," I said. "I'm willing to bet that Jake is neat."

"I think I'd have a better chance running across a unicorn, myself," Grace replied.

"At least it will make it easier to search," I said. "One thing we can be sure of; Jean didn't come in and straighten up after him. She could barely bring herself to tell us which door was his. They were close, weren't they?"

"They seem to have been," I said. "Do you want the closet, the dresser, or the desk?"

"I'll take the desk," Grace said. "That's going to be the hot spot, don't you think?"

I tended to agree with her, but I never really knew where I'd find a clue, so I started searching the other areas with equal enthusiasm.

"Check this out," Grace said two minutes after we got started. "I found his checkbook ledger. This is going to tell us quite a bit about him."

I started to look at it, but then realized that we had only a limited amount of time to search. "Tell you what. Why don't you set it aside, and we'll compare notes when we're finished. Who knows how long Jean is going to let us clean. She might change her mind any second."

Grace took a pillow off the bed and tossed it into one of the boxes we'd brought from the pantry. "There, we're packing. Happy now?"

I just laughed at my friend, but she had the right idea. As I started to work on the dresser drawers, I began to empty them as I searched, putting the clothing in boxes for donation — only after checking all of the pockets first. There was a very real possibility that the police's initial search had missed something important.

In the last drawer I opened, I found a photograph in a frame at the bottom below some folded shirts. I pulled it out and studied it, quickly recognizing the man as Desmond, though he had been younger when it had been taken. A nice-looking young lady with striking blond hair was beside him, and as I studied the edge of the photograph, I could see that someone, or something, had been removed. Carefully taking the photo out of its frame, I unfolded the snapshot and saw that there was a man on the other side of the woman, though the portion with his head had been torn away. The ragged edges of the photograph told me that it hadn't been a careful excision by knife or scissors, but rather a hurried and, from the looks of it, passionate removal. Who had caused that kind of anger? Then I remembered what Jean had told me earlier. There was a good chance that the missing man was Allen Davis, and that would make the woman in question Katie Wilkes. I started to put the photo back in its frame, but on an impulse, I stuck it into my pocket without saying a word to Grace. As much as I wanted her to see it, I'd already squelched one of her finds, so I couldn't very well point my first one out to her.

The rest of the drawers of the bureau had nothing of real interest, and I moved on to Desmond's closet. Inside it, besides hanging shirts, pants, jackets, and shoes, I found a small accordion file. That looked promising, so I pulled it out and started quickly scanning through the documents. Most were mundane things like old tax forms, clothing bills, and the like, but something caught my eye, so I pulled out the crumpled business envelope that had been uncharacteristically jammed into the folder.

It was a pretty sternly worded letter basically threatening Desmond with legal action if he didn't repay the funds his partner believed he'd stolen from their joint venture. The letter had obviously been wadded up at some point, though someone, most likely Desmond, had done his best to straighten it back out again later. I added the letter to the photo in my pocket, and then started transferring clothing into the boxes. "We're going to run out of boxes at this rate," I said.

"I won't be adding anything to the pile," she said. "The desk is full of mostly junk that isn't going to do any of us a bit of good."

"Is there anything of sentimental value in

141

there?" I asked. I wanted to be able to hand something over to Jean.

"I found some birthday cards from her to Desmond, and a few notes. Nothing major, but they might mean something to her."

"Probably more than we realize," I said. "The closet's nearly empty, and I already finished with his dresser. How can you go through life and not collect more things than this?"

"Some folks aren't the packrats we are," she said.

"I can't imagine not surrounding myself with things I love, or that remind me of good times I've had."

Grace nodded. "I'm with you. Let me give you a hand with what's left, and we can get out of here."

We were both in the closet when the bedroom door opened, and before either one of us could turn around, a shrill voice asked, "What do you two think you are doing?"

"Hello," I said as I backed out, with Grace close behind me. "You must be Jenny. We're so sorry for your loss." It was the same mousy brunette I'd seen in the photograph in the living room. I extended a hand to her, but she ignored it.

"Your donuts aren't going to cut any slack from me. I told Aunt Jean she was crazy to let you in here without someone watching you the entire time."

"Did you think we were going to take Desmond's socks, perhaps?" Grace asked, the bite clear in her voice.

"Who knows what you have in your pockets. I demand to see everything you both found here."

I refused to comply with that. "I'm going to try to forgive your rudeness given the circumstances, but we are here doing a favor for a friend, and I don't appreciate the line of questioning or the tone in your voice."

Jenny seemed to consider that before blowing up again, and then to my surprise, she crumpled onto the bed, barely able to hold herself erect. "I'm sorry. I know I can be a bit of a pain when I'm stressed, and if this wouldn't push me to my limit, nothing would."

"Were you and Desmond close?" I asked. I thought I knew the answer, but I wanted to see what she had to say about it.

"As kids we were inseparable, but people tend to drift apart as they get older."

"He and your aunt were close, weren't they?" Grace asked.

Jenny looked surprised by the question.

"Absolutely. She grew to depend on Desmond more and more every day. I wasn't sure it was entirely healthy for either one of them, but then no one asked me. Now that he's gone, it's up to me to step in and take his place."

"It's a lot to ask, giving up your life to come here," I said as sympathetically as I could muster for her.

"We do what we must," she said. "Now, if you'll excuse me, I'd like to have a few moments alone with Desmond's things."

"We don't mind staying and finishing up here," I volunteered. "It's a big job, and an emotional one, as well." There wasn't anything big about it, since we'd already finished nearly all the work, but I wanted to be certain that Grace had the opportunity to take the checkbook ledger, and anything else that she'd thought was important. I was beginning to wish that I'd allowed her to show me her find when we had the chance, but at least I'd held on to my discoveries. There was no way Jenny, or anyone else, was getting them from me.

"Thank you, but I've got it covered," Jenny said, and there was no room for debate in her voice. Grace and I were being dismissed, whether we liked it or not. "I'll show you out."

"No need," I said. "I'd like to say good-bye to Jean."

Jenny frowned. "I'm afraid that's impossible. She's resting now. I'll tell her you were sorry not to see her before you both left."

She escorted us to the front door, and I half expected her to grab our arms on the way out so we couldn't break free.

"Good bye," she said, and as Jenny closed the door behind us, I heard the dead bolt slam firmly into place. It appeared that our access to Jean Ray was now going to be limited by an overprotective niece, if that was all it really was. There might be a great deal more to it than that, but what could Jenny be afraid we might find? Grace and I were going to have to dig a little deeper into the woman's life, and I knew just the person we needed to ask for help. I doubted Jake would do a background search for us without more justification than we had, but I had a hunch that George wouldn't put up much resistance. He loved digging into people's pasts.

As we walked to her car, I said, "Tell me you kept his checkbook."

"Sorry, that would be stealing," Grace said. It was an odd time to start developing ethics of that particular sort. Before I could say anything else, she added, "However, I saw nothing wrong with keeping his ledger. Did you come up with anything?"

"I found a couple of things," I confessed, "but I'm not sure what to make of either one of them."

"I say we head back to my place so we can compare notes," Grace said. "After all, we can't really know what we should do until we've been able to come up with a game plan."

"I just love it when you use sports metaphors," I said with a smile.

"I've been in sales too long, I guess. We have more clichés than your average college football coach, though I never understood why." After Grace started the car and headed back toward her house, she asked me, "What exactly did you find, Suzanne?"

I dug out the letter and read it to her.

Grace whistled softly. "This guy has to go to the head of our list."

"I've got a feeling there's going to be plenty of names on it before we're through," I said as I showed her the photo. She took it from me and nearly sideswiped a car before I grabbed it back. "You can look at that when we land, I mean park."

"Are you implying that I'm a fast driver?" she asked with a smile.

"Imply? I don't think so. I didn't mean to leave any room for doubt in my voice at all. Slow down, I'd rather get there alive, if it's all the same to you."

She did as I asked, but still said with a grin, "Sissy."

"Ten out of ten, if my life's on the line," I said.

We got to Grace's house without further incident, and before she got out of the car, she asked for the photo again.

After I handed it to her, she shook her head. "Desmond wasn't happy with someone, that's for sure."

"The question is, was the feeling mutual?" I explained the scenarios that covered what I'd found, and how they matched what Jean had told me while Grace had been on her grocery run.

"Let's see that ledger," I said.

She handed it to me, and I flipped first to the last balance listed. "Wow, he had less than two hundred dollars to his name."

"Just because it's not in his account doesn't mean that he didn't take Jean's money and sock it away somewhere else."

"I didn't see any trace of it in his room, did you?" I asked. "I searched my area pretty thoroughly, too."

"I didn't find a dime," she admitted,

"which I find odd, as well. Who doesn't keep a little mad money hanging around?"

"Someone who can't afford to get angry," I suggested. "I'm curious about Jean's will, and nothing we've seen so far has made me any less interested."

"Do you think Desmond was killed for his inheritance? That's kind of premature, isn't it, given the fact that Jean is still alive."

I shook my head. "Think about it. If Jenny was afraid of being written out completely, she could have gotten rid of the one person in line ahead of her."

"Wow, who knew this Desmond had so many enemies? Who do we have so far?"

"Besides his cousin Jenny there's his former best friend, Allen Davis, his former girlfriend, Katie Wilkes, and his former business partner, Bill Rodgers."

Grace shook her head. "There are a lot of 'formers' on that list, aren't there? Are we excluding Gabby from that list completely?"

"No, as much as I hate to admit it, we can't strike her name off just yet." I considered it another moment, and then added, "Jean has to be included, as well."

Grace looked surprised by my suggestion. "Why would Jean want to see him dead? They were really close, by all accounts."

"It's what we've heard, not what we've

seen for ourselves," I said. "What if she caught him stealing from her, or something even worse? Don't let that demeanor fool you. Jean could be regretting her actions with those tears, not her nephew's death."

Grace nodded. "Got it. So, we trust no one."

I tried my best to smile at her. "Well, I don't think you had anything to do with it."

When the pause continued, I added, "Aren't you going to say the same thing about me?"

She grinned at me and said, "I don't know, Suzanne. Those *were* your crullers."

"But they didn't kill him," I reminded her.

"Okay, you're in the clear, then."

"Thanks, I think," I said. "Who should we speak with first?"

"I'm not entirely sure. There are a great many choices, aren't there?"

I nodded, and then went over the list again in my head. "Do we have time to do any more digging before your big date?"

She looked at her watch, and then said, "We'd better not risk it. Besides, we're going to need some time to find these people first. None of them live in April Springs, do they?"

"Not that I know of," I admitted. "Where did Desmond live before he came here to be with his aunt?"

"That's probably going to be the answer to the other questions, too. Let me make a quick call and we'll see."

I tried to ask her who she was calling when she held a hand up for me to be quiet. I didn't mind. I couldn't really, since I'd done it enough times to her over the years. When I heard her ask for Desmond's phone number and address, I knew she was calling information. Sometimes the easiest way was the best.

"He's listed as living in Talbot's Landing," Grace said after she hung up. "That's part of my sales territory. I know it pretty well, and it's just half an hour away."

"Then we get started tomorrow after work interviewing our suspects. Are you sure you have time to help?"

Grace smiled at me. "Are you kidding? While we're there, I'll pop in a few places and count it as a day of work."

"Isn't that stretching it?" I asked.

"All I have to do is go into one store in my territory to make it a work day. Is it my fault if it's an insanely easy requirement to meet?"

I laughed. "But you're not above taking advantage of it, are you?"

"Hey, I didn't make the rules."

"Agreed. Can you wait until eleven to go?"

She looked at me oddly. "Suzanne, I don't think you have to take off early. It can wait until noon."

I'd completely forgotten to tell her about my new working hours. "Sorry, I forgot to mention it. We close at eleven."

"Since when?"

I laughed. "Since tomorrow. I'm cutting my hours. I'll get to the shop at two-thirty or three every morning, make donuts till six, open the shop, and close by eleven. It's going to be like being on vacation compared to the hours I've been working."

"It will for a week or two, and then you'll get used to it again."

I looked at her. "Does that mean you don't approve?"

"On the contrary. I don't think anyone should have to work as hard as you do every week with so little reward."

"Hey, what can I say? It's my life. Now, will you drop me off at my Jeep? I can go home, and you can get ready for your date."

"It's a deal," she said.

When Grace dropped me off at the donut shop, I said, "Have a nice time."

"I plan to," she said with a smile as she drove away. I really hoped it worked out for her this time. Grace deserved to be happy.

For that matter, we all did.

I was expecting dinner when I got home, but found a note on the kitchen table instead.

> Out with Phillip. There are leftovers in the fridge. Love, Momma.

Wow, they were really getting to be steady in their dating, and if it was only three times a week, I was the crown princess of Donut Land. My mother had been reluctant at first to date the chief of police — or anyone, for that matter — but she'd seemed to take to it after she got over the initial setbacks the two of them had. I'd been ambivalent about their relationship at first, but the police chief had proven himself to both of us.

I foraged a little, and in no time found some leftover meatloaf, Brussels sprouts with cheese sauce, and sweet, cooked carrots. It looked like a feast to me, and I was warming it in the microwave when my cell phone rang.

"Jake," I said enthusiastically. "How's Asheville?"

"To tell you the truth, I'm not cut out to be a teacher," he said.

"Come on, you've got to love the adoring

attention of all of the coeds hanging on your every word."

He hesitated, and then said, "Some of them are a little more adoring than others."

I tried my best not to laugh. Evidently Ashley had found him after all. "What do you mean?"

"A girl young enough to be my daughter nearly assaulted me on campus today, she hugged me so hard, and then got away before I could dissuade her of an odd notion she had that she knew me."

"Did she say anything else? Maybe she just loved your lecture."

"She kept calling me Uncle Jake, no matter how hard I tried to convince her that we weren't related."

I couldn't help myself. I burst out laughing, and after a few seconds, Jake said, "It's not that funny. That girl needs some serious help."

"I'm sure she's perfectly lovely. After all, it's not every day a beautiful young brunette hugs you, is it? It had better not be, if you're struggling for an answer."

Jake paused a second, and then said, "I never said she was a brunette."

"I'm sure you must have," I said.

"Suzanne, I'm positive I didn't. Come on, confess."

"Okay, fine," I said. "She's my niece. At least she used to be back when I was married to Max. I ran into her and asked her to look you up when I found out she was going to UNC-A."

He sighed, and I was afraid I may have crossed the line, but then I relaxed a little when I heard him chuckle. "She flummoxed me, that's for sure. I must have turned twelve shades of red."

"I can't believe she didn't explain it to you," I said, admiring Ashley's willingness to fully commit to the gag.

"No, it was a hug-and-run. I'm happy that's been explained. Now, what other mischief have you been up to?"

I didn't want to tell him about Desmond's murder, but I really had no choice. There was no way I could keep it from him, not with his connections with state law enforcement, but it was too bad I had to kill the light mood between us.

"I'm afraid I've gotten involved in another murder investigation," I said.

After a brief pause, he expelled a breath of air, and then said, "Tell me what happened."

BASIC CRULLERS

Crullers come in many shapes, styles, textures, and tastes, depending on the recipe's country of origin, but here's one my family likes. Don't be afraid to try other recipes yourself!

Ingredients

Mixed
- 3 tablespoons butter, melted
- 3/4 cup sugar, white granulated
- 2 eggs, well beaten

Sifted
- 3 1/2 to 4 1/2 cups all-purpose flour (I prefer unbleached)
- 2 teaspoons baking powder
- 1 teaspoon baking soda
- 1/2 teaspoon nutmeg
- 1/2 teaspoon cinnamon
- Pinch of salt

Added

- 1 cup whole milk (2 percent may be substituted, but hey, these are donut treats!)

Directions

In one bowl, cream the butter and add the sugar and eggs. In another bowl, sift together the flour, baking powder, baking soda, nutmeg, cinnamon, and salt. Slowly add the dry ingredients into the wet, adding milk along the way, until it's incorporated. If you need more flour, add it now until the dough is stiff enough to work and not sticky. Roll it out to 1/2 to 1/4 inch thickness, and then cut out into shapes, traditional long rectangles, or fun squares, circles, or triangles. Fry in hot canola oil (360 to 370 degrees F) 3 to 4 minutes, turning halfway through. Dry on paper towels, then dust with confectioner's sugar or decorate with icing and sprinkles.

Yield: Depends on sizes and shapes of your crullers: 4–6 rectangles, 6–10 miscellaneous shapes

CHAPTER 8

It was time for me to come clean. "Do you remember when I told you about the cruller assault?"

"Of course I do. Flying pastries are a little hard to forget," he said.

"The man who threw them at Gabby was shot and killed last night between her shop and mine." I told him the rest of it, and then finished with, "Gabby is their number one suspect, and she's asked me to help her find the real killer."

"There's no chance in the world you said no to her, is there?" Jake asked.

"What do you think? When a friend asks me for help, I give it."

He paused, and then asked, "Are you two really friends?"

"Not like Grace and I are," I admitted, "but yeah, we've formed a bond over the years. I know she can be gruff and nosy and hard to get along with, but I still can't stand by and see her falsely accused of murder."

Jake took a deep breath, and then said, "Don't take this the wrong way, but are you sure it's not true? That missing money and diamond brooch could give her plenty of reasons to kill him, especially if he was making such a stink about it."

"I won't entertain the notion that she's guilty unless evidence that confirms it presents itself," I said. "For now, I'm working on the assumption that she's innocent."

"As long as Phillip Martin isn't looking at you as a suspect, we're fine," Jake said. "You have an alibi, don't you?"

"I'm afraid not," I admitted. "After you turned me down, I tried Grace, but she was on a date, and so was Momma. The only person who saw me was the pizza delivery guy, and he was at the house hours before Desmond was murdered."

"Suzanne, I'm so sorry. I should have come back to April Springs last night, or let you come here. I could have been your alibi."

"It's not your fault, Jake. Who knew what was going to happen, or that I'd need someone to swear that I didn't do it?"

"Still, it bothers me. Tell you what. I'll end my lecture series right now and come back to April Springs and help you look into the murder."

"I appreciate the offer," I said, "but no, thanks."

There was a touch of hurt in his voice as he asked, "Why not? We make a good team, don't we?"

"You know we do, and not just when we're investigating. Jake, I won't let you use this as an excuse to get out of something you committed to doing. Don't worry, Grace is helping me, and George, too. We'll manage."

"Well, I'm close by if you need me."

The microwave timer beeped, and Jake must have heard it. "Are you heating up leftovers for dinner again?"

"Momma's on another date," I admitted, "but trust me, her castoffs are better than most folks' first offerings."

"You don't have to convince me of that," Jake said. "What's on the menu tonight?"

When I told him, he asked, "Is there enough for two?"

I had to laugh. "You're staying in Asheville, sir, and that's the last time I'll discuss it with you. How's the food there?"

"Better than I usually eat," he admitted, "but nowhere near as good as your mother's cooking. She's been seeing a lot of the chief lately, hasn't she?"

"Yes, but it makes her happy, so I'm staying out of the way."

He chuckled. "That's got to be killing you. I know Martin's not your idea of the ideal boyfriend for your mother."

"She had to get back on the horse sometime, and he's at least got training wheels."

"I think you're mixing your metaphors there," Jake said. "I don't believe I've ever seen a horse with training wheels."

"You know what I mean. In a way, Chief Martin is a rebound fling after my dad died."

"He's been gone a long time, Suzanne," Jake said.

I didn't need to be reminded of that. "True, but this is the first man she's dated since, so I still think it counts. After she gets used to the idea of dating again, I'm sure she'll start playing the field." At least I hoped so.

"What makes you think this isn't serious?" Jake asked.

"I don't know. I just never entertained the prospect that it was," I admitted.

Jake must have heard something in my voice, because he was quick to drop the subject. "Hey, don't let your dinner get cold on my account. Go on and eat. I know how early you have to get up tomorrow."

"Not as early as today," I said.

"Why not?"

I'd forgotten to tell him, as well. When I brought Jake up to date on my changes, I could almost hear his smile over the phone. "Good for you. Now, if I can just get you to take a vacation every now and then, I'll be a happy man."

"Hey, I'm proud of myself taking baby steps," I said.

"So am I. I'll check in tomorrow, and Suzanne?"

"Yes?" I asked, hoping he'd tell me he loved me.

"Don't take any chances."

After we hung up, I realized that, in his own way, that was exactly what he'd said.

At least I was going to do my best to believe that.

I was just heading off to bed when I heard a car drive up. I peeked out the window and saw Momma being helped out of the chief's personal car. Chief Martin had purchased an older sedan specifically so he could take her out on dates without using the squad car or renting a vehicle every time they went out. I moved away from the window and into the hallway by the stairs, because the last thing I wanted to see was the two of them saying good night. I had no idea how long they'd linger on the porch, no matter how much the temperatures had been dipping at night lately.

To my surprise, he didn't even get a chance to walk her up to the front door. It burst open, and Momma hurried inside, as though she were being chased by a particularly aggressive bear. There was a look on her face I hadn't seen before: a mix of puzzlement, shock, fear, and unless I was mistaken, a little bit of joy.

"What's going on?" I asked as I rushed down the stairs to her. "Are you okay?"

"What? Of course I am. What are you still doing up?" Momma asked as she started to regain some of her composure.

"I'm sleeping in tomorrow," I said. "What happened? Did he get fresh with you?" I knew it was a ridiculous question for a daughter to ask her mother, but I was at a loss for what might have just happened.

"Of course not. Phillip has always been a perfect gentleman with me."

"Well, something surely spooked you," I said.

"It's nothing," Momma said as she took off her jacket and hung it up.

"Listen, I've seen nothing, and that's nowhere close to being it. Come clean. You can talk to me."

Momma sat on the couch, still looking a bit shell-shocked. Whatever it was, it had been big enough to throw her off her game, something I never would have believed if I weren't seeing it for myself.

"I suppose I must," Momma said, and then she started to stand. "We need coffee first. I'll make some."

I touched her arm. "Stop stalling."

She looked down at me, shrugged, and then said, "I suppose we have to talk about it sooner or later. Phillip just asked me to marry him."

"What!" I screamed. "You're kidding."

She looked at me with surprise. "Do you think it's foolish to believe that anyone would want to marry your mother?"

"I understand that completely, but I think he's nuts to ask you. You turned him down, didn't you?"

I looked long and hard at her, waiting, praying, hoping for an answer.

When she didn't volunteer one, I asked dully, "You didn't say yes, did you?"

"I told him I'd have to think about it," Momma admitted.

"You can't marry him!" I said as I jumped off the couch. "You haven't been dating all that long, and his divorce isn't even a year old. It's insane to act so rashly and even consider jumping into a marriage with someone you barely know."

"Are you going to tell me that we're too young, as well?" Momma asked.

"I know how old you are," I said, "I just wish you'd act your age."

She ignored my protests and calmly took my hands in hers. "Suzanne, I know you're speaking out of your concern for me, that you're worried that I might get hurt by doing something rash, but think about it. Have I ever in my life jumped into anything without thinking it through thoroughly first?"

I considered what she was saying and realized that it was true. My mother could drive me crazy sometimes with her endless analysis of a situation, but for once, I was glad about her caution. "I'm sorry," I said, calming down a little. "You just caught me off guard."

"If you think you were surprised, you should have seen my reaction. I bolted away so fast it was as though I were on fire. I must call and apologize for that."

I put my hand on hers before she could dial the police chief's number. "That can wait. The two of us need to talk about this first."

"Thus the coffee," she said as she pulled away. "I'm afraid neither one of us will be getting to bed early tonight."

"I'm fine with missing some sleep for an important cause, and I can't imagine anything more important than this."

While Momma went into the kitchen to make coffee — and to call Chief Martin, as well, I was sure — I slumped back down on the couch. I could easily believe the chief had asked her to marry him, and in a way, I was surprised that he hadn't proposed sooner. He was too eager when it came to my mother, always trying to pull the trigger too quickly. What really surprised me was that my mother was actually considering it. What would that do to us, and our dynamic? I knew one thing. If they got married and the chief moved in — and why would Momma leave our home? — I would have to move out. It wasn't that I hated him, we'd grown to at least tolerate each other lately, but I wouldn't intrude on a newlywed couple's space. The dynamic Momma and I had shared since my divorce would be over, and I feared we'd lose the closeness we'd fought so hard to achieve. It was the nature of the beast, after all. I could see our time together crumbling into a meal every now and then, maybe a movie, but not much else. It shocked me to realize just how much I clung to the fact that Momma and I had become a team, a pair of roommates who shared more than most grown daughters and their mothers.

Her joy would be a time of sadness for me, and I hated myself for thinking of it that way.

Momma came out with two coffee mugs, but I declined mine. "I've got to get up early," I said. "And we both know that I don't need any more stimulation tonight."

"Suzanne, nothing has changed, at least not at the moment."

I just shook my head. "I don't believe that for a second, and neither should you."

"You've made it clear how you feel," Momma said as she took a sip of coffee. How could she be so calm about all of this?

I took a deep breath and decided it was time to grow up a little. "I'm the first to admit that I've handled this all wrong tonight. Let me start over. I want you to be happy. That's all that matters to me," I said.

"Even if it means I marry Phillip?" she asked.

"Even then," I agreed.

"So, you're not going to try to talk me out of this anymore?"

I looked deep into her eyes and did my

best to mean what I was about to say. "It's your decision, and I respect what you come up with either way. For what it's worth, if you decide to marry him, you have my blessing."

She looked surprised by my declaration, but I knew in my heart that she realized I was being honest with her.

Momma hugged me, and then said, "I'm so glad you feel that way, but honestly, I don't know what to do."

I smiled at her. "That's easy. Take your time, weigh the pros and cons, and then make your decision. This should be like every other important judgment you've ever made in your life." I stifled a yawn, and then added, "If you'd like to discuss it more with me, I promise to be unbiased."

"Go on to bed, Suzanne. As you said, there's no need to make any decisions tonight." She hugged me, and then added softly in my ear, "I love you."

"I love you, too," I said.

As I lay in bed, I wondered what would happen. Things were changing all around me, and I seemed to be standing still. Grace could possibly be on her way to finding true love, and my mother just might be starting in an entirely different direction with her life. All the while, I made donuts, and spent

167

far too much of my time missing Jake.

One thing was certain.

No matter what happened, my life was most likely about to change, one way or another.

The next morning at the donut shop, Emma said, "You're being awfully quiet, Suzanne. Is something wrong?" She'd taken advantage of her sleeping-in time, but I was glad she was there with me now.

"No, not that I can think of," I said as I rolled out the last bit of dough for the glazed donuts we were making. I'd held out a small amount and had added bits of apple and dusted the dough with cinnamon and nutmeg before I cut the shapes out, hoping to improve on my apple-pie donut. It was a big hit when the weather got cooler, but I loved trying to tweak my recipes further now that I had my donut recipe book back, or a copy of it, at least. "Why do you ask?"

"If that dough gets rolled out any thinner, you'll be making pie crust instead of donuts."

I looked down and saw that she was right. I must have taken my anxieties about my mother's big announcement the night before out on my donuts. "Sorry."

I put my French rolling pin down and

took the solid donut cutter, rolling it across the dough to make cutouts for my filled donuts. Normally I wouldn't dream of adding anything extra to the dough itself, relying on fillings and toppings to make them special in their own way, but I wanted to experiment and see what would happen. They probably wouldn't proof right, or if they did, something would most likely kill them before a customer ever tasted one, but that was okay. For all I knew, they could turn out to be wonderful.

I cut the solid shapes out with the small hand roller, moving the circular cutter across the dough in one steady and fluid motion. I'd been so impressed the first time I'd seen the Bismarck, Solid, and Holed donut rollers, but using them now was just a matter of course for me. Plucking the cut shapes from the dough, I transferred them to a sheet and put them in the proofer along with the rest of the day's glazed donuts. Once they were all in, I helped Emma clean the work surface, and it was time for one of our truncated breaks. Along with our limited hours, I'd decided that we'd have to work more and rest less while we were there. As long as it allowed Emma to sleep in a little, she was all for it.

"We've got ten minutes," I said. "Care to

go outside?" It was our usual practice to go out in front of the shop on our breaks, no matter what the weather or temperature. In the summer, being out there was usually quite pleasant, but in bad weather, or frosty temperatures, we had to bundle up.

"I vote for outside," she said. "Always."

We got our coats on and stepped out into a perfect morning, still pitch-black, with more than a touch of frost in the air. It made me glad that Momma and I had a fireplace at the cottage, and we weren't afraid to use it. I knew a man who loved my donuts, and in exchange for a credit of coffee and treats throughout the year, he kept us supplied with seasoned oak firewood. I loved the barter system; and our woodpile never got low, and he never ran short on donuts.

"Brrr," Emma said as she pulled her jacket tighter. "Smell that," she commanded as she took a deep breath.

"Wood smoke," I said. "It smells like home, doesn't it?"

"I wish. Dad hates fires, and won't have one in the house. He says that owning a newspaper has made him jumpy about open flames for years."

"That's too bad," I said. "You could always come over and join us some evening." As long as I was still a resident in the cottage, I could make that offer. If Momma and the chief got married, I knew without being told what that meant to me. I'd be moved out before they got back from their honeymoon, and it didn't matter how hard they asked me to stay. Two was company, but I wasn't about to be a third wheel in my own place.

"I might just take you up on it." She inhaled again, and then asked, "Is there something else in the air, maybe? Could we get an early snow this year?" The last was not said with much anticipation, because besides a fun onetime ride on the back of a snowmobile, Emma was not a big fan of snow.

I, on the other hand, loved it.

"I'll keep my fingers crossed," I said, but when I saw her face fall, I quickly added, "But I don't think there's a chance we'll get any snow before Christmas, and it's not even Thanksgiving yet."

"I hope you're right," Emma answered.

The timer I'd brought with us went off, and as I killed it, I said, "We need to go back in. We don't have as much time as we used to, do we?"

She smiled at me as I let her in the door. "I can live with it, trust me. I love this new schedule, and I hope we won't be getting any complaints."

I had to laugh about that. "Emma, folks who would never dream about coming in before six or after eleven are going to howl like we cut off their air supply, you can count on it."

"And you're willing to put up with that?"

"Hey, I need the extra sleep just as much as you do, more probably. I'm looking forward to getting out of here at eleven every day, too."

"I don't know. I do all right on how much sleep I get now."

"Come back and tell me that when you're my age," I said with a smile.

We were rushed with our new schedule, and I knew it would take some getting used to, but ultimately it would be worth it.

I looked over the finished donuts sitting in their cases, missing only the raised apple ones I'd tried to make, unsuccessfully. The moisture content of the apple bits had most likely been too much for the dough to handle, but I wasn't going to give up. Maybe next time they'd be perfect. I still had plenty of things to offer to the world today, though. I was often tempted to take a photograph of my display case, but I wasn't at all sure what

I would do with it once it was taken. On a whim, I got my camera out of my jacket where I'd stowed it the day before to get some shots of the trees in the park. I took a few shots of the display cases, and Emma caught me doing it.

"What's going on?" she asked.

"I just wanted something for my scrapbook," I said, hoping the conversation was over.

"You scrapbook? You should talk to my mother. She loves scrapbooking."

"I meant to say if I ever decide to get around to making one," I said. I glanced at the clock and saw that we had a full ninety seconds before it was time to open.

Standing in front of the shop, his hands in his pockets and a hat pulled low over his face, I spotted George.

"I'll let him in, and you can get started on the dishes."

Emma smiled. "That's me. I get all the glamorous jobs around here."

"We could switch, if you'd like," I said, knowing full well that Emma was much more comfortable in back than she was waiting on customers up front.

"No, thanks. It's all yours."

"Come on in," I told George as I opened the door. "You look chilly."

"No, I'm fine," he said as he rubbed his hands together. "When did you start opening up at six instead of five?"

"This morning's our first day," I admitted. "I should have taken an ad out in the paper to announce our new hours."

"Folks will learn the new routine soon enough," he said.

"Coffee?" I offered, already knowing the answer.

"Yes, ma'am, please," George said.

"And a donut, too?"

"I've never said no to one in the past, have I?"

"I've got a hunch you won't start now. By the way, they're on the house."

He frowned. "Suzanne, just because I'm retired doesn't mean I can't afford to buy my own coffee and donuts."

I grinned at him. "Actually, I was hoping you'd be willing to work on Desmond Ray's murder case with me. The coffee and donuts are your salary."

He nodded. "That's excellent news. How about Grace? Will she be working with us?"

I didn't have the heart to tell him that we'd already started digging into it. "Absolutely, she's on board."

"And Jake?" George asked, clearly hoping that my state police investigator boyfriend was going to be helping us, as well.

"Not this time, at least not yet. If we need him, though, I'm sure we can ask for a hand."

"Good enough," George said as he took a big bite of donut. "You know something? These things taste even better when they're on the house."

"You're not freeloading; we're bartering your time and talent for mine."

"I like that even better," he said as he took a sip of coffee. "So, where should we get started?"

I couldn't leave him in the dark any longer. "Grace and I have already been doing some preliminary work. We've come up with four names, and I was hoping we could split them down the middle with you."

George took out his small notebook, much like the ones Jake and Chief Martin carried with them, and then said, "I'm ready."

"So far, we've been able to discover that Katie Wilkes, Allen Davis, Jenny Ray, and Bill Rodgers might have motives to want to see Desmond dead. Talbot's Landing seems to figure into some of it, so that might be a good place to start."

"I'm surprised," George said as he looked at the names.

"By how well we did?" I asked.

"More like the two you left off," he replied.

"Tell me who we missed," I said.

"One has to be Jean Ray, and the other Gabby Williams. Whether we like it or not, we have to keep them in mind."

"I understand that," I said. "They're on our list, too, but we know where we can find them."

George nodded. "Now, tell me about the four I don't know."

"Katie was Desmond's ex-girlfriend, Allen was his ex-best friend, Bill was his ex-business partner, and Jenny is his cousin, who happens to be working his old job now at Jean's place helping her out."

"Looks like there are some possible reasons for murder there," George said. "Any way you'd like to divide this list up?"

"I was kind of hoping you'd be able to dig into all of their lives a little so we can find out where they are, and what their stories are. I don't mean that you should confront any of them directly, or even speak to them yet. Are we clear about that, George?" I was being pretty demanding since one time when I'd asked George for his active help, he almost hadn't survived a confrontation with a killer. Surgeries, rehab, and a cane all reminded me of how close I'd come to losing him, and it was just recently that his limp had finally begun to fade away.

"Got it. I can do some digging, and they won't even know I was investigating them."

"Just how are you going to manage that?" I asked as three customers walked in.

"With my computer," he said as I walked over to the new customers.

"Hey, where have you been?" one of them asked. "We were here an hour ago for donuts, and no one was here."

"I was in back making them," I said. "What can I get you, gents?"

"Your store hours might be nice," he said.

I pointed to the window. "Six to eleven," I said. "Now, are we talking, or are we getting donuts and coffee?"

One of the other men said, "I vote donuts."

"I second it," the third man said, "and don't forget the coffee."

"Looks like you're outvoted," I said to the man who'd protested our new hours. "Tell you what I'll do. For the trouble, I'll throw three glazed donuts onto your order, on the house."

"Three apiece?" one of them asked with a smile.

I returned his grin. "One per customer, and the offer's only good for another ten seconds. Nine, eight, seven —" "Sold," the first customer said.

"I'll see you at eleven," George said as he walked out of the shop.

I hoped he kept his word. I knew there was a good chance that someone on our list was a killer, and it wouldn't do to make any wrong moves, at least until we had a better idea of who exactly we were dealing with.

CHAPTER 9

"Good morning, ladies," I said with a smile as Terri Milner and Sandy White walked into the donut shop around nine. "Are the kids in school?"

"Oh, yes," Terri said, her relief obvious. "I dearly love my twins, but I'd be lying if I didn't admit that school is a lovely diversion."

"I feel guilty. I have just one son," Sandy said.

Terri smiled at her best friend. "Let's just say we both deserve a break and leave it at that."

"You should bring them by soon," I said. "I'm planning to start making my pumpkin surprises any day, and I know they all love them."

"You don't have to tell us," Terri said. "There's a half-day next Friday, so we'll bring them by at eleven-thirty. Save a few for us."

"I'm sorry, but I won't be open then," I admitted.

"You're closing the donut shop?" Terri said loudly enough to get attention I didn't want. "I'll hate to see this place go."

"I'm not closing down," I said, louder than I needed to. "I'm just shortening my store hours so I can have a little bit of a life for myself." Louder again this time, I said, "No worries. Donut Hearts is doing great! As far as I'm concerned, we'll be here forever."

That seemed to satisfy the folks in the shop, and when I turned back to Terri, she said, "Sorry about that. I didn't mean to shout. I just can't imagine my life without your donuts in it. Tell you what. I'll bring the girls in on Saturday. Will you have them then?"

"I'll make them specially for you all," I said.

"We'll be here, too," Sandy said. "Who knows? If our husbands are lucky, we'll let them come, too."

I loved being around them both, and was glad that they'd adopted my donut shop as one of their favorite places. "The more the merrier. Now, what can I get you today?"

"Two coffees, and two glazed donuts," Terri said.

"I'll have the same," Sandy added with a grin.

"I was ordering for both of us, you big goof."

"In that case, cancel my order," Sandy said.

Terri looked at her friend oddly. "You did know what I was doing, right?"

"Now who's being the big goof? Of course I did."

After I served them, they took their favorite sofa by the window that looked out on the old railroad tracks, and Trish's Boxcar Grille Diner. There was a touch of fog in the air, and as I glanced out the window myself, it almost appeared as though the car on rails might actually be moving. It was just one more reason I loved my old depot, and couldn't imagine ever giving it up for anything.

Twenty minutes later, the front door opened, but instead of a new donut customer, it was James Settle, the ironworker and blacksmith who was intent on destroying part of our town's heritage. I had to move him to the front of my to-do list and find a way to stop him from tearing up our tracks even as I worked to solve Desmond Ray's murder.

"You think you're cute, don't you?" Settle

181

said angrily as he approached me.

"Well, I'd *never* say that I was beautiful, but I believe cute is fairly accurate." I turned to the two mothers and asked, "What do you think? Am I overreaching?"

"No," Sandy said. "I think cute is right on the money. Terri?"

"Definitely," she said. "I've always thought that about you."

"That's not what I mean, and you know it," Settle said.

I frowned at him, pretending to be upset. "So, you don't think I'm cute? That's not very nice, is it?"

He shook his head. "Blast it, woman, that's not what I mean, and you know it. How did you do it? Did you pay off that old fossil to keep him from issuing my permit? How many donuts did it cost you, or did you trade him something else?"

"Be careful, Mr. Settle," I said as I grabbed the nearest weapon I could find, a pot full of scalding hot coffee. "I don't appreciate your tone of voice, or the implication of your accusation."

He looked mad enough to spit nails for a moment, and then held up his hands. "I'm sorry. You're right, I was completely out of line. I apologize."

I certainly hadn't expected that. "Could I

get you a cup of coffee?"

"To wear, or to drink?" he asked, a slight twinkle in his eye now.

"That all depends on your mood and your attitude," I said.

He looked at me for a few seconds, and then said, "Why not? I promise to be good."

I poured him a cup, and he slid his payment to me as he said, "I don't know why you're so attached to those rails anyway," he said. "You can't even see them under the grass and the weeds, and I could really use them."

"I know they're there, and that's enough for me. They can't be the only old tracks you can use. Leave ours alone."

"Sorry, but I can't do that," he said. In a calm voice, he said, "You might have slowed me down, but you haven't stopped me. I'm driving to Raleigh to get that permit, so I doubt they can claim they're out of them there."

I'd thought about that yesterday and had called Henry to see if Settle could do just that. I smiled at him as I said, "I'll save you a trip. The permits can only be issued to an approved and duly appointed registrant with their office."

He didn't look at all surprised to hear it. "So, you did have something to do with it.

How else would you know that particular fact?"

He had me there, but I was going to ride the bluff as long as I could do it with a straight face. "You'd be amazed by what you can learn working behind the counter at a donut shop. I'm just full of trivial and useless information."

He took a sip of coffee, and then said, "It wasn't exactly useless this time, though, was it?"

I did my best to look innocent, but I had a feeling I was falling far short of my goal, so all I could do was trust myself to shrug in reply.

"Thanks for the coffee," he said as he finished it and slid the empty mug toward me. "I'm sure I'll see you around. I'm not going anywhere."

I was afraid of just that. "Come again," I said.

As soon as he was gone, Terri came over. "What was that all about?"

"It's nothing," I said.

"Suzanne Hart, I know nothing when I see it. Spill."

I brought her up to speed, and she nodded as I finished telling her about it. "I'll talk to my husband about it."

I knew that Terri's spouse was an accountant, hardly someone schooled in ways of handling situations like this. "You don't have to bother. Really."

She shrugged. "I know I don't have to, but I want to." Terri looked behind me and said, "I think we'll take one of those crullers, too. Sandy and I can split it."

I managed to hide my surprise and served her the lightly glazed cruller. I'd almost skipped making them since the incident with Desmond, but I couldn't bring myself to do it, given the fact that I had customers who adored them. I made two types, one light and airy, and the other dark and dense. They played well off each other, and I hoped someday I'd be able to look at them again without flinching.

It was nearly eleven, and I had seven customers still in the donut shop. I considered staying open since I hated to turn people out onto the street, but I knew if I didn't stand firm, I'd end up back to my old schedule soon enough, and I wasn't prepared to do that. "Last call," I said as I walked from customer to customer with the coffeepot.

"I can't believe you're chucking us out," Billy Richmond said. Billy — a tall thin man with a full beard and unruly ash-blond hair

— worked a midnight-to-eight a.m. shift, and he was too wired up when he got off work to go straight home, so he usually ran some errands, and then came by the shop before going home to bed at noon. I was sympathetic, since I had crazy hours of my own, but I wasn't about to let him talk me into staying open.

"Believe it," I said with a grin. "More coffee?"

"No," he said, answering my smile with one of his own. "It would just keep me awake all day."

After everyone was gone, Emma walked out front. "I wasn't sure you'd have the heart to do it," she said.

"I'm not about to give up an hour of newfound freedom," I said. "How do things look in back? Have you started cleaning yet?"

"I'm nearly finished, as a matter of fact. Now I'm just waiting for the trays out here," she said. We boxed the remaining donuts, less than three dozen in all, which was a good thing. After setting them aside, Emma took the trays, and I carried the rest of the dirty dishes to the back. While she was cleaning up there, I ran our reports, balanced the register, made out the deposit, and then started sweeping the floor out

186

front. By eleven-fifteen, we were walking out the door together, and I was suddenly loving our new store hours.

I was at my Jeep when I heard a car horn.

Grace and George were in her company car, and both of them were waving to me.

It appeared that my team was ready and eager to get started on our case.

"Are those for me?" George said as he pointed to the boxed donuts in my hands. I'd slid into the backseat and kept the donuts in my lap.

"In a way. I thought we might use them to get close to our suspects."

Grace laughed. "I love it. Suzanne, you're lucky you don't make chain saws. They'd be a little tougher to give away."

"Who doesn't love donuts?" I asked. I looked at George and asked, "Were you able to find anything out?"

"You bet," he said as he pulled out his notebook. "You were right. Katie Wilkes lives in Talbot's Landing, and so does Allen Davis. As a matter of fact, the two of them both work at the same place."

"That might make it tough to interview them separately," I said. "We don't want them conspiring, do we?"

"That's not going to be a problem,"

George said. "Davis is off today, and you can probably find him at Strike Out when you get to town."

"What is that?" Grace asked.

"It's a bowling alley," George explained.

I couldn't believe the detailed information he'd gathered, and I began to suspect that George had done some personal interviews without my blessing. "Hang on a second. I can see how you might be able to discover that two of our suspects work together, but how on earth could you possibly know that Allen Davis is bowling?"

"Would you believe that I used my cop's instincts and made a guess based on my years on the police force and my intense knowledge about the human condition?" George asked with a grin.

"Not a chance. Spill."

He replied, "It was easy. I Googled them both, and I found their FacePlace pages. Allen was crowing about going bowling today on his day off. Tell me something, ladies. Why do people feel the need to report their every movement to the world on the Internet for everyone to see? No one's life is that interesting, as far as I'm concerned."

"It is to them," I said. "Emma's been after me to have a Web presence, as she calls it, for our donut shop, but I don't want to get wrapped up in it. We're doing fine as it is."

Grace said, "It can be a useful tool in sales. My company's starting to get into it."

"You can have it," I said. "I like things plain and simple."

Grace laughed at me. "That's my best friend, the technophobe. Could it have something to do with the fact that you still don't know how to text on your cell phone?"

"Hey, I can do it. It just takes me a while."

Grace shook her head. "It would be simpler if you'd just call."

I laughed triumphantly. "My point exactly. So, where do they work when they're together?"

"They are both on the staff at Duncan Construction," George reported. "Katie works at a desk inside, and Davis is on one of the work crews."

I nodded. "How about Bill Rodgers? Were you able to find anything out about him?"

George consulted his notebook again. "You bet. He hangs out some in Talbot's Landing, but he's got a business in Union Square, so that's where he spends most of his time," he said.

"Those are on opposite ends of the county," I said.

George nodded his agreement. "That's why we need to split them up. Why don't you two ladies take Talbot's Landing, and I'll handle Union Square?"

"What about our other three suspects?" I asked.

That got Grace's attention. "Three?"

I ticked them off on my fingers as I explained, "We've got Jean Ray, her niece Jenny, and last but not least, Gabby Williams."

"When are we going to speak more with them?" Grace asked.

I shrugged. "We'll have to tackle them later. For now, it's time to split up and approach the three suspects on our list we don't know yet."

As George started to get out of Grace's car, I asked him, "Would you like a box of donuts to use as a bribe?"

"I don't see how that would work," he said. "I can't exactly represent myself as a donut maker, can I?"

"You can still use them to break the ice," I said.

He shrugged as he took a box, and then said, "I'll be lucky if any of these make it to Union Square."

I laughed. "Hey, knock yourself out. Half a dozen might work just as well as a full dozen."

He smiled as he walked to his car. I slid

the rest of the donuts on the seat in back, and then got up front with Grace.

"So," I asked. "Should we go to the construction place first, or the bowling alley?"

"I vote the alley. By the time we get there, the construction company employees will most likely be at lunch."

"Strike Out it is," I said. As we drove, I added, "I'm not going to ask you about your date last night, so I'd appreciate it if you didn't share any details with me."

Grace laughed. "At least you're being a good sport about my news blackout. How was your evening? Did anything interesting happen?"

I hadn't planned to tell her what had happened, honestly, I hadn't. Speaking the words aloud would make them feel as though they were real in some way.

But I couldn't help myself.

"Oh, yes," I said, and then began to tell her all about my mother's wedding proposal.

"I can't believe it," Grace said after I finished.

"How do you think I feel?" I asked.

She glanced over at me. "What are you going to do?"

"I'm not sure there's anything I can do," I replied. "Momma's going to have to do what's best for her."

"If she accepts his proposal, you can move in with me," Grace said. "I'd love to have you as a roommate, and there's plenty of space at my house."

It was sweet of her to say it, but I knew how much Grace loved having her own space. "Thanks for the offer, but I'm not ready to make any plans just yet."

She drove a little farther down the road, and then glanced over at me. "Do you think there's a chance she's going to turn him down?"

I thought about it, and then answered, "If you'd asked me two days ago, I would have been sure of my answer when I said there was no way she'd accept, but you should have seen the look in her eyes when she told me. It was pretty clear she wanted to say yes."

"So, what's holding her back?" Grace asked. "It's not out of respect for you, is it?"

I shook my head. "Momma knows I'll land on my feet if she decides to go through with it. I gave her my blessing to do what ever she thought would make her happy. I don't know that there's really anything else

I can do."

Grace glanced over at me, and she must have seen the pain in my expression. I was glad that I'd unburdened my cares to my friend, and even happier that she hadn't tried to joke me out of my sadness with quips about getting a new daddy.

If she had, I wasn't entirely sure what I would have done.

"Can we talk about the case?" I asked. "I really need a change of subject right now."

"Sure thing," Grace said, obliging me. "Let me ask you something. When's the last time you went to a bowling alley?"

I had to think about it before I answered. "It must have been when Max and I were dating before we got married. He thought it would be a hoot, but he wasn't all that pleased when I beat him by twenty-seven pins."

Grace laughed. "His ego must have been pretty badly bruised. I'm glad you didn't let him win to soothe his manly sensibilities."

"Are you kidding? Max's ego was always the size of a tractor trailer. It was fun knocking him down a peg, even if it was just for a few minutes."

"He didn't hold it against you?" Grace asked.

"Oh, no, but he didn't congratulate me,

either. It didn't take long before the excuses started flying. His shoes were too slick, his wrist was sore, and the lights were in his eyes. It was all I could do not to laugh in his face." I paused, and then added, "I probably shouldn't have married him after seeing the way he reacted sometimes, but Max had a way of blinding me to his faults that I still can't figure out."

Grace patted my arm. "Suzanne, you weren't the first woman he fooled, and we both know you were nowhere near the last. Max just has a gift."

"I'm glad I finally broke free, but I'm not sure I'd been able to do it if I hadn't caught him with Darlene." I said a silent thank-you to the dead woman in my mind. I'd never been a big fan of hers, but she'd deserved better than she'd gotten in the end.

We were silent for a while, and then Grace pointed out the window. "There it is. Care to Strike Out?"

"We don't really have to bowl, do we?" I asked.

"No, I think it might be better if we just pretend to be admirers."

We pulled up in front, and I grabbed a dozen donuts from the back. Grace looked at me and said, "I'm not sure those are going to work in there."

"Trust me, there aren't many men who can turn down my donuts."

Grace shook her head. "You're actually taking your treats into a place where they serve their own food?"

I shrugged. "It's a way to ask our questions. If anybody protests, I'll give them a donut."

"That's your answer to everything, isn't it? Donuts make the world go round."

"I don't know about that, but they do grease the wheels sometimes."

We walked into the bowling alley together, and though it was lunchtime, most of the lanes were empty. A group of senior citizens was bowling along one side of the thirty-six lanes, and a preschool group was bowling at the other, with bumper rails in place to keep their errant balls out of the gutters.

In the middle, as though outcast from the rest of the world, were three singles playing on their own lanes, two men and one woman.

"Which one is our man?" I asked Grace.

"I'm not sure. Hang on a second." She walked over to the bored girl in her early twenties sitting on a stool behind the cash register and asked her a question. The sullen girl pointed to one of the men, and Grace nodded. When she came back to me,

I said, "So, she knows Allen."

"She should. He comes here every week-end, and every day off. Do you want me to lead, or do you?"

"I'll do it," I said. We approached him and sat in the seats just behind where the bowlers sat. Allen was older than I'd expected, tall and lanky, with a fierce glare of concentration as he approached the line.

After a successful strike, he looked back and appeared to notice us.

It was as good a time as any to break the ice with him. "Hi. Are you Allen?" I asked.

Instead of answering, he just nodded. "If you want a free lane, there are plenty open."

"Actually," I said, putting on my brightest smile, "we're here to see you. We brought you donuts," I added as I held the box up.

He didn't look at all pleased to see us there, with or without donuts. "Fine, but it will have to wait three frames until I'm finished."

"That's okay with us," I said, and Allen dismissed us.

"Wow, he really responded to you, didn't he?" Grace whispered. "I thought he was going to jump over the chairs to get to those donuts."

"Hey, I said they usually work, not al-

196

ways," I said. "Besides, he's focused on his game."

"I honestly believe that you could set his shoes on fire and he wouldn't realize it," Grace said.

Allen bowled again and again and again, and after he got a strike on his last ball, he turned back to us. "I don't believe we've met," he said as he changed out of custom bowling shoes and slipped a colorful ball into its bag. It was pretty clear Allen was serious about his hobby.

"I'm Suzanne, and this is Grace," I said. "Here are your donuts."

I offered them to him, but he just stared at the box as though it were poisoned. "Why would you do that?"

"We're sorry for your loss," Grace said.

That earned us a scowl. "I don't know what you're talking about. I didn't lose anything, or anybody."

"We're talking about Desmond Ray," I said.

He turned away from us then. "Desmond being shot is not a great loss for me," he said. "You're wasting your time, and your donuts."

"I understand that you two were best friends once," I said, trying my best to look confused and hurt at the same time. Turning down the donuts had stung a little, but I'd get over it. I wanted the man to feel obligated to talk with us.

"That was a long time ago," he said, perhaps a touch wistfully.

"Until Katie came along?" I asked gently.

He looked at me as though I'd slapped him hard across the mouth. "What do you know about Katie?"

"We're going to see her next," Grace said.

"Don't bother her," Allen said, his voice taking on a more ominous tone.

"We might not have to, if you help us," I answered. "It's really entirely up to you." That was a clear lie, as we had no intention of leaving town until we'd spoken to her as well, but Allen had no way of knowing that.

"What do you want to know?" he asked as he sat down in his chair.

"When's the last time you saw Desmond Ray?" I asked.

"It had to be months ago," he replied. "He came around the office looking for her, and we ran into each other."

"Where were you the night before last?" I asked him.

"I was home alone eating a pizza and watching a movie."

If I didn't know any better, I could have sworn he was mocking me, since that was

198

my own alibi for the time of the murder, but there was no way Allen could have known that.

I wasn't certain how he'd be able to prove anything he'd said one way or another, but it was something to file away. "Had you spoken to Desmond since he moved in with his aunt?"

"No," Allen said. "I didn't have anything to say to him. We were finished."

"What caused the break?" Grace asked.

"If you really must know, I didn't like the way he treated Katie," Allen replied. "He was never good enough for her, if you ask me."

"And you are?" Grace asked. Sometimes she got a little too pointed with her questions, but there were times when pressing got results.

Not this time, but sometimes.

"We're done here," Allen said as he stood and retrieved his shoes and bag.

"That's fine," I said. "We'll just take the rest up with Katie."

Allen stood very close to me, and then said in a growl, "Stay away from her, if you know what's good for you."

"Is that a threat? We just want to talk."

"Think of it as fair warning," Allen said.

Grace piped in, "One more thing. Do you

own a handgun?"

He didn't answer, which was no big surprise to either of us.

As Allen walked to the door, I couldn't help calling out, with humor in my voice, "Hang on a second. Don't you want your donuts?"

He didn't even break stride as he walked off.

"What do you make of that?" I asked Grace.

"He's clearly not a big fan of your donuts."

"I'm not talking about that, and you know it. He doesn't have an alibi that can be checked, and he was pretty vague about everything but the way he feels about Katie."

"Sounds like Allen belongs right where he is on our list," I said. "Shall we go find Katie, or is Allen warning her about us right now?"

"There's only one way to find out," I said. "Let's go see if we can track her down."

Donut Toppings

There are lots of ways to finish up your donuts, and we are constantly experimenting with toppings. Some folks like it simple, while some go wild! Don't be afraid to play!

Some choices are:

Confectioner's sugar dusted over the top with a small sifter

3 tablespoons sugar, white granulated, mixed with 3 teaspoons cinnamon

Store-bought icing from a tub or tube

Chocolate glaze, made over a double boiler by melting equal parts semisweet chocolate and heavy cream.

A favorite candy with mint and chocolate melted and heavy cream

A glaze made up of 1 cup confectioner's

sugar, 1/4 cup of vanilla, and 1 teaspoon vanilla extract or 1 teaspoon orange extract combined until smooth.

After icing, sprinkles can be added, or any commercial candy you like!

CHAPTER 10

We got to the construction company after one wrong turn, and as we pulled into a spot in front of the large corrugated blue building, Grace asked, "How should we approach her?"

"We give her donuts," I said as I spotted a lone woman on a bench to one side eating a takeout meal. "Unless I miss my guess, Katie's right there."

"There may be more than one woman working here," Grace said.

I got out, grabbed the box of donuts that Allen had turned down, and said, "She looks just like the girl in the photograph, so unless she has a twin, that's got to be Katie." When I saw that Grace wasn't making a move, I asked, "Aren't you coming?"

"I'd love to, but we don't want her to feel like we're ganging up on her. I'll stay here and make some calls while you two talk."

I nodded, shut the door, and then approached Katie with my best smile.

"Excuse me, but are you Katie Wilkes?"

I could see that she was short even though she was sitting down, and petite enough to make me envious of her figure.

"Who wants to know?"

She was guarded, but not openly hostile. Maybe Allen hadn't called her after all.

I handed her the donuts, which she took without another thought. "I knew Desmond Ray, and I wanted to offer you my condolences."

If she was going to react badly, now would be the time. In a numb voice, she said, "I still can't believe he's gone." The tough attitude was gone completely, and her features softened in an instant.

I looked into her eyes and saw that she'd been crying. "I'm so sorry," I said. "I understand you two had just broken up."

Katie shook her head. "That's not true at all," she protested. "We were taking a little break to collect our thoughts about the future of our relationship, but Desmond and I both knew that we were destined to be together."

That wasn't anywhere close to the way I'd heard it, but it didn't seem the best time to contradict her. "I'm surprised you're at work today."

She shrugged. "I probably wouldn't be if I had a choice, but I need the money, and besides, staying home dressed in black isn't going to help him. I had to get out of my tiny apartment, so I figured I might as well come here."

It was time to ask the big question. "Where were you when he died?"

"I was taking a long walk," she said wistfully. "I love it when it gets brisk. Desmond used to walk with me sometimes, and strolling through town made me feel closer to him somehow while we were on a break. It gave me time to think, and realize that we belonged together."

"Were you alone?" I asked.

"It's hard to collect your thoughts if someone's talking to you," she said.

I couldn't just let it go. "Did you see anyone, stop to chat, or anything?"

The second I saw her reaction to my prodding, I realized that I'd pushed her too far. "Why do you want to know? Just who are you?"

"I told you already. I'm just an old friend of Desmond's," I said.

She looked at me suspiciously. "Are you one of the tarts he went out with sometimes?"

"No, we never dated," I said. It was an

interesting fact to pick up that Katie had rivals for Desmond's affection, and I added it to my mental file.

"Do you have a name?"

"I'm Suzanne. Suzanne Hart," I admitted.

"Funny, Desmond never mentioned you," Katie said. "How good a friend were you?"

"He came to my donut shop a couple of days ago," I admitted.

"You're the cruller lady," Katie replied, a look of illumination on her face.

"I prefer to be known as a donut distributor," I said, trying to get a smile and ease some of the tension between us.

"He wasn't a big fan of yours," Katie said.

"How could you possibly know that? Did you speak with him the day before yesterday?"

She hesitated just a second before she denied it. "Like I said, we were on a break. We were going to discuss getting back together tomorrow, but that's not going to happen now."

Before I could ask her anything else, she began to cry, maybe in earnest and maybe not, and a heavyset man with dirty jeans, soiled flannel shirt, and thick work boots came out of the building. He towered over her as he leaned down and asked softly,

"Katie, are you okay?"

"I'm fine, Chet," she said through her tears.

"Is this woman bothering you?" he asked as he studied me.

"Yes," she said through her sniffles. "I don't want to talk about Desmond, but she won't stop asking me questions."

Chet took a step toward me, and I could feel the force of his presence radiating like sunlight toward me. In a calm and still voice, he said, "You should leave."

"We were just chatting," I said. "I didn't mean to upset her."

"But you did," Chet replied, and took one more step toward me. I had to wonder if he would have tried to intimidate Jake that way if he'd been with me, but if Chet had had the audacity to try it, I knew my boyfriend wouldn't have backed down. I wasn't a state police investigator, though, and I really didn't have any justification for being there other than digging into Desmond's murder on my own.

"Fine, I was just going," I said. As I started toward Grace's car, I turned back to Katie and said, "If you want to help me find out who killed him, call me at Donut Hearts in April Springs any morning before eleven."

Chet wasn't impressed with my statement,

but he stopped moving toward me, which was a very good sign.

I figured the best thing I could do at the moment was retreat.

"Drive," I said when I got in the car. At least Grace was off the telephone.

"What happened?" she asked me as she started the engine.

"I'll tell you as soon as we get out of the parking lot." I looked back and saw Chet watching us intently.

I didn't take another breath until Grace drove out of the parking lot. I had a feeling that if I needed to approach Katie again, it wouldn't be at her place of work. Chet hadn't threatened me, but I'd still felt intimidated by his presence, whether because of his size, or the way he spoke, I couldn't say.

After I brought Grace up to speed on my conversations with Katie and Chet, she said, "It sounds as though he's a little overprotective of her."

"He's more than a fellow employee, I'd say, but I'm not sure how much more."

"Are there any other folks you want to rile up while we're in town?" Grace asked.

"No, I think that's it for now."

As we drove back home, Grace asked, "Did you believe Katie when she said that she and Desmond were on a break?"

"Either she was lying to me, or to herself," I said. "I'm not sure which answer I'd prefer, but either way, her name stays on our list."

Grace nodded. "So, it seems that both of our suspects had a reason to want to see Desmond dead."

"Hey, you know how this works. You get as many facts as you can, and then you go from there."

I wasn't looking forward to comparing notes with George. Grace and I hadn't added much to our knowledge in our quest to find information about who might have killed Desmond Ray.

Grace and I chatted aimlessly on the drive back, and as we entered the town limits of April Springs, I said, "I might as well go ahead and give George a call."

"You don't have to," Grace said as she pointed to a bench in front of the court house. I looked and saw George sitting there alone, resting in the sun and rubbing his bad leg. I'd thought he was fine now, but it appeared that his leg was still giving him some trouble.

Grace parked her car and we got out. We weren't being particularly quiet, but we didn't even startle George until I asked, "Is your leg hurting again?"

He opened his eyes, and then made a point to stretch, as though he'd been napping. How bad must it be if he was willing to let me think he'd nodded off instead of admitting to the pain? "What? I didn't hear you come up. I must have fallen asleep in the sunlight."

I wasn't going to let him have that particular lie. As I sat next to him, I said gently, "Give it up, my friend. I saw you rubbing your leg. You weren't asleep."

"Hey, he said he was napping," Grace said.

"Yeah, listen to your friend," George added.

I couldn't just let it go, though. In a softer voice, I said, "George, I'm just asking because I care about you. You need to tell me if I'm pushing you too hard."

"You know what? You are right now," George answered.

I had to laugh. "I'm not talking about interrogating you about your leg, and you know it. I mean asking you to investigate for us. Your health comes first."

He didn't like the implication. "Blast it all, Suzanne, I'm not a cripple, or an old man, either."

It was his pride talking, I knew it. It was

time to try another approach. "George, would you tell me the truth about your leg if I asked you nicely?"

"Maybe," he said.

After a long pause, I realized what he was waiting for. "How's your leg holding up?"

He nodded. "Usually it feels pretty good, but when it's going to rain, it throbs a little."

"Is it going to rain soon?" Grace asked as she sat on the other side of him.

George grinned. "If my leg's any indication, we'd better get ready for the next Great Flood. I hope there's another Noah building an ark somewhere nearby."

I was so pleased he'd admitted his discomfort that I decided to drop it. As long as he was being honest with us, I'd worry less about him.

"I hope you had better luck today than we did," I said.

"Couldn't you find either one of them?" he asked. I saw his hand go back to his leg, give it a quick squeeze, and then drop it just as quickly when he realized that I was watching him.

"We found them both, but they weren't exactly cooperative," I answered.

Grace grinned as she added, "It was hard for us to make much headway, even with her donut bribe. Allen wouldn't even take them, and Katie didn't budge an inch after she accepted them without question."

"Come on, I can't believe you two didn't get anything out of either one of them."

I shrugged. "Both their alibis were loose and impossible to prove one way or the other."

George thought about that for a moment, and then nodded. "I might be able to do something about that. I've still got a few favors coming to me from the police department, so I'll be able to see if either one of them has a registered weapon. I'll check the rest of our suspect list, as well," George said as he jotted a few notes down in his notebook.

"Is there anything else?" he asked as he finished writing.

"That's about it," I said. "There's really not much left to say."

"Tell me anyway," George said. "I'm not ready to get up yet. This sunshine just feels too good."

I wasn't sure if that was strictly true, or if George's leg was hurting him to the point where he couldn't walk without a limp, and he refused to do that in front of us. But either way, I decided to humor him. "Well, we found a man who was willing to run us off just because he thought we were making

Katie a little uncomfortable."

Grace shook her head. "Now is not the time to understate things, Suzanne. I saw the look on his face as you walked back to the car; you didn't."

George seemed interested in that fact. "Could he be a suspect, as well?"

"I suppose it's possible," I admitted.

George took out his notebook and asked, "What did you learn about him?"

"Not much," I said. "His first name is Chet, but I didn't get a last name. He's huge, he works construction, too, and he's overprotective of Katie."

"That's a lot," George said as he jotted the information down. "I can work with that. In an hour, I'll have a last name to match his first."

Grace asked, "You're not going there yourself, are you?"

I hoped not. George could take care of himself, but I wouldn't send Jake up against Chet without backup, and he was a lot younger than George, and more fit, as well.

He smiled. "Why go there when I've got everything I need at the tip of my fingers on the Internet? I've got to tell you, since I was injured, I've spent a lot of time on my computer. It's amazing what you can un-cover out in cyberspace, if you just know the right places to ask your questions."

"That's excellent," I said. "We've shared our information with you, so now it's your turn. What did you discover?"

"Less than you," he admitted. "Bill Rodgers was in Charlotte today so I never got to see him. I can't even find out a way to talk to him, let alone learn where he was when the murder occurred."

"So, we haven't had a good day, have we," I said.

"Don't worry. It's early," George said.

I glanced at my watch. "I don't know what you're talking about. It's nearly five," I said.

He must not have seen my smile, because it was clear he hadn't realized that I'd been kidding. "I don't mean in time, but in the course of our investigation. We've got some things we can start checking, and new people to investigate." George stood then, and I saw him steady himself on the back of the bench where we were sitting before he trusted himself to walk just yet. "If you ladies will excuse me, I've got someplace I need to be."

He walked away, fighting not to limp as he did it, which just made it that more obvious.

"He's hurting, isn't he?" Grace asked me.

"A lot more than he's willing to let on," I

admitted. "I'm worried about him, but talking to us was a big step, and I didn't feel like I could push him any harder than I did."

"You were a little tough on him, Suzanne," Grace said softly.

I looked at my best friend. "I admit it, I was. But I knew he'd try to kid us and deflect all day if I didn't get to the heart of it. Being blunt was the only way I knew I could get his attention."

"Wow, just don't try to get my attention anytime soon," Grace said with a smile.

"Don't worry, you're safe, for now," I answered. "What time are you going out tonight on your date?"

Grace glanced at the town clock high above us. "Actually, I don't have much time before I have to get ready. Sorry to bail on you again."

I grinned at her. "Are you kidding? I'm thrilled about it."

"Come on, I'll give you a ride back to your Jeep," Grace said.

"Thanks, but it's not that far to walk, and besides, George was right. The sun feels good, and we won't have that much longer until it really starts getting cold around here. I think I'll hang out here and take it all in while I still can. Have fun tonight."

"Always," Grace said. I sat back down and

watched her get into her car and drive away. There was a big grin on her face, which I wasn't sure she could tell that I saw. I was really happy for her, and I hoped it worked out with this guy. She deserved to find a little happiness in her life.

I was still sitting on the bench taking in the warmth of the day when a shadow passed over me, blocking out the sun.

I was surprised when I looked up to find Jean Ray standing there.

"Hello, Jean," I said. "Care to join me?"

"If you wouldn't mind," she replied.

I made room for her on the bench, and as she settled beside me, she said, "I've been making arrangements for Desmond all day. It's really exhausting."

"You shouldn't have to do that alone," I said. "Would you like me to help?"

"Thank you for the kind offer," Jean said, "but Jenny has stepped in, and I must admit, she's been a force to reckon with. I'm not sure how I could have done it all without her."

"It's good to have someone you can rely on," I said, purposely keeping my voice level. If I let Jean have any idea what I thought of her niece, I was afraid I would alienate her from me, and having her on my side would be a lot better than having her against me.

"I worry about some of the things she's saying, though," Jean said.

I couldn't wait to hear what that might be. "Anything in particular that's bothering you?" I asked.

"I shouldn't say," she told me, but I could tell that there was a part of her that really wanted to share it with someone else.

"I'm here for you, Jean, and I won't judge you or her, no matter what you tell me. I'd like to think that we're friends."

Jean appeared to think about that, and then finally nodded. "You're right. Suzanne, I can't tell you how much joy your quaint little shop has brought me since you opened it."

"I'm glad to have you there anytime," I answered, and then added, "Jean, you can trust me, you know that, don't you?"

"Of course I do, but it's probably just nothing. My imagination tends to get the better of me lately."

"What's troubling you?" I asked.

She was about to answer when Jenny hurried up to where we were sitting. "There you are," she said, scolding her aunt. "When I turned around a minute ago, you were gone. You can't just wander off like that."

"I needed to rest," Jean said, her gaze

shifting to me as she said it.

"Of course you did. You must be exhausted," Jenny said. "Let's go home."

Jean sounded weary as she asked her niece, "Would you mind getting the car, dear? I'll sit here and wait with Suzanne."

Jenny appeared to consider that, and clearly didn't find it to her liking. "It's not that far, and besides, we have one more stop to make along the way. I promise, we're almost finished, and then we can go back home."

I didn't like the possessive way Jenny kept saying the word "home," and it was clear that Jean hadn't cared for it, either.

"I don't mind staying with her," I said.

"Nonsense," Jenny said, putting more force into her words. "Let's go, Aunt Jean."

She put a hand under her aunt's arm, and Jean stood. Before Jenny could drag her away, Jean turned to me and asked, "Suzanne, I hate to impose, but could you come by the house for a visit tonight?"

"I'd love to," I said.

Jenny frowned. "I'm afraid that won't work, Aunt Jean. Some friends of mine are bringing over dinner tonight, and I don't know how long they'll be there."

"Tomorrow then," Jean said.

"We'll see. It's going to be awfully busy,"

Jenny replied. She turned to me and said, "We'll call you."

As Jean was being led away, she glanced back at me one last time. It was clear she was uneasy about something, and I had a hunch what it was. Jenny had been in town less than a day, and she was already running her aunt's life as though it were her job. Was that why Jean was upset, or was there more to it than that?

I was going to find out, and I wouldn't let Jenny stop me from seeing her aunt now that I knew she wanted to talk to me.

The sun was beginning to set, so I decided to walk back to my Jeep. I was three feet away from it when my cell phone rang, and I was delighted to learn that it was Jake.

"Hey, stranger," I said. "How did the day's lecture go?"

"Better than I had any right to expect," he said with a laugh. The chuckle told me more than his words. He'd had a good time and was happy about it, something I didn't get to hear all that often in his voice. It was the nature of the business he was in — dealing with death and all of the dark things that occupied the worst parts of the human condition, to be saddened by it all — but for the moment, there was a real lightness in his voice that I loved to hear. "It turns out that teaching can be fun, once you get the hang of it."

"Since you've just been doing it a few days, it didn't take you long, did it?"

"Okay, I'm no pro yet, but I can't tell you how nice it feels not to be hunting down bad guys for a change. How was your day?"

"Let's see. I got up way too early even with my new hours, spent the day making and selling donuts, and then ran into dead end after dead end in my investigation. It was peachy, just peachy."

"Don't give up, Suzanne, you're too good at this to just walk away."

"From donut making, or sleuthing?" I asked with a laugh.

"Either one," he said. I loved that Jake had given up his early opposition to my amateur investigations and was now more accepting of the idea that I could mine information that was unavailable to the police.

I was about to thank him for the compliment when I heard a familiar woman's voice speak to him. "Come on, Jake, we're going to be late for dinner."

"Was that Ashley?" I asked.

"She wants to make up for tricking me, so she's offered to take me to dinner tonight."

I could imagine her asking, but I was a little surprised that he'd accepted. I was about to comment on that when he said, "I'm sorry, Suzanne, but I've got to go. Talk to you tomorrow."

He hung up before I could even say good night. There was something about that exchange that left me less than satisfied with the situation, and I needed to talk to someone about it. I saw that Grace's official date hadn't started yet, so I took a chance on calling her so I could talk about it with her.

Thankfully, she picked up on the first ring. "Where are you?"

"I'm at my Jeep," I answered, a little confused by the question.

"Oh, it's you."

"Hey, I deserve better than that, don't I?" I asked.

"He's two minutes late," Grace said.

"Wow, you're one tough gal to date. You might want to cut the guy a little slack," I said.

"We've got reservations," she said, "but I might be able to get them pushed back a little. What's going on, Suzanne? Did something happen?"

"Yes, but not with the case." I felt so silly saying it that I wondered why I'd called her in the first place. "You know what? Forget it, Grace. It's not important. Have a nice night."

"Suzanne Hart, don't you dare hang up that phone. Now tell me, what's going on?"

I took a deep breath, and then said, "Jake just called. Our conversation was kind of abrupt, because he had to go to dinner."

"That's understandable," Grace said.

"With Ashley," I finished.

There was a longer pause than I liked, and the silence just seemed to drag on and on. I finally asked, "Grace, are you still there?"

"I am. I'm just trying to figure out what to say," she said.

I didn't like the sound of that. "You don't think there's anything to it, do you? Tell me I'm just being paranoid."

She paused again, and then said, "Jake cares deeply for you. He's not about to throw that away, especially with your niece."

"You know, technically she's Max's niece, not mine."

"You know what I mean."

"So, I don't have anything to worry about?"

Grace was a little more somber than I liked when she answered. "I don't know that I'd say that, either. It might not be a bad idea to visit him at the campus tomorrow."

I didn't like that idea at all. "I've got work

to do, and an investigation to run. Besides, if I just show up, he'll think I don't trust him."

"Do you?" Grace asked.

"Of course I do." At least I thought I did.

"Then there's nothing to worry about." I heard a doorbell ring in the background, and she added quickly, "Sorry, Suzanne, but I've got to go. He's here."

I was about to say good night when she hung up on me, as well. There seemed to be a lot of that going on lately, and I had to admit, I wasn't a big fan of it.

As I drove back home, I knew in my heart that Jake was faithful to me, no matter what the temptation. I was just being silly, but it still didn't help ease the anxiety I felt about his dinner plans. While I knew without vanity that I was at least a little attractive, I'd be lying if I didn't admit that I was no raving beauty, even when I'd been in my early twenties, and that was some time ago. Ashley was, for want of a better word, a knockout, and while I didn't dream for one second that she'd set her sights on Jake, I probably would have felt better if she was back in her dorm studying instead of having dinner with my boyfriend.

CHAPTER 11

Momma was out again — presumably on another date — when I got home, and I couldn't face more leftovers, so I got back into my Jeep and drove to Trish's diner. I knew I could just as easily have walked the short distance through the park, but it was dark out, and I was feeling more than a little vulnerable at the moment. I knew what the real problem was. As much as I loved my independence and freedom, sometimes I got lonely, and tonight was definitely that kind of night. I wanted to be around people who were laughing, arguing, having deep discussions, just living their lives. I knew that I could get so wrapped up in my life that sometimes I forgot there was another world out there going about its business without a single thought or care about mine.

After fighting the temptation as long as I could, I tried calling Jake to see if his dinner was over, but when I did, the call went straight to voice mail. That was just about more than my overactive imagination could take at the moment. I almost turned around and drove back home, but I was still hungry, so I decided to keep going.

Trish was working the front when I walked in. "Hey, Suzanne, how are you?" She took a second look at me, and then added, "Is everything okay?"

I glanced around the diner and saw several couples out together, young and old, and the only place to sit was at the bar. "I'm fine. You're busy. I'll come back another time."

She touched my arm before I could go. "You're not getting away that easily. There's always room for you here. Why don't you sit right here and we can chat while I work?"

I couldn't just leave, not that way. "Okay. Thanks."

"What can I get you? After you order, we can talk."

"I'll have the special, whatever it is," I said.

"Don't you even want to know what we're serving tonight?" Trish asked. "You really are off your game tonight."

"Okay, what is it?" I asked.

"Country-style steak, green beans, and mashed potatoes."

"That all sounds great," I said.

Trish gave her cook the order, and then poured me a glass of sweet tea without asking. She knew well enough that I had usually had Coke with my burgers and sweet tea with everything else, though I changed it sometimes just to be different.

As Trish slid the glass in front of me, she said, "It won't take a minute, but you still have time to tell me what's going on."

I saw an older couple approach the register with their bill. "You really don't have time for this, and nothing's wrong, anyway. I'm just feeling a little sad, blue, and alone. I bet you never feel sorry for yourself, or all alone in the world, do you?"

Trish's smile dampened for a moment. "Trust me, I have more than my share of dark days, too."

"How do you cope with them?" I asked her.

"Mostly, I just come into work, get busy, and after I start dealing with the folks who come in, my problems just fade away."

"And what happens when they don't?" I asked.

"I have a piece of pie," she said.

"I'm serious, Trish. I'd really like to know."

She looked at me steadily. "Suzanne, I wouldn't lie to you."

There was a bell from the kitchen, and

she returned a second later with my plate. As Trish slid it in front of me, I took in the rich aroma of the gravy-laden steak, saw the real butter melting on top of the mashed potatoes, and marveled at the bright green tones of the beans.

"What do you think?" Trish asked me.

"It looks good enough to eat," I said.

Trish laughed, and then patted me on the back. "I'm really glad you came in tonight."

"You know what? I am, too," I said.

I finished my meal, good to the last forkful, and was about to ask her for the bill when she whisked my plate away and put a large slice of apple pie down in front of me.

"I couldn't possibly eat this," I said.

"I'll put it in a box, then," Trish said as she started to take it away.

I put my hand on the plate to stop her. "Well, maybe I could manage one bite," I said.

Trish laughed, and then said, "Good for you. I knew deep down that you were my kind of gal."

"Hey, someone who makes treats for a living can't afford to turn her nose up at pie when she gets the chance."

"Don't sell what you do short," Trish said. "You make a lot of people in April Springs happy with those donuts you make. It's not a little thing, bringing some joy into the world."

"I know, and I love it. I'm just having one of those evenings."

She looked stunned by the admission. "Still? After eating a slice of my world-famous apple pie?"

I realized that I was feeling better, though whether it was due to the food or the company, I couldn't say.

It made me glad, yet again, that I lived in a small town.

I was trying to get interested in a movie on television, but my thoughts kept skipping to a thousand different places. No matter where they went, though, they always returned to Jake. I trusted him, but that didn't mean I wasn't curious about why he wasn't answering his phone.

When the actors in the movie began discussing something that had just happened — something that I'd clearly missed — I turned off the show and thought about going to bed, even though it was early, even for me.

I'd just stood when the front door opened, and Momma came in. "Suzanne, how was your evening?"

I considered telling her about Jake and his

dinner with Ashley, but honestly, I didn't feel like rehashing it with her. "I'd love to tell you it was uneventful, but I'd be lying."

"Do I want to know?" she asked as she hung her jacket up.

"I don't think so. Can I get a free pass tonight?"

Momma must have seen something in my eyes, because she nodded and said, "Of course you may."

"How was your date?"

"It was quite lovely, actually," she said, and though I knew Chief Martin wouldn't have described it that way in a million years, I was certain that he would have been pleased to hear it nonetheless.

"How goes the decision-making process? Come to any conclusions yet?"

She laughed, a surprising reaction as far as I was concerned. "That's funny, you sound just like Phillip."

"I bet his request for the information was a little more urgent than mine," I said with a grin. I couldn't help getting a little tweak in.

"I'll tell you what I just told him. I'm not ready to make a decision one way or the other. If you must know, I think he's relieved that he didn't get an outright refusal, and he's taking my delay as encouragement more than anything else."

"Who can blame him? You certainly shocked me when you didn't say no right away."

Instead of being upset, Momma just nodded as she sat down on the couch. After I joined her there, she said, "At first, I thought he was insane when he proposed. We've known each other our entire lives, but we've only been dating for a few months."

I saw a look in her eyes that surprised me. "But now?"

She glanced at me a moment, and then asked, "Do you want the truth, or would you like to hear what you want to hear?"

That answer wasn't as easy as it should have been, but I knew what to say. "The truth. Always the truth."

I hoped I meant it, but even if I wasn't entirely convinced that it was true, I was still glad I'd said it.

"The idea of being with him has some real advantages," she finally said. "As much as I love having you here and sharing this home with you, the prospect of spending the rest of my life with a man who clearly adores me isn't to be discounted lightly."

"I guess the real question is, how do you feel about him?"

She took a deep breath, and then let it

out slowly. "That *is* the heart of the matter, isn't it?"

"Do me a favor, Momma."

"For you? Anything," she said as she touched my shoulder lightly.

"Don't turn him down because you're worried about me. Grace has offered me a room at her place, so if you decide to marry him, I won't get in your way, and I certainly don't want to be used as an excuse for you to say no, if marrying him is what you want to do."

She looked shocked by the declaration. "Why, that never even occurred to me."

It was time to lay my position out on the table. "Momma, I can't stay here when you're trying to build a new life with someone else. It's nothing against you or the police chief. I just don't want to get in the way."

"Suzanne, I would never bring another man into this house. Your father and I spent our entire married life here together, and I won't do anything to touch those memories. I thought you understood that if I say yes, I'll be the one moving out, not you. The house will be yours, and yours alone."

That was a blockbuster, and I wasn't sure how to react. "Momma, are you sure? This is the only place you've lived all your life.

How could you leave?"

"I don't have to tell you that getting married involves some sacrifices for both people."

I looked around our homey place filled with love and memories. "But it's a lot to give up," I said.

"And at least as much to gain," she said. "No matter what happens, this is your home. Do you understand that?"

"I do now," I said, surprised to hear her say it. "I don't know what I'd do if you weren't here, though. The place would feel as empty as my heart would with you gone."

She hugged me, and I returned it.

"I love you," she said.

"I love you, too." I pulled away, and then said, "I meant what I said. I just want you to be happy. Everything else is just details to work out later."

She nodded, and then looked hard at me. "Here I've been so wrapped up in my life that I missed it completely."

"Missed what?" I asked.

"You're troubled, aren't you? Talk to me, Suzanne."

How did she do it? Did my momma have some kind of radar for when my heart was weary, my step unsure? No matter how I tried to hide my unhappiness from her, she always found a way to see it, and many times, more clearly than I did.

"It's Jake, isn't it," she said, not as a question, but as an answer.

"Yes," I said, "but I'm just being silly."

"Nonsense. When it comes to matters of the heart, especially for Hart women, it's never silly. Now, tell me all about it."

I took one last stab at holding her off. "What about my free pass?"

"Rescinded," she said with a smile. "Now talk."

"Well, I may have done something really stupid. I pointed a beautiful young brunette college student at Jake, and they're having dinner together right now." At least I hoped they were still eating.

"I'm going to need more details than that," she said.

"I told you I ran into Max's niece Ashley at the Boxcar, right?"

"Certainly."

I took a deep breath, and then admitted, "Well, I asked her to run up to him on campus, hug him, and call him Uncle Jake."

Momma frowned her disapproval. "Why on earth would you do that?"

"I thought it would be funny," I answered.

I expected to get the scolding I deserved, but instead, she just shook her head. "Sometimes things can blow up in our faces, can't they?"

"I'm really hoping it didn't this time," I said.

Momma patted my hand. "Suzanne, Jake cares for you very deeply. I cannot imagine the circumstances where he'd cheat on you, especially with a young woman who is essentially still a little girl."

"She may not be as old as I am, but if you'd seen her, you'd never think she was a little anything. Ashley was always pretty, but she's turned into a real beauty."

"Still, Jake wouldn't do anything with her. I'm sure of it."

It felt good hearing her say that. "I am, too, but then again, I was sure of Max, and look how that turned out."

Momma pulled her hand away and frowned as she looked at me. "Max has no right to be mentioned in the same breath as Jake. They are two completely different men, as opposite as you're ever likely to find. Don't paint your new boyfriend with the same brush you use for your ex-husband. If you do, that will be your major mistake, not introducing him to Ashley."

"I know you're right, but it's so hard. Once you've been cheated on, there's no way to keep from being a little jumpy." I sighed, and then added, "If there is, I haven't found it, anyway."

"I'm happy to say that I never experienced that myself, but you've got to find a way to let the past stay where it belongs. It's the only way you'll ever have a future."

"Hey, are we still talking about me?" I asked with a grin.

My jibe could have gone either way, so I was relieved when Momma just laughed. "Perhaps a little of both, if I'm being honest myself. Have you tried to call Jake again?"

"Yes, but his phone goes straight to voice mail," I said.

"Which could mean any number of things," Momma said. "Sometimes your imagination can get the best of you, Suzanne."

"I know, but there's nothing I can do about it." I stifled a yawn, and then asked, "Would you like to play a game or something?"

"Thank you for the offer, but it's late, and we both need our rest," she said as she stood.

"I'm not sure I'll be able to sleep tonight," I admitted.

"You at least owe it to yourself, and all of your customers tomorrow, to try. After all, you don't want to put blueberries in the strawberry donuts now, do you?"

"Well, that would make them blueberry donuts, wouldn't it?" I asked with a laugh.

"Good night, Suzanne."

"Good night, Momma," I answered. I walked up the stairs, and she went into the master suite downstairs.

As I lay in bed trying to sleep, I tried to imagine our cottage without my mother's presence all around me. If she did marry the police chief and left to start a new life with him, I wouldn't move downstairs, I promised myself then and there. This was my bedroom — it had always been such, with the exception of four years away at college and the time I'd wasted with Max — and I wasn't about to move. Besides, if I did that, I'd miss my lovely views of the park. That had directly led to some problems in my past, but for the most part, it had been a joyful place to live, and I wouldn't change rooms just because I'd get a little more space. Then again, if Jake and I ever decided to get married, there wouldn't be enough room for us both upstairs, and I'd be forced to move down with him.

"Whoa, slow down, girl," I said to myself. I wasn't exactly certain that he was still my boyfriend at the moment, let alone a potential mate. I wasn't just putting the cart before the horse, I didn't even have a cart yet, and barely a horse.

I had to laugh at the nonsense of it all, not letting myself consider the fact for one moment that because of the way Jake had lost his wife and child, he might never want to get married again. Goodness, he couldn't even tell me that he loved me.

With mixed emotions, I finally drifted off to sleep, wondering what tomorrow would bring, and if I'd ever hear from Jake again.

Emma came in late the next morning, despite our new hours, and I wasn't in the best of moods to begin with.

"You're kidding, right? You know what the new schedule is, don't you?" I asked her as I added bits of orange slice candy to my new orange glaze. I'd tried adding real orange chunks the first time, but they'd absolutely ruined the glaze. Nobody who came into my shop was really concerned about healthy fruits and vegetables anyway, at least not during their visit to Donut Hearts. The candies added a real boost to the glaze, and I decided to increase the orange extract to the next batter I made for orange cake donuts, as well.

"I'm really sorry," she said as she put on her apron. "It couldn't be helped."

"You didn't oversleep, did you?" I asked with a hint of a grin as I turned off the small mixer. There was no reason to take my bad mood out on her.

"Believe it or not, I couldn't get my dad to wake up, and it took forever to get here."

"What's your father got to do with you being late for work?" I asked, being careful to keep my voice light.

"He had to drive me over here so he could have my car today. His is in the shop."

I finished mixing the last batter and asked, "I'm just curious, but why couldn't your mom do it?"

"She's out of town again, and honestly, who can blame her? Didn't I tell you about that? I really am sorry."

Emma looked so pathetic I had to laugh. "It's okay. Can you empty the orange glaze into one of our small containers?"

She looked at my latest creation, then took a spoon and sampled from the bowl. "Man, that is sweet," she said as she put the spoon in the sink.

"Is it too much?" I asked. I hoped I hadn't ruined the glaze. It wasn't that expensive to replace, not that I liked to just throw money away, but the time it would take to make a new batch was in short supply at the moment.

"Are you kidding? I think it's perfect."

"Good. I need to get started on the cake donuts, so if you'll take care of the icing, I can get started."

Emma skimmed the icing tank as I started measuring ingredients, and we were soon working in steady rhythm. The recipes took my full attention, so we really didn't have time to chat, something I was just as happy about. I'd checked my messages upon waking up, and there was still nothing from Jake. What was that man up to? No matter what it might be, I'd hoped to hear from him so I could at least know where we stood.

As I loaded the dropper and added batter rings to the fryer, I thought about how much my life revolved around Jake's presence in it, and while I really didn't believe that he'd ever cheat on me, I knew that if he did, it would be just once. After what I'd gone through with Max, no one would ever get a second chance to cheat on me again. That might seem a little too stern for some women, but it was something I couldn't, and wouldn't, budge on.

"Stop it," I said aloud, frustrated and tired of making up scenarios where my perfectly loyal boyfriend cheated on me.

Emma poked her head around the corner. "Stop what?"

"Sorry, I was talking to myself," I said as I flipped the donuts with the skewers I used in the hot grease.

"That's fine, as long as you don't start answering," she said with a grin.

On our break outside in front of the donut shop, Emma asked, "You're not still mad about me coming in late, are you?"

Her question caught me by surprise. "What? Of course not. Why do you ask?"

Emma didn't want to tell me, I could see it in her eyes, but she finally confessed, "You've been a little distant all morning, that's all."

I hugged her. "I'm sorry I worried you. It's not you, it's me."

When she pulled away, she asked, "Now why do I usually hear that from soon-to-be-ex-boyfriends instead of you?"

I had to have showed something when she said that. In a voice that was filled with anguish, Emma asked, "Suzanne, did he break up with you? Is that what's wrong?"

"Don't be silly," I said. "Of course not. I'm just a little out of sorts."

Emma's relief was obvious. "I'm glad of that. I'm counting on you and Jake."

"Why is that?" I asked as a car passed by

us in the darkness, on its way to who knew where.

"You two are going to make it. I believe it with all my heart."

I laughed slightly, and then added quickly so she wouldn't take it the wrong way, "You should count on yourself. You're the only one who can't disappoint you."

"Are you kidding? I let myself down all the time," Emma said with a smile.

"You are an amazing young woman, and you know it," I said.

"Thanks. That means something coming from you."

"Any reason in particular?" I asked her.

"I thought you knew. You're my role model," she answered with a grin.

"Then, girl, you've got more problems than I realized."

At four minutes to six, my cell phone rang. I thought about ignoring it since I could see George waiting outside for me in the cold, but I couldn't bring myself to do it.

It was Jake.

I took a deep breath, and then said, "Hey there, stranger. That must have been some dinner last night."

He paused, and then asked, "What are you talking about?"

"The last time we spoke, Ashley was hauling you away to eat dinner. I tried calling you later, but it always went straight to voice mail." Goodness, I hated what I was saying, even though I was trying to keep my tone light and breezy. I had to save this, and quick. "Did you two have fun?"

Jake laughed, evidently missing my internal angst. "Fun? I'd hardly call it that. We sat down, and three minutes later she was off with her friends. To be honest with you, if she hadn't bolted, I was going to get a mysterious telephone call to give me an excuse to leave myself."

"Does that mean you didn't find her company charming?" I asked.

Jake took a deep breath, and then said, "Don't get me wrong. She's a lovely young woman, but we had nothing to talk about. I'm not sure which of us was more bored, but if I had to bet, my money would be on me."

I had to laugh. All that worrying and fretting had been for nothing. "I'm so glad you called," I said. "But why didn't you answer your phone last night?"

"My battery died, and I left my charger in my apartment. It took me until midnight to find one that was compatible, and I set my alarm so I could wish you a good morning before you opened for business. Do you have any big plans today?"

"You know me. There's always something going on around here."

His laugh was full and genuine. "That's one of the things I . . . like most about you. Well, I'll let you go, I'm sure you're chomping at the bit to start selling donuts. May I call you later?"

"That would be delightful," I said. He'd almost said "love," I could hear it in his voice. That was progress, at any rate.

After I hung up, I walked quickly into the kitchen, where Emma was up to her elbows in soapy water. "I'm going to open now. I just thought I'd give you a heads-up."

"Hang on a second," she said as she looked at me. "What changed?"

"When?"

"Just now," she said. "You were down in the dumps, and now you're practically skipping around the kitchen. Jake called, didn't he?"

I rolled my eyes at her, and then laughed. "I don't have any idea what you're talking about."

"Role model," she said, laughing in kind.

I didn't respond as I walked back out into the dining room of the donut shop. I did feel better having spoken with Jake, and

243

there wasn't anything wrong with that. I didn't need a man to be happy, I knew that in my heart, but sometimes they were surely nice to have around.

If he'd ever stay in April Springs long enough, I added.

Then again, maybe this arrangement was perfect. There was certainly no risk of us ever getting tired of each other when he was in town so infrequently. None of that mattered, though.

Jake was in my life, a state that I preferred infinitely more than if he hadn't been.

For the moment, all was good in my world.

At least it was until I opened the door and heard what George had to say.

SUPHGANIOT (SORT OF)

This is a traditional Jewish holiday recipe that's fun as a change of pace from our usual donuts. The flavor is more subtle, the dough different to work, but worth the effort.

Ingredients

Mixed
- 1 egg, beaten
- 1 container yogurt (5 ounces), plain or vanilla
- 2 tablespoons sugar, white granulated
- 1/2 teaspoon vanilla extract

Sifted
- 2 cups flour, self-rising
- A pinch salt

Directions

Beat the egg in a large bowl, and add yogurt, sugar, and vanilla, mixing until incorporated. In another bowl, sift the flour and salt, and then add the dry ingredients to the wet. After this is mixed, cover the bowl and put in a warm place for 30 to 45 minutes. This allows the ingredients to fully incorporate, and the dough will rise a little in the process. Using a small cookie scoop or your hands, make small balls the size of walnuts. Fry in hot canola oil (360 to 370 degrees F) 2 to 3 minutes, turning halfway through, although they will most likely roll themselves. When they're golden brown, dry them on paper towels and adorn however you like.

Yield: Depending on the size of the dough balls, from 6–10

CHAPTER 12

"Come in," I told George as I unlocked the front door and flipped on the all of the front lights. We left it semilit inside when we were baking, so that no one would think we were open, but could have some hope that we would be soon. The place looked really bright with all the overhead lights on, and it always took me a few minutes to get used to it after I opened the shop to our first customers.

"Can I get you some coffee?" I asked George as he sat at the bar.

"I'll take your biggest mug," he said, "as long as I'm still on the payroll."

"You know it," I said. "Hey, George, would you try something for me?"

"Sure, I'll be your guinea pig," he said. "As long as it doesn't include any ingredients that I don't like."

We'd gone through some tastings before with additions that George wasn't all that fond of. There had even been one time when I was just punishing him a little.

"How do you feel about orange?" I asked.

"I love it," he said. "I have a glass of juice every day."

"This isn't nearly as healthy as that," I admitted, suddenly reluctant to make him try the new glaze and added extract in the orange donut recipe.

"Okay," he said a little warily. "What's in them, then?"

"Orange slice candies," I said.

"In the donuts?"

"No, in the glaze," I answered.

He thought about it a moment before answering. "Sure, why not?" he finally said.

As I served him a donut, a large man and a much smaller one came into the shop together. I knew them both too well, though the time of year was out of synch for them.

"Gentlemen, I didn't realize you like donuts when you aren't plowing the streets of April Springs." I glanced out the window and added, "In fact, I didn't realize your truck would even run without a snowplow attached to it."

Bob, the big one of the two, laughed heartily and slapped his skinny companion on the back hard enough to wake him up next week. "That's why I've missed this place. She's a real jewel, isn't she?"

Earl just nodded. Ever since they'd been coming to the shop, the smaller man had said barely a handful of words, but he could put away at least as many donuts as his hefty friend, and that alone gave him a special place in my heart.

Bob pointed to the donut George was about to take a bite of and said, "That looks good. I'll take a dozen."

Earl held up a hand. "Me, too," he said.

"Hang on a second, guys," I quickly explained. "That's an experimental donut. I'm not sure it's even ready to go onto the menu."

"What are you waiting for?" Bob asked.

"For him to approve it," I said as I pointed to George.

"That's a big responsibility, my friend," Bob said to George almost reverently.

"Tell me about it," George answered.

Bob was clearly interested in hurrying the approval process. "Well, don't just sit there. Take a bite and tell us all what you think."

George took one bite, then another. "It's a little sweet for my taste, but I've got a feeling some folks will love it." "That's good enough for us," Bob said. "Two dozen, to go."

"I only made nine of those donuts today,"

I confessed. "Are you sure you want to try them?"

"We're sure," Bob said. "Round out the rest any way you please. We're hauling gravel today from the quarry, and there won't be any time to stop for lunch."

After they paid and left, George said, "That's a pair of odd birds."

"Bob and Earl are good people," I said. "They always plow out my parking lot first when it snows, and I keep them supplied with donuts and hot coffee. George, when you came in, you had a dour look on your face. What's going on?"

"I'm afraid I've got some bad news," George said.

"Did something happen to Jean Ray?" I asked.

He looked puzzled by my question. "Not that I know of. What makes you ask something might have?"

"Just call it a hunch," I said.

He wasn't buying that, though. "Suzanne Hart, I've known you long enough to be able to tell when it's more than a guess. Come on, give."

I recounted my experience on the bench by the town clock the day before, and George frowned when I got to the point where Jean had looked back at me.

"I don't like it," he said.

"I'm not pleased about it myself. I plan to go by her place this afternoon. Hopefully, Jenny will be out so the two of us can talk in private."

"Don't count on it," George said. "From the way it sounds, that girl will barely leave her aunt's side."

"Then I'll just have to come up with a diversion," I said. "Care to help me with it?"

"I'm afraid I can't," George said. "I stopped by to tell you that I've got a little situation I have to take care of, so I'll be out of town for the next several days."

"What happened?" I asked, not caring if I was being nosy. George was like family to me, and what happened in his life mattered to me.

He bit his lower lip, and then admitted, "My brother's sick, and he's asked to see me. I have half a mind not to go, but what can you do? Family is family, and I can't say no to the man."

"You two aren't very close, are you?" I asked.

"No, as a matter of fact, it's just the opposite. Hey, how did you know that?"

"In all the time I've known you, you've never mentioned him, not even once."

George nodded. "I knew you'd make a good detective someday."

"Coming from you, that's a compliment," I said. "Any idea how long you'll be gone?"

He shrugged. "That depends mostly on him, but I have a long drive ahead of me, and I'd better get started."

I poured a cup of coffee for him in my largest travel cup, and then jammed half a dozen donuts in a bag. "These are for your trip."

He took them, though it was clear he was reluctant to do it. "I haven't earned these yet, Suzanne. The least you can do is let me pay for them."

"Trust me, you're worth every bite and each sip," I said.

George smiled at that, and then got up. He was nearly out the door when I asked, "George, do me a favor, okay?"

"If I can," he answered.

"I know it might sound odd, but would you call me when you get there?"

He got an odd look in his eyes, and I felt silly making the request.

"Forget it," I said. "You don't have to call."

"I will," he said. "To tell you the truth, it's nice to have someone care whether I make it there or not. Thank you."

Before I could answer, he left the shop. I

hadn't even asked him where he was going, but I knew one thing. I'd be happier when he was back, and it wasn't just because Grace and I would miss him in our investigation.

It was a little past ten and donut sales had been brisk, though the shop was empty at the moment. We had lulls like that all the time, and instead of wasting them, I took advantage of the chance to clean up, refill the napkin holders, and straighten things up in general. It was amazing how many napkins we went through in the course of a day, but like anything else, it was just a cost of doing business. I'd been in places where the owners tried to discourage using too many, but I always felt unhappy about being afraid that I wouldn't have enough, so I tried not to let it bother me when little Timmy used a dozen napkins when one would have been perfectly fine. At least they were cheap. I'd found a supplier who offered me a good product at a great discount, a combination that was better than a birthday present, as far as I was concerned.

I was filling the last holder when I heard the door chime behind me. I turned around with a smile, but it quickly faded when I saw who it was.

Standing right in front of me, with no counter, no security, and absolutely no way to defend myself but a half-empty box of napkins, was Chet, the man mountain.

From his expression, it was clear that he wasn't all that happy about being in my donut shop.

That made two of us.

I tried to put a table between us as I said, "Listen, you told me to leave her alone, and I did. There's no reason to come in here and make another fuss. As far as I'm concerned, there's no problem, okay?"

"That's what I wanted to talk to you about," Chet said.

"Her ex-boyfriend was murdered. The police must have interviewed her by now, and I'm trying to help Desmond's aunt figure out what happened to him. Jean lost someone she loved, so she has that right."

Chet held his massive hands forward, as though trying to ward off my words. "Can I get a chance to talk, too?"

"Go ahead," I said, searching over his shoulder for a sign that someone, anyone, was about to come into the shop. Cops loved donuts, so where were my friends on the force when I needed them? I'd even welcome a visit from Chief Martin, something I was certain would shock him if he knew about it. At least Emma was in back, not that she'd be able to do anything to stop Chet if he decided to do something to me. But at least some backup was better than none at all.

"I came by to say that I was wrong," Chet said simply.

"About what, exactly?" I asked.

To my surprise, Chet smiled softly. "I'm the first person in the world to admit that I'm overprotective of Katie, but I never should have treated you that way. I'm sorry. I don't know what got into me."

I looked into his eyes and saw that he was sincere. "Are you in love with her?" I asked softly, without realizing that I was pushing things way too far.

Chet's face began to cloud over, and I wondered if that was how I was going to die, right there in my donut shop.

"No, of course not," he said with a little too much force for my taste. "We're just friends."

Wow, this guy's mood changed faster than the weather. "Okay, I was just asking."

"I like her, but we're nothing more than buddies. I look out for her, that's all. There's never been anything between us, at least not like that." Chet was overexplaining, and I had to wonder if he wasn't just protesting a little too much.

"Got it," I said as I moved back behind the counter. It was probably a little crazy, but I felt better having something between us more substantial than a box of napkins.

He looked at me, and then nodded as he said, "I just wanted to make that clear."

Chet started to go, and then turned back around to face me. What was going to happen now?

"I'm here, I'm hungry, and you sell donuts," Chet said. "Would you mind making me up a dozen to go?"

I grabbed an empty box, and then asked, "Anything in particular?"

"No, you choose. Just make them good."

How was I supposed to know what he liked? I quickly picked a dozen of my most popular varieties, and then sealed the lid with tape.

"Would you like coffee, too?"

"No, I never could stand the stuff," he said as he slid his money across the counter to me.

"I've got hot chocolate, too," I said.

Chet grinned. "You know what? I haven't had any of that for ages. That would be great."

I poured a to-go cup and he took a sip as I made his change.

"That reminds me of my mother," he said. "She used to make cocoa this good, but I haven't had any since she passed away."

"I'm sorry for your loss," I said. It appeared that this man had a heart that matched the rest of him.

"She's been gone a while, but I still miss her. Is your mother still alive?"

"She is," I answered. "We live together, in fact." Now, why on earth had I told him that?

Chet nodded as he put his change away. "You're lucky."

"I think so, too."

Chet took the box and headed for the door again. But the man just refused to leave. He stopped yet again, turned to me, and asked, "You're finished with Katie, right?"

I wanted to tell him yes with every fiber of my being, but I knew if I lied to him now, he'd just come back. I had a feeling that Katie Wilkes was in the thick of things, so I couldn't give her a free pass. "Chet, think about it. If I can help the police see that Katie wasn't involved in Desmond's murder, her life will be a lot better than it has to be right now. I know what it's like to be under a cloud of suspicion, and trust me, it isn't any fun. In a very real way, I'm actually doing her a favor."

He looked curious about my answer. "What makes you think you can help her?"

"I've had some luck helping the police out in the past," I admitted. "If Katie talks to me, I've got a real shot at doing some good here."

Chet frowned for a moment. "But she already talked to you."

"Not enough. There are some hard questions I need to ask her, and she has to tell me the truth. Maybe then I can be of service to her. It's going to start getting hard on her soon, trust me."

"It already is," Chet admitted. "She cried all afternoon after you left."

"You need to convince her to talk to me, for her own sake."

Chet seemed to think about it, and then shook his head. "I don't know if I can do that."

"Have her call me," I said. "My number here is on the box." I walked over, took out my pen, and then jotted my cell phone number down, as well. "She can reach me at one of those numbers any time, day or night, but I should warn you, I go to bed around seven-thirty, so I might be slow to answer after that."

Chet nodded, and then walked out of the

donut shop with his donuts and cocoa in hand.

Four minutes later, Chief Martin walked in. I grinned at him and said, "I have to say, your timing is lousy."

"What?" he asked with a frown. "What are you talking about, my proposal to your mother?"

I didn't want to get into my earlier conversation with Chet any more than I wanted to discuss his plans to marry my mother. "What brings you here this morning, Chief?"

"It's this thing with your mother," he admitted. "She's got me tied in knots."

"I'm not sure I'm the one you should be talking to about it. What's between the two of you should stay that way," I said as I polished the counter, even though it was already clean.

"I'm not talking about her, confound it. I mean the two of us." He pointed a finger from me to his chest, and then back again.

I finally got it. "Hang on. Let me get this straight. Do you think I'm the only reason my mother hasn't accepted your proposal?" There was no softening my words now.

He looked at me defiantly. "Well, are you?"

Why was I surprised? "Believe it or not, I gave her my blessing."

"You're kidding," he said, clearly stunned by the news.

I shook my head and explained, "I want Momma to be happy, and if that means you're in her life, then so be it. I'll admit I wasn't crazy about the idea at first, and I still think you pulled the trigger *way* too soon, but like I said, it's between the two of you."

"Do you really mean that?"

"I wouldn't lie to you, not about that," I added hastily.

Chief Martin shook his head as he bit his lower lip. "If you aren't the problem, then what is? What is she waiting for?"

"Would you rather have a quick no, or a possible yes that takes a while?" I asked.

"You know the answer to that," he said with a grin.

"Then if I were you, I'd stop pushing. Give her time to make up her mind. The worst thing you can do right now is press her for a response. I can guarantee you that if you push her, she'll push right back."

He chewed that over, and then said, "Yeah, I guess I can see that. Thanks."

After he was gone, Emma came up front. "I can't believe you just did that."

"What did I do?"

She stared at me as she said, "You just

gave the police chief advice on winning your mother; you realize that, don't you?"

I shrugged. "I meant what I said. I want her to be happy. That's all that matters."

Emma nodded. "You must." She looked around the empty dining room and asked, "Did anything else exciting happen while I was in back washing dishes?"

"I'm guessing that you didn't hear my earlier conversation with Chet, did you?" I asked.

"No, but I had my iPod in, and it was a little loud."

So much for what little reinforcements I had at the shop. I was just glad that our conversation had turned out okay.

It was just before eleven and I was overjoyed that we'd be closing soon when the door chimed, and, Max walked in. I'd already boxed up the two dozen donuts we had left and had taken the trays to Emma. If we planned it right, we'd both be out of there in ten minutes, and then Grace and I could continue our investigation into Desmond Ray's murder.

Max looked at the empty display cases behind me. "You're sold out already? Is business just that good, or are you cutting back on your production?"

"Why can't it be a little bit of both? How are you doing, Max?" I said as cordially as I could manage. "It was really nice seeing Ashley again."

He frowned. "It might have been if she hadn't spent the entire time riding me about you."

"I knew there was a reason I liked that girl," I said.

"About the donuts. I don't suppose you have any in back, do you?"

"I might be able to round up a dozen or two," I said. "Why, are you staging another play?"

He nodded. "Open tryouts are in half an hour, and my actors love it when I bring your donuts by."

"What's the production this time?"

"We're doing *Young Love in Autumn,*" he said. Max loved to go against type by producing plays intentionally written for young actors using his seniors at the center. They were quite good, and folks were still talking about the rendition of *West Side Story* they'd once done.

"I can't wait," I said. "Be sure to save me a ticket up front."

"I will, in exchange for those donuts," Max said, running a hand through his hair and smiling that deadly smile of his.

"Save it for Emily Hargraves," I said with a laugh. Emily was a friend of mine, and a fellow business owner in April Springs. Her newsstand was just down the street, Two Cows and a Moose. It was popular not just for what she offered for sale, but because of her three stuffed animals who ruled over the place, always dressed in season-appropriate attire that matched Emily's whimsical mood.

"Emily won't give me the time of day anymore, and you know it," Max said.

"Well, I always said that girl had both good sense and taste."

"About the donuts?" Max reminded me.

"Here you go," I said as I slid them across the counter. When I quoted him the price, he said, "I thought we were bartering these for good seats."

"No, thanks. I'll take my chances at the box office," I said.

Max paid, and after he was gone, I locked the door behind him.

"We're all clear," I shouted to Emma in back.

She must have been standing at the kitchen door. "Everything's washed and put away, ready for tomorrow. You run the reports, and I'll sweep up out here."

"You've got a deal," I said.

As I ran the cash register reports and started counting out the money in the till, Emma looked around and asked, "What happened to the extra donuts?"

"Max bought them all at the last second," I said.

Emma nodded, but I noticed that she was clearly a little disappointed by the news. "Is there something wrong with that?"

"I was hoping to get a few for myself," she said. "It doesn't matter."

"You could have grabbed them in back when you had the chance," I said.

"I thought about it, but it never occurred to me that we'd be sold out."

I looked at her a second, and then asked, "Emma, those donuts weren't for you, were they?"

She grinned. "Okay, they might have been for someone else."

"A young man, perhaps?"

"Perhaps," she said, her smile suddenly intensifying.

"Sorry about today, but you have my blessing to grab some tomorrow."

She nodded, and then went about her cleaning. Emma was in love with the idea of falling in love, and it was difficult to keep up with the young men in her life. I didn't envy her the roller coaster of emotions that was the result of her love life, and I was especially happy to have Jake in my life. He was everything that Max was not, and in the best ways possible.

The reports and the cash on hand matched perfectly, an event that never failed to surprise me. I made out the deposit just as Emma finished up, and I began to turn out the lights.

"See you tomorrow," I said as I let us both out, and then locked the door behind us.

There was a handsome young man standing across the street, and his smile lit up the day when he saw Emma.

She practically skipped across the street to greet him, and I realized that my assistant most likely wouldn't change places with me, either. We had chosen our own love lives, as was fair and right.

As I drove to Grace's house, I wondered if she was happy with her new man, but I wouldn't ask, no matter how much I was dying to know.

When I got to her house, though, I realized that I didn't have an option about asking her about anything.

Her car was gone, and there was a note taped to the front door for me.

Hey, Suzanne. Had to run to Hickory.

Tried to call, but your phone was busy. Back tonight. Be careful.

It appeared that I was on my own.

CHAPTER 13

I didn't really have any choice about what to do next. I was going to have to keep digging by myself, no matter how crazy it might sound. I'd have to be a little more careful than I had been in the past since no one was watching my back, but I couldn't let that stop me.

I was driving back through town so I could go to Talbot's Landing when I passed Gabby Williams's shop. Gabby was standing in front of her place, looking more than a little lost. On a whim, I pulled in to see what was wrong.

She looked insanely happy to see me. "Suzanne, I just walked over to your shop, and you were closed. I didn't know what to think."

"I changed my hours," I explained. "It's nothing to get alarmed about."

"I wasn't really *that* worried," she said, though I knew that wasn't the case at all.

"Was there something you needed to see me about?" I asked.

"How is the investigation coming?" she asked, lowering her voice, though we were the only two people around.

"We're making some progress," I said, "but it's still early. How are you holding up?"

"My customers are staying away from my shop in droves," she answered, nearly in tears. "They all must believe I killed Desmond."

"Take it easy. It could just be a slow day."

Gabby scoffed at that. "Don't try to kid me into believing that. I saw the foot traffic at your donut shop drop when you were a suspect, so I know what's happening to me now. You've got to do something."

"You don't mean that I should help you drum up some business, do you?"

She looked at me like I'd lost my mind. "I'm talking about solving the case."

"I can only do what I can do," I said, quoting one of my mother's favorite expressions.

"Then what are you going to do next?" she asked.

I shook my head, wondering how I'd gotten myself into this. "I'm going to Talbot's Landing to interview a few more people."

Gabby paused a moment, and then nodded. "That sounds good. I'm going with you."

"Gabby, that's not necessary," I said, knowing how most folks would react to her relentless pushing and prodding.

"I'm not selling anything here. Why shouldn't I go with you?" She looked into my Jeep, and then added, "Besides, Grace and George aren't around, and it's not safe for you to go alone."

"Sometimes I have more luck that way," I said, which was true. If I showed up somewhere with George or Grace in tow, it had to feel like we were ganging up on the people we were questioning, and while I knew that bullying worked for some investigators, I wasn't a fan of it myself. I liked to ask a lot of questions, but I had to believe I knew when to ease up, or lose my access to people completely.

"Nonsense. I'm going," she said forcefully.

I had to stop this before it got out of hand. I took her hands in mine, and then said, "Gabby, as much as I appreciate your offer, there are two reasons it's a bad idea. One, these people aren't going to want to talk to me if you're there, given the fact that you're a person of interest in the case."

"What's the second reason?" she asked.

I wanted to say that it was because she'd

269

drive me crazy, but I wisely didn't. "You need to keep the shop open, even if you don't get a single customer to come inside. Folks in town need to see that you have nothing to hide from, and if you abruptly close ReNEWed, they're going to think you're admitting you had something to do with Desmond's murder."

"That's preposterous," Gabby said.

"We both know it, but think about it. Remember, I kept my shop open, even when things looked bleak for me. You've got to do the same."

She nodded. "I can see that you're right, but that doesn't make waiting around here any easier. I feel so helpless."

What an odd word for Gabby to use to describe herself. I could imagine her as a thousand things, but helpless would never make the list. "Put on a happy face, and act as though you haven't a care or concern in the world," I said. "That's the best thing you can do for your reputation."

"Thank you, Suzanne," she said. "I'll try my best."

I decided to leave while I still could. "Keep your chin up," I said as I got into the Jeep.

Gabby surprised me by giving me a thumbs-up sign.

I had to laugh as I drove out of town. She was trying, I had to give her that.

I just hoped I'd be able to help her as I'd promised.

The drive to Talbot's Landing was longer than it had been the day before, even though I knew that was ridiculous. It was just that without Grace to chat with, the miles seemed to creep past. I almost found myself wishing that I'd agreed to have Gabby join me just for the company.

Almost.

It did give me time to think about the case. As I wondered aloud who might have some insight into Desmond's life, I realized that the folks around him who weren't biased might be able to shed a little light for me.

I'd looked Desmond's address up before, so I drove there when I got to town instead of going in search of other clues. If I was being honest with myself, I wasn't looking forward to going back to Duncan Construction, even though the two people I needed to talk to both worked there. Chet did, too, for that matter, and I was beginning to wonder if it might be smarter to wait for him to call me rather than just show up. He had my cell phone number, so there wouldn't be any delay getting his message, if there ever was one. Besides, if I went to Desmond's old place first, at least I could delay the decision until later.

The address was for an apartment complex, and fifty years ago, it might have been nice, but the ravages of time and scores of tenants didn't make it look like much now. The building trim was in need of painting, and if there was a budget for landscaping, someone had to be stealing from it. I walked up the cracked sidewalk, found a list of residents just inside with the super's name on it, and rang the bell.

An older woman with a ready smile opened the door.

"I'm looking for the building super," I said. "Is he home?"

"He's a she, and she's standing right in front of you," the woman said as she held out a hand. "My name's Steve."

"Steve? Really?"

She laughed. "Well, it's actually Stephania, but my dad wanted a boy, so he shortened it to Steve as soon as I could talk. I wasn't sure about it at first, but I kind of like it now. What can I do for you? If you're looking for an apartment, I hate to tell you, but we're booked full."

"Actually, I'm looking into a past tenant's

life, and I'm hoping you can help me."

She looked a little startled by my confession. "You aren't a cop, are you?"

"No, ma'am." I thought of one of the elaborate stories that Grace and I used occasionally, but I just couldn't bring myself to lie to this woman for some reason. "It's about Desmond Ray."

"I heard about that," Steve said, saddened by the mention of his name. "I can't believe someone just shot him down like a rabid dog. What's your concern in the matter?"

"He was killed beside my shop," I admitted.

That made Steve take a step back. "You can't be Gabby Williams."

"No, I'm on the other side. I'm Suzanne Hart."

"The donut lady," she said as she nodded.

"That's me. How did you hear about Gabby?"

"The scuttlebutt around here is that she's the one who killed him," Steve said.

"You can't believe everything you hear," I said.

"Or read, either. I know that. I just didn't have a compelling reason to think otherwise."

I couldn't hold off one question any longer. "Excuse me for saying so, but you're not exactly what I pictured when I rang your doorbell."

"Why, because I can speak in complete sentences, or because I'm a woman of a certain age?"

I had to laugh at her question.

"What's so amusing?" she asked.

"I don't have a chance whether I pick A or B, do I?"

Steve nodded. "You've got a point. I just hate stereotypes."

"I do, too," I said. "You have to admit, though, you aren't exactly the norm."

"I don't know; it makes perfect sense to me. I've always been good with my hands, Dad made sure of that. I like all different kinds of people, and I hardly pay any rent at all. It's ideal, as far as I'm concerned."

"The way you explain it, it makes perfect sense. So, will you help me? Is there anything you could tell me about Desmond that the police don't already know?"

"Suzanne, I've never been all that fond of speaking ill of the dead."

"I understand completely," I said, "but it might be the only way his killer pays for what he or she did."

She looked around, and then said, "I've kept you standing out in the hallway long enough. Would you like some tea?"

"That would be nice," I said.

Steve led me inside, and I found a well-furnished living room with an easel in one corner. "Do you paint?"

"Just about everything," she said.

After she brought us both cups of warm tea, Steve said, "So, you think it might be a woman, don't you?"

"It's a possibility," I admitted as I took a sip. It was warm, fragrant, and rich, nothing like I'd ever had before. "This is really good."

"It's my own blend," she said as she took a drink herself before setting it aside. "Did you have any particular woman in mind?"

She was testing me to see if I'd done any other digging, and I didn't have a problem obliging her. "Katie Wilkes comes to mind, offhand."

Steve nodded. "I think so, too, but it's important that you don't forget the men."

I was willing to go a little further, but I didn't want to supply her with my complete list of suspects without getting at least something in return. "You mean someone like Bill Rodgers."

"Bingo," she said. "If I had to go after anyone, it would be one of them."

"Could you tell me why?"

"Katie was the jealous type, and I told

Desmond once that he'd have to chew his own leg off to get away from her if he ever decided to break up with her. She had a way of latching on to that boy that was nearly criminal."

"Did they fight much?"

Steve nodded. "All the time. Nothing Desmond did was good enough for her, and she was constantly accusing him of stepping out on her, though I couldn't imagine it. Desmond was no saint, but he wouldn't have done that."

"How sure of that are you?" I asked.

Steve shrugged. "Not as certain as I probably should be before saying it, but you've got a way to make me want to share."

I laughed. "Bartenders and donut makers are both good listeners."

"I'll take your word for it, since you're the first of either I've ever met. Desmond tried to break up with Katie twice while he was living here, but somehow it never seemed to take hold."

"How can that be?" I asked, honestly curious.

"She kept stalking him, and she must have found a way to wiggle back into his good graces. I told him he was a fool, I'm sorry to say, but he said he knew what he was doing. The last time I spoke with him he told me he was moving, and that he thought he'd finally managed to break free. It was odd, though. I offered to check his apartment and give him his security deposit back if it merited it, but he told me to keep it for myself."

"Why did he say that?"

She frowned at me as she answered. "He told me that he was about to come into some money."

That opened up quite a few interesting possibilities. Was he planning to get it from his aunt, or perhaps from another source? "Did he happen to say where it might be coming from?"

"Not to me, but Pam might know."

"Pam?" I asked.

"The woman in number eighty-two."

"Were they ever a couple?" I asked.

Steve just laughed. "I doubt it. Pam just turned eighty, but the two of them were close for some odd reason."

It might pay to have a chat with her. "Do you happen to know if she's home right now?"

"Pam never goes anywhere. We like to say that if she didn't see it out of her peephole, it never happened."

"Got it. Now, how about Bill Rodgers?"

Steve's face clouded up. "He came by

looking for Desmond the day after he moved. He was screaming at me, ranting about losing his money, and saying that Desmond was going to pay for what he'd done, one way or another."

"It was a serious threat, then?"

"It alarmed me enough that I called the police," Steve admitted.

"What did Chief Martin say?" I asked.

She looked confused. "Who's that?"

Then I remembered that her police chief had to be different than mine. "Sorry, that was a slip. What did the police do?"

"They made a report, which is often what they're best at." She took another sip of tea, and then her telephone rang.

"Excuse me," she said.

"By all means."

She answered it, spoke briefly, and then hung up. "Sorry, but I've got to go. There's a leak in one of the faucets upstairs."

I stood, as well. "Thanks so much for the tea, and the conversation."

"It was my pleasure," she said with a smile. As Steve led me through the door and out into the hallway, she said, "Hang on one second, would you?"

I assumed that she was retrieving some tools, so I did as she asked. Sure enough, she came out a minute later with a small toolbox in her hand. "I took a chance and spoke with Pam. Since that's where the leak is, she's agreed to speak with you, as long as I'm there, too."

"That was so sweet of you," I said. "Thank you."

"I'm glad to help you out, but I'm really doing it for Desmond. He wasn't my favorite tenant by any definition of the word, but I still think of him as one of mine, and I look out for every last one of those folks as best I can."

"I understand." As we climbed the steps, I asked, "Is there anything I should know about Pam?"

"Treat her like a peer, not a little old lady. She's sharper than the two of us put together, and if you handle it right, you could learn a lot."

"Thanks again," I said. "If you're ever in April Springs, come by my shop and I'll treat you to a donut."

"I might just do that," she said.

"I hope you do."

We didn't even have to knock on the door to Apartment 82. A spry older woman with a face that was a roadmap to a hard life opened the door the second we hit the landing.

Steve said, "Pam, this is Suzanne. She's a

donut maker."

Pam smiled, showing a full set of bright white teeth. "You didn't happen to bring any with you, did you? I dearly love a good éclair."

"I'm sorry, but if I'm back this way again, I'll be sure to grab one just for you."

Pam shook her head. "That would hardly pay enough to cover your delivery costs."

"I hadn't planned to charge you," I said with a smile. "I feel as though I already owe half a dozen to Steve, so it wouldn't be any trouble to throw an éclair in, as well."

She smiled at that. "In that case, I'd be delighted."

I had to remember to bring donuts and an éclair the next time I came this way, whether it was related to the case or not. "No promises when it might be, though," I said.

"That's not a problem. I adore surprises."

Steve asked, "Is the leak in the bathroom or the kitchen?"

"Kitchen," Pam said. "Sorry to bother you."

"It's no bother. It's what I do."

After Steve started examining the sink, Pam said, "I'd offer you some tea or coffee, but I need water for that."

From under the sink, Steve sang out,

"Working on it, dear."

I laughed, enjoying the company of these two bright women. "Don't rush on my account. I've had plenty of both today."

"Tell me," Pam said, "I've always wondered about something. What time do you have to get up every morning to have donuts available for sale in your shop?"

"I used to go in really early, but I pushed my start time ahead to three A.M. so I could get a little more sleep every day. I may not even go in until three on some days."

Pam was amazed. "And you do that every day? Surely you take at least one day off a week to rest."

"No, ma'am. If I'm in April Springs, I'm making donuts."

"My goodness, I don't know where you find the energy." As she settled onto a chair in her dining area, Pam motioned for me to take the other. "I find two chairs perfect for my needs. I never liked a great deal of company, so if anyone else comes by, they have to fend for themselves."

"I'm sorry to bother you," I said.

"Nonsense. Stephania spoke quite highly of you, so you're now instantly moved into the 'friend' category, and I can't seem to replace those fast enough. That's one of the hazards of getting older."

281

When I didn't say anything, she waited a few moments, and then smiled. "Good. I just hate it when people tell me I'm not all that old. Balderdash. I'm ancient, and I know it, but I refuse to be treated like it. Now, you wanted to know about Desmond. He was a mixed bag at best, I'm afraid."

It was clear that Pam had no compunctions about speaking ill of the dead. After all, to be fair, who else would she have to talk about when most of her friends were deceased?

"Could you tell me about him?" I asked.

"He was tall, deeply tanned, and had a mop of dark hair."

"Actually, we met. He came into my shop the morning he was killed," I admitted. I knew quickly enough there was no dancing around with this woman and the truth. I had a feeling that she'd see right through any pretext I tried to use.

"You poor dear. Very well, we'll dig a little deeper then. Desmond was a bit of a cad, playing with that girl's emotions like he did. He was very hot and cold about her, and she had a temper that wouldn't tolerate his games. One moment she'd be threatening to kill him, and the next they'd be locked in an embrace, barely coming up for air." She paused, and then said, "You're probably wondering how I see so much. The keyhole is a remarkable way to observe the world while being undetected."

"It's great for spying, too," I said without thinking it through. I needed this woman's observations, and I'd just insulted her.

I was about to apologize when she burst out laughing. "Exactly. Call it what it is, an old woman's answer to television. The insulation on the inside walls isn't great, so I was privy to both sights and sounds. It was certainly better than what's being offered on the idiot box these days."

I couldn't disagree with her. "What else did you see?"

"The day before Desmond moved out, a rather large man with meaty hands came by and pounded on the door so hard I thought it might splinter under his touch."

That could possibly be Chet, though I knew the description wasn't enough to tag him for the action. "What happened?"

"Desmond either wasn't home, or he was wise enough not to answer. Then the pounding began on my door."

"What did you do?"

Pam laughed, her clear eyes sparkling. "I didn't hide under my bed like a coward waiting for the end. I threw open the door, of course. The gentleman identified himself as Brett, and went on to ask about Desmond. When I told him I had no idea where he was, he said that I should tell him to straighten up, or he'd take care of him. I couldn't imagine what had provoked him so."

I had a pretty good idea of that myself. "Could his name have been Chet, by any chance, instead of Brett?"

Pam seemed to consider it, and then nodded her head. "Yes, I believe you're right. It *was* Chet. I must be slipping."

I certainly hadn't seen any evidence to back that up since I'd been there. "Is there anything else?"

"No, but isn't that enough? Now tell me, how on earth do you make a living charging so little for your donuts?"

"Have you ever been in my shop?" I asked. If she'd visited Donut Hearts, I certainly didn't remember it, and I had a feeling that Pam was a woman who would prove difficult to forget.

"No, but if you're charging the going rate, you must either have a phenomenal volume, or the wolf is never far from your door."

"Let me put it this way," I said with a grin. "He's there so often I keep a bowl of water available at all times just in case he gets thirsty."

"Got it," Pam said.

Steve reappeared and said, "That should do it."

"You fixed it that easily?" Pam asked.

"Hey, sometimes a good tightening up is all anything needs."

"You are a miracle worker," Pam said as she pressed a small pretty box into Steve's hands.

"It's not necessary, you know," Steve protested, but her tenant wouldn't hear of it.

"Suzanne, you must take one, as well."

"But I didn't do anything," I replied.

"You brightened my day, and that's surely worth a token of my esteem. Feel free to come by any time. You are always welcome. Now, if you ladies will excuse me, I need a nap."

Steve and I walked out, and then down the stairs. Steve smiled at me and waved her box in the air. "If I were you, I wouldn't open that."

"Why? What's wrong with it?"

"She bakes little bricks she calls brownies, and no one leaves that apartment without a box of them. If you're crazy enough to try one, you'll break a tooth."

"Thanks for the heads-up," I said. "What do you do with them?"

"There's an old well at the back of the property I'm slowly filling up. When it's topped off, you won't be able to blast them out with a stick of dynamite."

As I handed her my box, I said, "Do me a favor and add this to the pile."

She placed my box on top of hers. "Will do. She means well, that's what counts. You made her day; you know that, don't you?"

"She seems like a lot of fun. I meant what I said about the donuts. If you come by before I get back here, I'll pack a few éclairs for her, if you'll deliver them for me."

"It would be my pleasure. It was nice meeting you, Suzanne."

"And you, as well."

I walked back out to my Jeep, and on a whim, I looked back up at the apartment building. Pam was standing there at her window, her curtains drawn back, and a smile on her face. The moment she saw me, she waved good-bye.

I waved back, and then drove toward town.

I hadn't eaten lunch yet, and neither Chet nor Katie had called, so I didn't feel right going to Duncan Construction without some kind of invitation. I couldn't even stop by to see Allen Davis, since my interview with him hadn't gone all that well, either. That was the problem with trying to get folks to talk to me who weren't under any obligation to do so.

Food might help, and even if it didn't clear my head, I was hungry, and that was enough. Maybe I'd have time to figure something else out, but at the very worst, I'd get a meal out of it.

ELBOWS

This is my take on a popular treat called Kneecaps. They are small, sweet fried donuts, and when covered with powdered sugar, they're really good. While Kneecaps have an indent in the middle for whipped cream, these do not.

Ingredients

Mixed
- 1/4 cup warm water
- 1 envelope active dry yeast (.25 ounce)

- 2 eggs, beaten
- 1 cup whole milk
- 1/4 cup butter, creamed
- 1/4 cup sugar, white granulated

Sifted
- 4–5 cups all-purpose flour
- 1/4 teaspoon salt

Directions

Add the dry yeast to the water and set aside. Cream the butter, and then add the beaten eggs and sugar. In a separate bowl, sift the flour and salt together. Add the yeast to the wet mixture, and then slowly alternate adding the milk and dry ingredients until the mixture is smooth. Add more flour if needed to make the dough workable, then place in a greased bowl, cover, and let rise in a warm place until doubled, approximately an hour. Punch the dough down and roll out on floured surface 1/2 to 1/4 inch thick, cut out donut rounds, and cover the rounds and holes for another half hour. Fry in hot canola oil (360 to 370 degrees F) 3 to 4 minutes, turning halfway through. Drain on paper towels, and then dust with confectioner's sugar or ice and decorate.

Yield: 6–8 donuts and holes

CHAPTER 14

At least there was a diner right downtown. Diane's Dairy and Dogs was the epitome of a greasy spoon, but I didn't mind. Sometimes I liked getting a bite at those kinds of places. Old cinder-block walls had been painted white at some point, I was sure, but now they had faded into a dull yellow. The front of the diner was full of windows, allowing anyone passing by to see what the day's specials were by looking at the plates of food on the tables. Two ceiling fans spun lazily above, barely stirring the air, and the booths and barstools hadn't been reupholstered in red vinyl for two or three decades. For all that, the place was jammed with customers. There weren't any hostesses at this diner, either: it was clearly a seat-yourself type of establishment.

I sat at the bar, then looked at the menu, safely shrouded in plastic.

A middle-aged woman three times my size

walked over to me, and I could have sworn she called me sweet pea.

"Excuse me?" I said.

"Sweet tea?" she repeated, a little slower the next time, as though I were either hard of hearing, or a little touched in the head.

That was a great deal better than a very bad term of endearment. "Please, but no lemon," I agreed.

She drew a glass, slid it in front of me, and then looked at me expectantly, her order pad drawn like a weapon.

"What's good here?" I asked as I glanced at the menu.

"Most of it," she admitted, though she wouldn't go further than that. "But not all."

Okay, that hadn't worked. "What do you sell a lot of?"

"Dogs," she replied.

I was willing to live life on the edge, but I wasn't interested in risking it by ordering one of their hot dogs. I looked at a chalkboard with the day's specials, and saw vegetable soup and grilled cheese. I pointed to it and said, "I'll have the special."

She nodded, jotted something down, and then walked away.

The man beside me, dressed in a business suit, smiled and said, "Diane isn't much of a talker, is she?"

"That's good to know," I replied. "I was afraid that it was something I said."

"No, she pretty much treats everybody like that."

I was getting ready to introduce myself when he returned his focus to his newspaper, pretty much ending our chance of having a conversation.

That was okay, too. In three minutes, Diane brought me my food, and I hesitated a moment before tasting the soup. How bad could it be, anyway?

I took a small taste, and felt a flood of delicious warmth wash over me. The veggies were tender and perfect, and the seasoning was excellent. It was so good I nearly forgot about my sandwich, but when I did get around to taking a bite, I nearly spit it out. No, they couldn't have ruined it that way. I peeled back one of the slices of toasted bread, and sure enough, there was mayonnaise spread on it. I'd seen it a few places in the South before, and I knew that some people loved their grilled cheese sandwiches that way, but I couldn't be counted among them. I pushed the sandwich aside, took a healthy swallow of tea to wash the taste of the sandwich out of my mouth, and then returned to my soup, where my attention belonged. When the bowl was finished, I thought about asking for more, but then I realized that if I did that, I'd have to explain why I hadn't eaten the sandwich. A great many waitresses at diners all across the South took it as an affront if you didn't like something being served, though I wondered if Diane would even notice.

I was about to ask for my check when I noticed something sticking out from under my plate. There, on a small green lined sheet, was my bill. She must have slipped it there when she'd put my sandwich down. I slid a dollar under my bowl, nodded to the man beside me, and then walked to the register. The tea had been good, not great, so I hadn't asked for a to-go cup.

As I paid an older woman with bright henna hair, I had a sudden thought. George had told me that Rodgers hung out some in Talbot's Landing, so maybe I'd get lucky and find him there. It would surely save me driving to the other end of the county. "Do you happen to know a man named Bill Rodgers? He doesn't live in town, but I heard he comes here sometimes."

"Of course I know Bill," she said as she made my change.

"Do you know where I might find him?"

"I do," she answered. "Next in line, please."

As a large, heavyset man handed her his bill along with a ten, I stepped to the side and asked, "Would you mind telling me where?"

"Closer than you think," she said. "You just had lunch with him."

And then she pointed to the man with the newspaper I'd been sitting beside the entire time.

At least no one had taken my seat, though it had been cleared of its dirty dishes.

"You weren't finished?" Rodgers asked as I sat back down. "Sorry about that. I told Diane you'd cleared out."

"I'm done with my meal, but I was hoping we could talk for a second."

Before I could introduce myself, or explain why I was there, he looked at me and said, "Ma'am, I'm sure you're a perfectly nice woman, but I'm not interested."

I started to protest when he held a hand up and cut me off. "It's not you, it's me. I'm just not in the mood to date right now."

"I'm not asking you out," I said. "My name is Suzanne Hart."

He shrugged. "That doesn't ring any bells." After a long pause, he finally admitted, "I'm Bill Rodgers."

"I know who you are," I said, though the knowledge had just been gained a moment ago. "I need to talk to you."

"Why?" he asked, clearly curious.

There was no other way to do it. I said, "I saw Desmond Ray the day he died."

Rodgers's expression grew suddenly suspicious. "You're not a cop, are you?"

"Actually, I'm a donut maker," I said.

"So, why do you care about Ray?"

"I heard he wronged you, and I wanted to hear your side of the story. While it's true that I'm not with the police officially, we've worked together in the past, and I know the two of you had a business deal that went sour recently."

"Lower your voice," he commanded. "I won't talk about it with you, not here."

"Then where? I don't have a lot of time, Mr. Rodgers." That wasn't exactly the truth, but I didn't want to be led along, either.

"I'm busy at the moment," he said.

"Then now's good for me," I said, quite a bit louder than I had before. A few folks at the diner looked our way, and Bill Rodgers got the message. Either he talked with me now, or I'd spread the word that he was a suspect in Desmond Ray's murder.

"Let's go," he said, grabbing his bill and throwing a ten at the woman at the register.

"What about your change?" she asked.

"Put it in the tip jar," he told her, and I had to hurry to follow him outside.

"Let's walk," he said, and then started off down the street.

After we'd taken a dozen steps from the diner, I said, "Okay. What happened between you and Desmond? What exactly was the deal you two were involved in?"

"I was a fool to invest with him, and I got exactly what I deserved. Desmond burned me, but I didn't kill him. Honestly, I was upset, but I wouldn't commit murder for a thousand dollars."

"Is that all that was at stake?" I asked. When I'd heard how he'd reacted to the bad deal, I'd just assumed it had involved a great deal of money.

"It was enough to sting a little," Rodgers said. As he walked, he slowed for a moment, and then added, "If I'm being honest about it, it wasn't the money; it was the principle."

"That doesn't exactly cancel you out as a suspect," I said.

"No, but I was here in town from seven to midnight the night he was killed, and I've got the mayor, the police chief, a mortician, and a handyman as my witnesses. We were playing poker, and I never left the table, let alone the town."

If that were true, it would clear him. "Do you mind telling me what business deal the two of you were involved in?"

"As a matter of fact, I do mind."

We were beside the building that acted as the police station, courthouse, and town hall. I stopped, and in a moment, Rodgers stopped with me. It was clear I'd gotten everything I was going to out of him.

"Thanks for talking," I said. "I'm sorry to have bothered you."

"That's it? Really?"

"Unless there's something else you want to tell me," I said.

"No, nothing I can think of. Good-bye."

"Bye," I said, and then crossed the street. Surely either the mayor or the chief of police would be in, and I could confirm his alibi and strike his name from our list.

The police chief confirmed it, and the mayor seconded the fact that Bill Rodgers couldn't have killed Desmond Ray, at least not on the night it happened.

At least I'd managed to cross one name off my list.

I was driving out of town when my cell phone rang. It was a number unfamiliar to me when I glanced at it, so I said, "Hello?"

"Suzanne? This is Katie Wilkes. I need to talk to you. How soon can you get to Duncan Construction?"

I glanced at my watch. "I can be there in four minutes," I said.

She seemed shocked to hear the news. "Are you in town?"

"I am," I said. "Is there anything you'd like to tell me now while we're talking on the phone?"

"No, it can wait," she said.

I drove as quickly as I dared to Duncan, wondering what Katie had to tell me. I had to give Chet credit. He'd managed to do what I'd failed to accomplish. It appeared that Katie Wilkes was ready to talk.

She was sitting on the same bench in front of the construction company where I'd seen her earlier, only this time, Chet was sitting beside her instead of trying to chase me off.

Chet walked over to me when I parked, though Katie kept her place on the bench.

"Thanks for doing this," I said.

"I got you this far. The rest is up to you. Watch yourself, okay?"

"I'll do my best," I said.

I wasn't sure how much I'd be able to push her with the jealous man-mountain standing nearby, but I had to try.

"Hey," I said as I approached and sat next

to Katie on the bench. "Are you ready to talk?"

Chet decided to stand, which was fine with me, since there was no room for him on the seat with us.

"It's about Desmond," she said.

Yeah, I kind of figured that, though I didn't say it. "What about him?"

She looked uncomfortable as she admitted, "I didn't tell you the complete truth before when we talked."

"You weren't taking a walk that night?" I asked, being careful to keep my voice level and calm.

"No, I was walking," she said, "I just wasn't alone the entire time."

"Who was with you?"

She stared at the ground before answering. "I'd really rather not say."

This girl was killing me with her evasiveness. If she wasn't ready to talk, why had she called me? "I'll do my best to keep it quiet," I said, "but you really need to tell me, or the state police. I can have an inspector here in two hours." I could, too, if I could manage to drag Jake away from campus to intimidate one of my suspects. It was mostly a bluff, but I was hoping that Katie wouldn't realize it.

"There's no need to bring in the cops,"

Chet answered for her, a frown creasing his forehead.

"I'm just saying," I said as I stared up at him. "She needs to tell someone. Why not me? I'm a lot easier to deal with, trust me."

Katie seemed to consider that, and then said, "Chet, would you mind getting me a glass of water?"

"Sure thing," he said without hesitation, and headed quickly inside.

As soon as he was gone, she said, "I was with Mr. Duncan, and I didn't want Chet to hear it."

"I thought you were still in love with Desmond?"

"I am, I mean, I was," she said. "Harry was helping me sort things out, that's all. There's nothing going on between us. He's just a friend."

"Then why did you feel the need to send Chet away?"

She stared at the ground as she admitted, "He gets jealous, even though I've told him a thousand times that we can never be anything more than just friends."

"So, you're saying he doesn't have any reason to believe otherwise?"

"Believe me, I haven't led him on," she said.

"I need to talk to Harry," I said.

"You don't trust me?" she asked.

"Katie, I have to have confirmation. You said yourself that he wasn't with you the entire time. I need more specifics if I'm going to tell the state police that you have an alibi." Jake was a member of the state police, so technically it was true.

"Shh," she said as Chet came back out with a glass full of water.

"Thank you," Katie said as she took a large gulp.

Chet looked at her as though she were the only woman in the world for him, and Katie would have to be blind not to see it.

I stood, and then started toward the office.

Chet asked me, "Where are you going?"

I was at a loss, but Katie spoke up for me. "She wants to get a quote to see how much it would be to build a new donut shop."

On the face of it, if you didn't know how anemic my bottom line was at my shop, it was a good lie, and it gave me the perfect excuse to approach Harry Duncan. I considered the fact that Katie was a strong liar on the spur of the moment, as well, so I wasn't sure just how far I could trust her. It had been my experience in the past that people who lied so well usually had a great deal of practice doing it.

Chet seemed to accept her explanation, and Katie joined me, while her large friend made his way to the back where I could see that the heavy equipment was stored.

"Thanks," I said. "That was clever of you."

"I didn't want to make Chet suspicious," she said.

"That's probably wise."

She started to go into Harry Duncan's office when I put a hand on her arm. "If you don't mind, I'll go in alone."

"I just wanted to let him know that he could tell you anything," she said.

Katie had a point. There was little chance that Duncan would talk to me without her blessing. On the other hand, I didn't want her to give him any signals about what to say. "If you want to use him as your alibi, you need to tell him that he can tell me anything, and then not say another word. Do you understand?"

She nodded. "I don't blame you for being careful. You don't want me leading him to say what I want, do you?"

"That's right."

"Good enough."

Katie knocked on the office door, and we both heard a man say, "Hang on. I'm on the phone."

After twenty seconds, he said, "Okay, I'm

off. Come in."

We waited a second, and then walked in side by side.

"Harry, you can tell her anything," Katie said, and then turned around and left the office.

"What's this about?" he asked.

"Where were you the night Desmond Ray was murdered?"

"That guy was a cancer around here, between Allen and Katie. I hate to speak ill of the dead and all of that, but I've got a feeling the world's a better place with him gone."

His phone rang, and as he reached for it, I said, "If you want to help Katie, tell me what you know about her alibi. If you answer that call, I'm going to assume that it's her telling you what to say, and I won't be able to tell the state police that she's in the clear."

He stared at the phone for ten seconds, and when it finally stopped ringing, he looked almost relieved.

Before he could say anything, Katie peeked in and said, "That was your *wife.* I tried to tell her you were busy, but she made me put her through anyway."

"Don't worry about it. I'll deal with her later," he said.

After Katie left, I asked, "You're married?"

"So, what if I am?"

There was a little boy's defiant tone in his voice as he answered my question.

"What did your wife think of you spending time with Katie?"

"She's fine with it," he said with a shrug. Unlike Katie, he was a terrible liar, and I was sure his wife had no idea what was going on. As a former betrayed spouse, my heart went out to her, but I had to find out if Katie was in the clear before I worried about a stranger's relationship with his wife.

"Did you see her the night of the murder?" I asked.

"My wife? Of course I did. I see her every night."

"I'm talking about Katie," I said, a little more strongly than I should have.

He took too long to answer, and when he finally did, it was clear that he was lying again. "Sure I did. We were together all night."

"Where exactly were the two of you?" I asked, not convinced at all that he was telling the truth.

"Around," he said. "She needed to talk, so I offered to listen."

I shook my head. "Sorry, but it's not good enough. I need one specific detail that Katie just told me before I'll believe either one of you."

One look in his eyes told me that he didn't have an answer to that. I could almost see his mind working as he decided how to handle me. He finally decided to go with righteous indignation. "Believe me or not. Frankly, I don't care. I don't have time to play games with you. I have a business to run."

As I stood, I said, "I just hope you have a better answer when the state police come."

He laughed at the threat. "Bring them on. I've got three lawyers on retainer. I'm not afraid of the police."

As I left the office, Katie said, "He confirmed my story, didn't he?"

"As a matter of fact, he didn't."

She shook her head, her face flushing. "The fool is lying to you, trying to protect his marriage."

"And leaving you out in the cold in the process," I said.

"I'm telling the truth," she said more forcefully.

"It's not up to me, anymore."

She stood, and then stormed into her boss's office. I thought about sticking around to hear what was being said, but Chet walked in, so I took that as my cue to walk out.

Whether Katie had lied to me or her boss had, one thing was certain. Her alibi hadn't gotten any better since the last time we'd spoken, and quite possibly, it had just gotten a great deal worse.

The drive back home was uneventful, which was nice. It gave me a chance to think about what I'd seen and heard on my visit. With Bill Rodgers off my list and Chet added to it, I was left with the same number of suspects as I'd had before, though the exact roster had changed. I briefly considered Harry Duncan, and wondered if he might have had something to do with Desmond's death, but in the end, I doubted that it was possible. If something had happened to Katie, I could see him as a suspect, especially to keep her from revealing too much to his wife, but it didn't make any sense for him to have harmed Desmond Ray. I needed to focus more on Katie and Chet. I hoped that Grace would be able to help again tomorrow. I knew she had a job to do, and for that matter, so did I, but my investigations usually went so much better when I had her with me. I was just lucky that she didn't have a nine-to-five job where she could never get away. Her supervisory duties and her sales territory still left her time to lend me a hand when I needed it, and that was especially the case right now, since George was off visiting his brother.

Momma's car was in the driveway when I got back to the cottage, but that didn't necessarily mean that she was still home. She'd been seeing Chief Martin nearly every night since the proposal, and the lights blazing inside didn't mean anything, either. Some sinister things had happened in our park over the past few years, and we both had no problem paying a larger electric bill if it meant that people believed we were at home. It may have given us both a false sense of security, but neither of us was willing to give it up, no doubt much to our power company's delight.

The second I walked inside, all illusions that she might be gone were instantly dismissed. The house was filled with the aroma of turkey and pumpkin pie, a combination of scents that could weaken even the strongest man's knees.

"Hey, I'm home," I said as I hung up my jacket in the hallway. "If you tell me I'm not invited to the feast, you're going to break my heart."

Momma stepped out of the kitchen and

smiled. "How can you not be invited? You're the guest of honor."

"Where's the chief?" I asked. "Will he be here soon? I'm starving."

"It's just the two of us tonight," she said.

I glanced at the table and saw that there were just two place settings, and I suddenly felt guilty about our earlier conversation. "I don't want to crowd him out," I said.

"Don't worry, I did it all on my own. I've missed spending time with you, so I thought a nice dinner would give us a chance to catch up."

"Let me wash up first, but is there anything I can do?"

She smiled at me. "It's all taken care of. Have a seat, and I'll bring the food out."

When I got back from the powder room, the turkey was in its place of honor, flanked by mashed potatoes, green beans, Brussels sprouts and cheese sauce, and jelled cranberry sauce. "Wow, what is this, a dry run for Thanksgiving?"

"Call it what you'd like. The turkey was on sale, so I thought this might be fun."

"I'm not complaining. Trust me."

As we sat down, Momma asked, "Would you like to say the prayer?"

I did as she asked, and mentioned George's brother as well. As we began to fill our plates, Momma asked, "What's wrong with George's brother?"

"He's dying," I said. "George left town this morning." I suddenly realized that he'd failed to call me upon his arrival. Then again, I hadn't asked him where he was going, so I had no idea when he might get there. "Momma," I said, "I know it's not usually done, but would you mind if I gave him a quick call before I eat? I'm worried about him."

"You have my blessing," she said. "Give him my love, as well, would you?"

"I will," I said. I stepped out on the porch, dialed his number, but there was no answer.

"That was quick," Momma said when I rejoined her.

"He didn't pick up. I'll try him later." I tried to put George and his problems, along with the case I was working on, out of my thoughts. Momma had prepared a feast, and I wasn't about to disrespect the time and effort she'd put into it, especially since she'd done it just for me. "Let's eat."

We had a wonderful meal, and I made the mistake of not pacing myself, so there was barely room for pie, but I managed to have a sliver somehow.

"That was nothing short of amazing," I said.

"I'm glad you enjoyed it." She looked at the bountiful supply of food still on the table and then added, "I'm afraid we'll be eating leftovers for a month."

"Not if Jake gets a chance to help," I said.

As Momma and I began to clear the table, she asked, "Have you spoken with him today?"

"He called at six this morning," I said with a smile.

"Judging from your expression, it went well."

"His cell phone was dead, and he didn't take his charger with him. Everything's good."

"I'm so glad," she said.

I had to give her credit for not saying that she told me it would be. Momma was happy for me, and that was all that mattered. As she began putting things in Tupperware, I started on the dishes. I was happy that she didn't try to stop me.

Once she was finished with the leftovers, she picked up a towel and began to dry. It was nice working side by side with her.

"If anything changes around here, I think I'll miss this most of all," I said.

"What, my cooking?"

"No, just doing everyday things with you. In case you didn't realize it, I'm a big fan of hanging out with you."

I looked down at her and saw a tear in the corner of her eye. "Having you here after your divorce has given me a new lease on life," she said. "If you hadn't been there pushing me all along the way, I would never have taken a chance on dating again. You've helped me remember something about myself that I'd nearly forgotten."

"I would have fallen apart when Max cheated on me if you hadn't been there to help me get through it, Momma. I don't think I've ever thanked you enough for that."

"It's so lovely that my daughter has turned out to be my best friend, as well," she said.

I felt a tear of my own begin to well up, and the last thing we needed was a shared crying jag. "Right back at you," I said with a smile. "Hey, is there any pie left?"

She laughed at me, and then said, "You can't be serious."

"I don't know, after we finish the dishes, another sliver of it might just hit the spot."

"I don't know where you put it," she said.

"The same place every other woman does," I replied, "mostly my hips."

"How is your investigation coming along?" she asked.

Momma rarely inquired about my extracurricular activities. "I'm treading water at the moment, at least that's what it feels like."

"These things take time," she said.

"Is the chief making any progress on his end?" I asked.

She shook her head. "I wouldn't know. When we're together, we find other things to discuss besides our work."

"Okay, forget I asked."

Momma added, "When Jake is finished lecturing, is there any chance he'll be able to lend you a hand? I know you can take care of yourself, but I feel better when he's around."

"That makes two of us," I said. "I'm a big fan of the man myself. He's got two more lectures, and then he'll be finished. I hope he'll be able to come to April Springs for a few days, but with his job, he never knows where he's going to be next."

"You're good at enjoying the time you've got, though."

"We do our best," I said. "I can't tell you how honored I am that you chose me over Chief Martin tonight."

Momma smiled softly. "It won't hurt him to miss seeing me for one night."

"Are you kidding? Missing this meal alone would kill him if he knew about it. I wouldn't tell him what we just ate, especially the pie."

"There's no need. I told him he could have a slice tomorrow, and you'd think I told him he'd just won the lottery."

"He did," I said. "So, do you have any plans for the rest of the night?"

"That all depends on you," she said.

"I'm wide open," I answered, and my telephone rang.

"It's George," I said as I checked the caller ID.

"By all means, take it."

I stepped back out onto the porch, both for privacy and the fact that we got better reception out there. My room had two bars, but the rest of the house was hit or miss.

"George, how was your drive?"

"Well, I made it in one piece," he said. He sounded really tired, but I knew better than to say it aloud.

"Where exactly are you?"

He laughed gently. "I didn't tell you? I'm in Alabama."

"That's quite a drive from here."

"Tell me about it," he said.

"Have you seen your brother yet?" I hated to ask the question, but I wanted George to know that he could talk to me about it.

"Just for a second. Sorry, I should have called you earlier, but I had a lot to deal with. I just didn't feel like chatting, you know?"

"We don't have to talk now," I said. "I'm just glad you made it there okay."

I started to hang up when he said, "Hold on. I've got something for you."

"How could you do any digging while you were on the road?" I asked.

"I told you, I called in some favors. I found out about the gun permits, if you're interested."

"Of course I am, but we can wait and talk about this tomorrow. I know you're dealing with a lot right now."

He paused, and then in a voice older than I'd ever heard from him, George said, "To be honest with you, I could use the distraction."

"Then by all means, fire away."

He laughed a little. "That's cute. Fire away with the gun permits."

I hadn't meant to be amusing, but I wasn't about to deny credit for it. "What did you find out?"

"Three folks on your list have permits," he said. "Care to guess which ones?"

"I'd rather you just tell me," I said.

"One belongs to Katie Wilkes, Allen Davis has one, too, and the third one is held by Gabby Williams."

CHAPTER 15

"Gabby? You're kidding me." I couldn't see her with a gun, and if she did have a weapon to match that permit, why hadn't she said something to me about it when we'd talked about my investigation?

"It's for a .44, which is not a little gun at all. Then again, Gabby is big enough to handle it without any problem."

I felt my heart sink a little as I started to ask the question I was afraid I already had the answer to; which caliber of gun had been used to kill Desmond Ray.

I never got the chance, though.

"I'm sorry, Suzanne," George said. "They're calling me back into his room."

I couldn't even pass on Momma's love, he hung up so quickly.

"Suzanne, what's wrong? Did he die?"

It took me a second to realize that Momma was speaking to me. "What did you just ask me?"

"George's brother. Is he gone?"

"No, but it's not looking good."

"I'm so sorry," Momma said.

I was, too, as much for George as I was sorry for Gabby. I had to find out if her gun, or one like it with the same caliber, had killed Desmond Ray, but who could I ask? No one, I realized. I was just going to have to wait for George, no matter how long it took.

"Do you feel like taking a walk in the park?" I asked Momma.

"It's a little chilly, isn't it?"

It was more than that, but I didn't care. For some reason I just had to get out of the house. "Come on, we can bundle up, and when we get back, we can have a fire."

I half expected her to say no, so I was delighted when she agreed. "Why not? It might do us both some good to get out and get a little fresh air."

As we stepped out onto the porch, twilight was nearing. The clocks would be changing in a few weeks to daylight savings time, and soon we wouldn't have light this time of the evening. Most folks enjoyed sleeping in, but I got up so early that it really didn't matter all that much to me. I didn't know anyone else who would be able to tell two-thirty from three-thirty in the morning, either.

I started to tell Momma about Gabby's gun permit, and a few other facts about the case I was working on, but before the words could leave my lips, I bit them back down. This wasn't a night for murder and mayhem. I wasn't at all sure how many more evenings Momma and I would have alone, and I didn't want to ruin one of the last ones by talking about what had happened to Desmond Ray.

We strolled around the big loop in the park, my gaze going for a moment to the Patriot's Tree, a mighty oak that had seen its share of death over its lifetime. Even with everything it had experienced over the many years it had stood there, the tree had remained; strong, silent, resolute.

I glanced back at the cottage and thought I saw something in the shadows.

"What's that?" I asked Momma as I pointed to our front porch.

"What?" she asked as she looked, too. "I don't see anything."

Whatever it had been — if it had been anything at all — was now gone. The trees around our place sometimes projected the oddest shadows, almost creating optical illusions in the waning moments of daylight.

"I'm sure that it was nothing," I said. "I

must be tired. My eyes are starting to play tricks on me."

"Are you getting enough sleep?" she asked, always and ever my mother.

"Probably not," I admitted.

"You should turn in early tonight and try to catch up," she said.

"I'll be fine," I answered. "Honestly, I'd rather stay up and hang out with you. Who knows how many more nights we'll have?" The last part just slipped out unbidden.

"Suzanne, I relish our time together, as well. Even if other things change, I promise you, that won't."

I put my arm in hers as we walked back to our cottage. "Momma, what did you teach me about making promises I couldn't keep?"

"What makes you think I won't keep that one?" she asked.

"I know you mean to, but life has a way of getting in the way, doesn't it?"

She stopped, and since our arms were locked, I stopped, as well. "Suzanne," she said. "Look at me. As long as I'm breathing, I'll always have time for you. Is that understood?"

"Yes, ma'am," I said with a smile. I knew that if she accepted the police chief's proposal a great deal would change, but not everything. Momma and I would stay close; I was sure of that. We'd both worked too hard to reconnect after the Max part of my life had ended.

When we got up on the porch, I looked around for some kind of sign or calling card that someone had been on our porch, but there was nothing but some early fallen leaves. Before long, the park would be filled with tones of orange, red, and yellow, and soon after that, we'd be walking on a carpet of brightly fallen leaves. This, too, was fleeting, and I made up my mind to enjoy every last moment of it, and I had a feeling that my mother felt the exact same way.

"Do you have any interest in a game?" I asked Momma when we walked back inside. I felt much better with the solid door locked between us and the rest of the world.

"Certainly," she said. That was when I noticed her book on the coffee table.

"I have a better idea," I said. "Let's light that fire we promised ourselves, and then read a little before bed. I've got a new book I've been dying to start, but I never seem to be able to stay awake long enough to make much progress."

"What's the title?" she asked. My mother was an avid reader, almost exclusively traditional mysteries. Some folks called them cozies, but she didn't care what sub-genre they were listed under. It was the puzzle of the crime and the people involved that mattered to her, in equal parts. There wasn't any gore, and not much blood, in her books, and that was just the way she liked it.

"It's new to me, but not the world," I said. "I've been browsing through some of Bill Bryson's books. Have you read them?"

"He's certainly funny, isn't he? Which book are you on?"

"*A Walk in the Woods*," I said. "Somebody at the donut shop left it behind one day, and when no one claimed it, I took it home. I've been lugging it back and forth every day, just in case the owner shows up, but I can't imagine anyone minding if I dip into it a little bit myself."

"Do you have any new mysteries coming up for your book club?" That was one activity my mother had endorsed when Jennifer, Hazel, and Elizabeth had come into my shop, and my life.

"We had to cancel this month's meeting because of an illness, but we're all set for next month."

"It sounds perfectly lovely."

I was sure it would be, especially for her. Why hadn't I thought of inviting Momma to our group before? My mother loved reading and discussing books, and I knew the three women in my group would welcome her gladly. My lack of an invitation may have been because I'd wanted to keep that little bit of my life for myself, but with the idea that Momma and I would no longer be living together looming larger and larger, it would be a way to keep her close.

"You could always come with me the next time," I said.

"No, as lovely as the invitation sounds, I really shouldn't."

"Why not?" I asked. "It sounds like something you'd really love."

She took my hands in hers. "Suzanne, I dearly appreciate the offer, but you need to keep these ladies for yourself. We share enough of our lives together. This should be yours, and yours alone."

"Okay, but if you change your mind, let me know." I looked at the fire, which had taken hold and was burning brightly, and said, "I'll be back in a second. I just want to get my book."

"I'll be here," Momma said.

As I got to my room, I picked up my "borrowed" copy, and was starting back toward the door when my telephone rang.

"Jake," I said. "It seems like forever since

we talked."

He laughed, and I could picture his smile as he said, "It was just this morning."

"I know, but it seems longer than that. How was today's lecture?"

"More of the same," he said. "I can't imagine how difficult it must be to come up with something new to say day in and day out."

"And did Ashley audit you again?"

He laughed. "No, I believe that particular joke has run its course."

"You have to admit, it must have been a little flattering to get that kind of attention."

He snorted. "I'll do no such thing. Enough about me, now. Tell me about your day."

I recounted what I'd learned, what I suspected, and what George had said. When I was finished, Jake whistled softly. "You don't waste any time."

"Funny, I don't feel as though I'm making any progress at all," I admitted.

"You're kidding, right? You found out more today than most police forces could have managed with all of their resources. There's something to be said for the direct approach from an indirect source. I may have to write a paper on it."

I couldn't see my boyfriend as an academic. "Really? Have you got the scholarly bug now that you've been guest lecturing?"

"Not a chance," he said. "I was just imitating some of my new acquaintances here. Apparently publishing papers is very important in this job."

"So, you're not tempted to take on a sideline as a guest lecturer?"

"Not a chance," he said. "When it comes down to it, I'd rather do than teach. What's your next move?"

"I'm not exactly sure," I replied. "I've been thinking about talking to Gabby about her gun, but I don't want to do it if I can help it."

He hesitated, and then asked, "You need the caliber of the bullet, don't you?"

"Yes," I admitted. "But I can't figure out a way to find out what it was."

"Don't go anywhere. I'll call you right back." He hung up before I could say anything else, and two minutes later, my phone rang again.

"That didn't take long," I said.

"What can I say? The chief likes me."

"I wish I could say the same thing."

Jake laughed, and then said, "To be honest, I think he's happy that I'm in Asheville and not there mucking things up with you." The humor went out of his voice as he added, "I hate to tell you this, but it was a

.44, just like the one Gabby owns. There's something else you need to know, too, and it's not good."

"How can it get any worse than that?"

"Gabby told the chief that she couldn't find her gun when he asked her about it. She thinks it might have been stolen, but not being able to produce it is putting her in some hot water. If you can think of anything to do that can help her, I'd do it, and fast."

"Thanks, Jake. You don't happen to have any ideas, do you?"

He whistled for a moment under his breath, something I'd just recently learned meant that he was thinking deep thoughts. "Well, I think you're on the right track. I don't believe for a second that Desmond's murder was random in any way. Go back over your list and try to find out who had the best reason to want to see him dead. At this point, you can't afford to ignore anyone, no matter how unlikely they may seem as a suspect."

"I haven't forgotten any of them, trust me."

"Maybe it will come to you in your sleep," he said.

I yawned as if on cue, and he laughed. "It sounds as though it's not that far off. Are you going to bed now?"

"No, Momma and I are reading downstairs in front of the fireplace."

"Have a good night, then."

" 'Night, Jake," I answered. "Thanks for calling."

As I walked downstairs, I thought about what he'd said. It all made sense, but maybe I hadn't taken it far enough. There were more suspects than I'd paid attention to lately, and not everyone in the world who owned a gun had the requisite permit. For some reason I kept thinking about Jenny Ray, and what she gained by Desmond's death. For the moment, she had control over her wealthy aunt's life, and now that her closest living relative was dead, Jenny was most likely next in line to inherit. That made me realize that I'd failed to visit Jean as I'd promised. That took priority, and no matter what else I did, I had to go by her place tomorrow as soon as I closed the donut shop for the day. I could dig around a little into Jenny's life as well by asking her a few questions while I was there. That settled that, so with a game plan in mind, I walked back downstairs with my book so Momma and I could share a little time together.

She was fast asleep on the couch, and I

didn't have the heart to wake her. Taking the fallen book from her lap, I marked her place, then set it aside. I grabbed a blanket, gently eased it over her, and then went back upstairs.

It appeared that our bonding time, at least for now, was over, and I needed sleep easily as much as she did.

Tomorrow was going to be a big day, I could feel it in my bones, and I needed to be at my best if I was going to have any luck catching a killer.

Even if it was Gabby Williams.

Early the next morning was uneventful enough, but then again, we weren't open yet, so most of what Emma and I did at the donut shop was pretty routine. It was nearing five-thirty, though, when all of that changed.

We were in back applying glazes, icing, and sprinkles to a variety of donuts when we heard someone pounding at the back door. It was too early for a delivery, and I wasn't willing to open it unless I knew for sure who was back there. It was too easy to get ambushed, and I wasn't having any of it.

"We're closed," I shouted through the thick door.

"I know you are," Gabby shouted back. "Let me in."

Before I could unbolt the door, Emma asked, "Should you really do that?"

"You don't trust Gabby?" I asked.

"Let's just say I'll be glad when they catch the killer, no matter who it turns out to be." Emma must have realized how that sounded, but she was clearly in no position to take it back.

"I feel the same way, but I can't just leave her out there."

"Why not?" Emma asked.

I shook my head and fought to hide my smile. Even with all I'd learned about Gabby recently, and some of it was pretty bad, I couldn't see her gunning me down in my own shop. I might be wrong, but I wasn't uncertain.

I opened the door, and as I did, I heard Emma's grunt of disapproval.

I couldn't change the way she felt, though.

"It took you long enough," Gabby said when I finally let her in.

"In case you hadn't noticed, we're busy making donuts here," I said, matching her tone. I'd learned long ago that was really all she respected, someone willing to fight her fire with fire.

"Sorry," she said as she took off her coat.

"I was going to wait until eleven, but I can't stand it." She looked at Emma, and then asked, "Suzanne, is there somewhere we can talk?"

"I can set up the front if you'd like," Emma volunteered.

I wasn't about to run her off, though. "No, you keep working on the donuts." I turned to Gabby and asked, "Does this really have to be in private? If it does, then we can go up front and talk while we set up." If she was going to snub Emma and demand a private audience with me, Gabby was going to have to convince me that it was important. Besides, a small part of me was glad that we'd be by the windows, where anyone passing by could see us. It wasn't that we got a lot of foot traffic at that time of morning, but if Gabby was feeling homicidal toward me, it might just be enough to stop her from acting on her impulse.

"Yes, I'm sorry, but it is."

"Then you can work with me while we talk."

Gabby followed me out of the kitchen and into the front with the displays and the dining area, and then asked, "What can I do?"

"We swept last night, so you can put the

328

stools back on the floor and wipe the tables down."

She began to do as I asked, but paused and said, "I don't know how sanitary it is to store barstools on tabletops."

"Everything is clean, and besides, we're wiping the tables down, too, aren't we?"

"I suppose so," she said.

"Did you come here to criticize my hygiene and work practices, or was there something else on your mind? I thought you said that it was important."

She stopped what she was doing and looked at me. "Suzanne, I haven't been entirely up front with you."

"Are you talking about your missing .44 revolver?" I asked.

Gabby looked surprised that I'd already heard the news. "How did you find out, and so quickly? Martin hasn't been feeding you information about me, has he?"

"No. Don't forget, I'm good at what I do, too." I said that with a clear conscience. Martin hadn't told me anything, Jake had. Just because he'd gotten the information from our chief of police didn't mean that I had a direct pipeline myself to our local law enforcement.

"It looks bad, doesn't it?" she asked.

"I suppose it could be worse," I admitted.

"Give me one example," Gabby said.

Without thinking, I supplied one. "Someone could have a photograph of you standing over the body with a smoking gun in your hand."

"I don't even want to think about that."

"The gun, the photograph, or the body?" I asked.

"Suzanne, I shouldn't have to tell you how dangerous it is running a business alone. That gun made me feel safe, and I don't regret getting it."

"Where did it go, then? It's not doing you much good at the moment."

It might have been a cheap shot, but I took it anyway. Misplacing a handgun was not like losing a set of car keys. She should have known better, and acted more responsibly with it. Who knows what it had been used for once it left her presence?

"I don't know what happened," she said, slumping down on a stool and burying her head in her hands. "I didn't even realize that it was missing until Chief Martin came to the store yesterday demanding to see it. It's a wonder that I'm not in jail."

"If we don't do something quickly, trust me, that status isn't going to last," I said.

"Do you still believe me?" Gabby asked as she looked at me, hope filling her gaze.

"I don't think you're a cold-blooded killer," I said. I decided not to add, "I could be wrong, though" to my declaration. It wouldn't be politic to accuse Gabby until I had rock-solid proof, or unless there was no other choice.

"Thank you, Suzanne," she said as she stood quickly, moved toward me, and wrapped me in her embrace.

I tenderly pulled away. "Gabby, this isn't getting us anywhere. I need to open the shop, but as soon as we're finished at eleven, I'll take up my investigation again. In the meantime, lay low, and do your best to stay out of trouble."

"That shouldn't be too difficult. I'm not even opening today," she said.

Before I could remind her that it might be better if she kept her presence obvious on Springs Drive, she quickly added, "I can't take the stares and the whispers. I'm going home and locking the door behind me."

Then again, if Gabby looked as guilty to everyone else as she did to me at the moment, contact with the outside world might be the worst thing she could do. "Maybe you're right. That could be a better choice."

Gabby nodded and said, "I thought so. I'm going back home, Suzanne." She started for the kitchen so she could go out the back, but I peeked outside, and no one was in sight.

"Why don't you go out this way?" I suggested.

"If it's all clear, why not?" She did as I asked, and soon disappeared into the darkness.

When I walked back into the kitchen, Emma asked, "You didn't leave her out front all alone, did you?"

"Relax, she's gone," I said. "You really should give Gabby a break."

"Maybe so, but if you heard some of the things my dad said about her, you'd be jumpy, too."

"What has he been saying?" I asked. It wouldn't surprise me if Emma's dad, as the town newspaper publisher, got information before any of the rest of us, and that included the chief of police.

Emma just shrugged. "I really couldn't say."

"Come on, you can tell me," I said.

"No, I'm sorry, but I can't. I'm still living there until I can afford to go away to college, so I can't make any waves."

"I understand completely," I said. Emma's relationship with her father was strained enough as it was, and I didn't want to add any more pressure to an already volatile situation. I glanced at the trays and saw that they were ready. "Can we put these out for sale?"

"You bet," Emma said. She glanced at the clock, and then added, "We're not due to open for another twelve minutes, though."

"Tell you what. Let's be real sports and go ahead and open early, just this once."

"That's fine with me," she said. "I'll get started on the dishes after we finish setting up."

After we had two coffeepots brewing and the display shelves stocked, we were ready for business.

The only problem was that we didn't have a single person waiting to get in. Apparently our customer base had already adapted to our new hours, and I wasn't sure if I was glad about it, or unhappy that they'd changed their habits so quickly.

At just past seven, Terri Milner dropped in. "Suzanne, I'm desperate, and I really need your help," she said.

"Sure, I'll do whatever I can," I said.

"It's my day to supply snacks for the twins' party at school. I made cupcakes last night, but when I got up this morning, the dog had eaten or licked every one of them. They're ruined."

"That's bad," I said. "How many treats do you need?"

"Two dozen," she said.

"I can handle that, no problem. We could do glazed or cake, so which would you prefer?"

Terri frowned. "That's the problem. The theme is Being Green, so everything we serve has to be colored green. What am I going to do?"

"Give us five minutes, and we'll have you covered," I said. "Green icing is easy enough to make, and we'll ice a variety of donuts for you to take."

"No," she said with a look of pure dread on her face. "They all have to be as nearly identical as you can make them. Otherwise, the children will fight over who gets which donut."

I didn't know if that was true or not, but the customer was always right, particularly when they were paying for the privilege. "Fine, twenty-four donuts, each one exactly like the next."

The relief on her face was clear. "You're a real lifesaver," she said.

"What can I say, I do my best. Can I get you some coffee while you wait, and maybe an éclair, as well?"

"Oh, yes," she said. "That would be delightful."

After I poured Terri a cup of coffee and served her the treat, I peeked in the kitchen and found Emma doing dishes, her iPod earbuds in. After grabbing a tray of two dozen unglazed cake donuts, I took them into the kitchen and set them down near the glazing and icing station, all without being observed by Emma.

It took me three tries to get her attention. I finally had to tap her on the shoulder, and she dropped a stainless steel bowl on the floor when I did.

"You scared the life out of me," she said as she pulled her buds out.

"Your music may be too loud. What do you think?"

"Sorry," she said as she pulled the earplugs out. "I just love this song. What's up?"

"I need enough green icing to cover those donuts, pronto," I said as I pointed to the tray.

She dried her hands. "Do I even want to know why?"

"Why not? It's for Terri Milner's twins."

She nodded. "I don't even want to know why they want them. I'll have them ready in a jiff."

I walked back out front to tell Terri we were working on her order when I found

James Settle, the blacksmith coveting our railroad rails.

"Did you come to make more trouble?" I asked.

"No, ma'am," he said with a smile as he held up his palms to me. "I just want coffee and a plain cake donut."

"Okay, that works for me." I did as he asked, and was surprised to see Terri approaching.

"I'm sorry, but they won't be ready for a few more minutes," I explained.

"That's not why I'm here." She turned to the blacksmith and said, "Are you still interested in those train tracks?"

"Of course I am," he said. He looked at me quickly, and then added, "I'm sorry, but it's true. I got the rights just yesterday."

"You're not taking our rails without a fight," I said.

"He doesn't have to," Terri said. "My husband has a client who has a few rails he'd like to get rid of. They were in the way of a building he was putting up, and he didn't want to sell them for scrap if he could find a good home for them."

"Does he know I'm going to cut them up?" the blacksmith asked. "I wouldn't want to take them under false pretenses."

"All he cares about is that some of their

history is preserved. If you're interested, here's his number."

"Do you happen to know how many he has?" Settle asked.

"I'm afraid there aren't many, maybe forty or so."

"That's more than I'd be able to harvest here." Settle frowned for a moment, and then added, "I can't pay a lot for them. Do you know how much he wants for the lot?"

Terri smiled. "My husband told me that I could work out a deal for them myself. You make bookends out of them, right?"

"Among other things," the blacksmith admitted.

"I'm sure a nice set of bookends for his office, and another set for my husband, would be repayment enough. Would you be willing to do that?"

"It would be my pleasure. Thank you so much," he said as he took the phone number from her.

"Don't thank me," Terri said. "I did it for Suzanne."

He turned to me and said, "Then thank you. Tell you what. I'll make you a set of bookends, too."

"You really don't have to. I'm just glad to help, if it will keep our tracks where they belong."

James Settle smiled, and then pulled a document from his pocket. "We can make sure of that right now."

"How can we do that?"

"This document gives the bearer the rights to those tracks for the next twenty-five years." He took a pen and signed his name, wrote something else, and then handed it to me. "Now it's your decision what happens to them, not mine."

"I'm going to frame this," I said, and I meant it when I saw that he'd transferred the rights to me.

Settle left whistling just as Emma brought two boxes to the front. She opened the box lid and showed them to Terri. "How do these look?"

They were the brightest shade of green I'd ever seen in our shop. I thought they looked absolutely hideous, which meant the kids would probably love them.

"They're perfect," Terri said. "You guys are wonderful."

As she reached for her purse, I said, "These are on the house."

"That's not right. You just saved me."

"Terri, you did me a much greater favor by brokering that deal for those railroad tracks. Trust me."

She frowned for a moment, and then nodded. "If you're sure."

"Positive," I said.

After she left, Emma asked, "What was that all about?"

"It was the barter system at work in all of its glory," I said with a grin.

I put the document safely under the cash register, and then went about the rest of my morning selling donuts. It might have been a small victory in the scheme of things, but it was one I would gladly take.

For the next twenty-five years, those tracks would stay right where they were, a reminder of things past.

ANCIENT CRULLERS

Okay, let me start with a disclaimer. This recipe was passed on to me by someone else, and honestly, I'm not a big fan, though I know folks who are. It's more like fried pie crust than cruller, in my opinion, but if you've got a bare minimum of supplies (say a snowstorm or flood has kept you in your house with no grocery store within reach) you might want to give these a try. I cut them into triangles, just for fun.

Ingredients
- 1 egg, beaten
- 1 tablespoon sugar, white granulated
- 1 tablespoon lard
- 1 tablespoon whole milk
- 3/4 cup all-purpose flour

Directions
This is not complicated, just a little harder than making donuts out of canned biscuits,

with the added disadvantage of not being nearly as good! Don't forget, you've been warned. Beat the egg in a bowl, add the sugar, lard, and milk. Once that's incorporated, add the flour. If you need more to make it workable, that's fine. Roll the dough out 1/2 to 1/4 inch thick. Fry in hot canola oil (360 to 370 degrees F) 1 to 2 minutes, turning halfway through. Once they're drained, a little icing makes them easier to eat.

Yield: 6–10 triangles

CHAPTER 16

As soon as we closed the donut shop for the day, I gave Grace a call.

"Hey, should I come over?" I asked. "I gave Emma a dozen donuts just now, but I've still got two dozen donuts left, and you're welcome to any you'd like." Grace had once turned down every donut I offered, including the healthiest ones I knew how to make, but over the past several months, she'd come to realize that even with her healthy lifestyle, indulging in a donut every now and then wouldn't hurt her. I thought it might be because of the murders we'd investigated together. There was nothing like seeing death up close to make you realize how important the little things were, including minor indulgences from time to time.

"Sorry," she said. "I should have called you earlier, but I've been crazy busy. I've been driving through Haley's territory all day, so I can't help out with the investigation until sometime after three."

"Is something wrong?"

Grace sighed. "No, everything's fine, but I've got a young woman who has applied to be a district trainer, so before I can pass her name on to my boss, I have to do spot checks in her territory, and then we're meeting for a lunch evaluation."

"So, she doesn't even know you're coming?"

"She doesn't have a clue. I had our secretary call her just now to meet me, and we'll go over what I found at lunch."

"That sounds cruel."

"Hey." Grace laughed. "She asked for the scrutiny. There are no worries, though. Haley's stores have all been as spotless as she is. I hate to put you off until then, though."

"Don't worry about me. I can handle things until you're free," I said.

"Just don't take any chances until we can get together, okay?"

"I make no promises," I said with a grin. "Call me when you're free."

"You've got it," she said.

I hung up, and after I dropped by the bank to deposit our day's receipts, it was time to go see Jean Ray, whether Jenny liked it or not. I wasn't happy about that situation, or the fact that I'd forgotten Jean completely yesterday.

It was time to make amends.

Jenny answered the door when I knocked, something I'd been afraid might happen. I had a dozen of my spare donuts with me, keeping the last dozen in my Jeep just in case, but I doubted they were going to get me past the door.

"I brought you these, as promised," I said as I tried to shove them into her hands.

No great surprise, Jenny wouldn't take them. "Who exactly did you promise?"

"Didn't your aunt tell you? Jean and I made plans to see each other today."

Jenny frowned at me. "I'm afraid that's not possible. She's resting," Jenny added as she tried to shut the door on me and my donuts.

I wouldn't budge, though. "Jean, are you there?" I shouted past her. "It's Suzanne. I came for our donut party."

"Quiet," Jenny snapped. "You'll wake her."

"I wasn't asleep," Jean said from behind her. "Now, be gracious and let my friend in, or you won't be here long yourself."

The steel in Jean's voice was remarkable. This was a different woman than the one I'd spoken to last. What had happened in the interim?

Jenny gave me a quick glare, and then stepped aside. "Of course. Won't you come in, Suzanne?"

I smiled brightly at her. "I'd be delighted. Thanks for asking."

"Shall we have those in the living room?" Jean asked.

"That sounds good to me," I agreed as I followed her in.

Jenny trailed us, but Jean turned to her and said, "We'd like some coffee, and after you've made it, you're welcome to join us."

Jenny didn't say a word; she just nodded and walked into the kitchen.

I put the donuts down, took Jean's hands in mine, and then asked softly, "What happened? You're a new woman."

She replied in hushed tones, as well. "I realized that I was tired of being taken care of, so I decided it was high time I took responsibility for myself. Jenny tried to push me one too many times, and I had my fill of it, so I pushed back." The pride shone on her face, and it must have been in mine, as well. "She hasn't completely learned who the boss is yet, but she's starting to catch on."

"I'm surprised you even let her stay," I said.

"The poor girl has nowhere else to go," Jean confided, still speaking in a low voice. "She broke down and confessed it all to me this morning. What could I do? Like it or not, we're all the family each of us has now that Desmond's gone."

I had one question I had to ask her, though I hated doing it. "I know it's going to sound horrible, but could she have killed Desmond to get to your money?"

I thought there was a good chance I was about to be thrown out, but Jean shook her head and admitted, "I considered the possibility myself, and if Desmond had been done in with anything but a gun, I might have given it more credence, but the way he was killed let me know right away that Jenny was innocent."

"How do you figure that?" I asked.

"Didn't you know? Her parents were gunned down in a mugging that went horribly wrong. She detests guns, and so do I. I can't imagine ever owning one. I inherited a collection from my father, but the day Jenny's folks died, I got rid of every last one of them. Besides, Jenny's not a killer. A bully, perhaps, though I'll break her of that, but not a murderer."

"What did you do with the guns?"

"I gave them all to the police," she said.

346

"They were happy enough to take them, but not as glad as I was to be rid of them."

That answered questions about two of the suspects on my list. Jean had no reason to lie to me, since she didn't know she was on my suspect list, and it would be easy enough to check with Chief Martin to see if she'd donated the guns as she'd said. Although I wouldn't strike off either one of their names yet, at least until I could confirm her story.

Jean, Jenny, and I had our coffee, and against my better judgment, I ate a cruller, as well. I'd packed one without thinking, and the last thing I wanted to do was remind Jean of the incident with Desmond in front of Gabby's shop. I was enjoying our chat when my cell phone rang.

"Excuse me, but I've got to take this," I said.

"Of course, be my guest," Jean said.

I stepped away from them and said, "Hello?"

"Suzanne, you've got to come quick."

It was Gabby, and from the sound of her voice, something big had happened.

"What's going on? Where are you?"

"I'm at my house," she said. "The police just found my gun!"

"I'll be right there," I said.

I made my excuses, gave Jean one last hug,

347

and then headed to Gabby's house to see what exactly she'd gotten herself into this time.

Two squad cars were pulled up in front of Gabby's place, and Officer Stephen Grant was standing outside on the porch with her.

I got out of the Jeep and approached them. "What's going on?"

Officer Grant said, "Hey, Suzanne. Everything's fine. There's no need to panic."

"That's what you think," Gabby said. "If this isn't a good time to lose my mind, I hope I never see one better."

I touched her hand lightly to comfort her, and then looked at Officer Grant. "Is it true that you found her weapon?"

"It was behind her nightstand in her bedroom," he said. "We just found it. The chief's checking it out right now."

"I need to speak with him," I said.

Officer Grant stepped in front of me, blocking me from Gabby's front door. "He knew you'd come running, so I have specific orders to keep you out here until he's finished. Sorry," he added softly.

"It's not your fault," I said. I pulled Gabby to one side of the porch and asked, "What are they going to find?"

"How would I know? I have no idea how

it got back there."

"Could it have fallen off your nightstand and you didn't realize it?"

She thought about that, and then nodded. "I suppose so. I don't remember the last place I saw it, so how could I say for sure one way or another?"

"Gabby, has anyone been in your house lately besides you, especially right before Desmond was murdered, or since then? Someone could have taken it to kill Desmond, and then brought it back here to frame you for murder. Think hard, it's important."

She seemed to consider it, and then shook her head. "No one's been here."

"Are you positive?"

"I am. There are no spare keys, and no signs of a break-in."

That was bad. If her gun had been used to kill Desmond, it might just be enough to convince a jury that Gabby was a killer.

Chief Martin came out two minutes later, and he immediately spotted me standing there with Gabby on the porch. "Why am I not surprised to find you here?"

"Gabby and I are friends," I said. "She called me, and I came. What did you find out about the gun?"

"That's confidential," the chief said.

"Come on, who am I going to tell? Be a sport. Can't you see what this is doing to her?" I pointed to Gabby, who looked as wild-eyed as I'd ever seen her.

"Fine, but neither one of you is to breathe a word of this. That gun hasn't been fired in years. There's dust in the barrel, and no signs that it's ever been cleaned, let alone shot. I'll send it to the ballistic lab the state police run, but I'm willing to bet good money that it wasn't used in the murder."

Gabby nearly collapsed against me until I could guide her to a nearby chair. "Are you all right?" I asked.

"I knew I didn't do it, but the thought that someone else might have used my gun to kill Desmond was just about more than I could take."

I turned to the police chief. "Would it be okay if she went back inside?"

"That's fine," he said. "We're finished here."

A thought occurred to me. "You did have a warrant for this search, right?"

"We didn't need one," he said with a smile. "Gabby invited us in herself."

I waited until she settled down some before I left her alone. Gabby was finally breathing normally again, and her color was returning to normal. "If you don't need me, there are some things I need to do, and the sooner the better."

"Go on. You've been a true friend," Gabby said as she squeezed my hand.

This bonding we were doing was either going to change our relationship forever, or would soon be forgotten by both of us. I wasn't sure which, and if I was being honest about it, I didn't even know which outcome I'd prefer. How odd it would be to have Gabby on my side all the time, instead of never knowing where we stood.

As I left her place, I started thinking about the long list of suspects I'd had. They'd dwindled down considerably, so that now there were just three names left: Katie, Allen, and Chet. All three lived in Talbot's Landing, and all three worked at Duncan Construction. I looked at my watch and saw that I had another hour before Grace would be free, so I texted her that I was going to Talbot's Landing, and started off alone to see if I could catch a killer on my own.

There was just one place where I could find my final three suspects, and I had to go there alone. I considered telling Chief Martin about my theories, but that was all they were, without real proof to back them up. George was out of town, and I couldn't wait for Grace to be free.

But I knew it could be reckless going to Duncan Construction alone. I dialed Jake's number as I drove, and it went straight to voice mail. I left a message laying out my suspicions and what I was up to, just so there'd be some kind of record in case something happened to me. I knew that I probably should have waited for Grace, but I also knew from experience how her lunches could stretch out into dinners, and I had a feeling that if I didn't move on this, and quickly, something else bad might happen. I had no reason for the premonition, but I'd learned not to ignore them over the years. Besides, I was going to Talbot's Landing in full sunlight in the middle of the day, surrounded by loads of other people.

What could happen?

I had a dozen donuts left, and I wasn't afraid to use them. I approached the front desk of Duncan Construction and asked for Allen Davis. While I was waiting, Harry Duncan came out of his office. He looked surprised to see me.

"Did you finally bring us some donuts?" he asked.

"Special delivery," I said with a smile.

Harry rubbed his hands together, took

them from me, and then chose a chocolate glazed cake donut. "I love these things." He took a bite, and then retrieved another before he said, "Sally, take the rest of these to the break room, would you?"

"What about the phones?" she asked.

"I'm not too proud to answer a telephone myself. Go ahead and take one for yourself."

"I just might," she said. I loved guessing what kind of donuts folks might like before they chose one, and I had a hunch Sally was a straight-up glazed kind of gal. I was disappointed when she pulled out an éclair, glazed with chocolate and littered with sprinkles. Well, it wasn't an exact science, after all.

As soon as she was gone, Allen came out of his office and looked around. "Where's Sally?" Then he spotted me. "What are you doing here?"

Harry said, "Davis, that's no way to speak to a woman who just brought us treats."

He lowered his head a little and said, "Sorry."

"That's better," Harry said. "Now, whatever she wants to know, you tell her. Do you hear me?"

"I do," he said.

Sally came back, and Harry retreated to his office, taking his donuts with him.

"Let's talk outside," Allen said, glancing over at Sally.

That was fine with me. I didn't want her eavesdropping, either.

Once we were out of the building, Allen said, "Sorry about that, but if she hears a word of what we're discussing, it will be all over the building before I clock out this evening." He frowned at me as he added, "I don't know why you're here. I already told you, I don't really have an alibi for the night Desmond was killed."

"You have a gun, though, don't you?" I asked.

"No I don't," he replied.

"Don't lie to me, Allen. I found out about your permit."

He shook his head. "You should have kept digging. I sold my gun to Harry two months ago. He must not have registered it yet. If you don't believe me, go ask him."

"You could have another gun somewhere," I said.

"I could, but I don't."

"Then if you don't have an alibi for ten the night of the murder, you're still a suspect."

"Hang on, I didn't know there was a specific time of death given," he said. "Nobody told me it happened at ten."

I looked at him skeptically. "Are you telling me you have an alibi after all?"

"Come with me," he said with a grim smile.

I followed him inside, and to my surprise, we walked into Harry Duncan's office. Before he could protest, Allen said, "I need you to tell this woman two things."

Harry looked oddly at me. "You seem to have an affinity for my company lately."

I took the opportunity to ask what I needed to know. "I'm really sorry about this, but could you tell me if you ever bought anything from Allen?"

Harry nodded. "I got a gun from him a few months ago for protection."

"Do you know where it is right now?"

The boss went to his office safe, and after opening it, he showed it to me. "I keep it here for protection."

Jake had told me about sniffing the barrel of a gun to see if it had been fired recently, but there was no need. This one was coated in grease, much of it crusted over after drying out. "It's a mess, isn't it?" Harry said. "I really should clean it up."

"Who else has access to that safe?"

"Nobody knows the combination but me," he said. "Not even Sally. And that's more than two questions."

"Just one more," Alex said, looking far too smug for my taste. "Do you know the day and time you called me about the missing keys to the gate at the warehouse?"

"I'm not likely to forget it. It was the night that fellow was murdered in April Springs."

Harry was convincing, there was no doubt about it. "And the time?"

"Ten o'clock on the nose. He made me miss the news, but I had to get in there, and if it meant dragging his fanny down here with me, that's what I was going to do."

I had one more chance. "When did he show up?"

"Seven minutes later," Harry said. "I know, because I timed him."

I'd just lost another suspect.

That left two, and they both worked at the same company.

"Is that it?" Harry asked.

"It is with Allen, but I'd like to talk to you a little more myself."

He turned to Allen and dismissed him. It was clear the man wanted to stay, but one look at Harry's frown kept him from asking.

After he was gone, Harry said, "Your donuts bought you some time, but I believe it's all used up. If you'll excuse me, I've got work to do."

"Even if it means you can help me find a killer? It's one of your people, I'm sure of it."

"I just confirmed Allen's story, and even alibied him. What else do you want from me?"

"An audience with Katie Wilkes, and a man named Chet."

CHAPTER 17

"Do you mind telling me why?"

"I'd rather not," I said.

"Why not?"

"The one who's innocent is going to be tainted in your mind forever if I say much more, and it's just not fair. I have to ask a few more questions before I'm sure."

"I don't think I can let you do that," Harry said as he stood.

"But it will help you, too," I protested.

"Only if I believe that one of them is guilty, which I don't. Ma'am, I don't mean to be rude, but you've worn out your welcome here, and I'll ask you kindly to leave."

"Fine," I said as he loomed over me. I couldn't really blame him. He had no idea what my credentials were. As far as Harry knew, I was just a nosy woman who made donuts and asked lots of questions.

That didn't mean that I was going to give

up, though.

I walked toward my Jeep, but then dashed around the side of the building the moment I got there. My last two suspects had to be somewhere nearby if they were working today, and if I couldn't get to them from the front door, I'd just have to use the back.

The back door was unlocked, so I let myself in. I'd had to pass the gated storage area, but there was no need for a key at the moment. The gates were wide open. Off to the right on the next property was a large field of dried corn stalks waving in the breeze, and it appeared that someone had created a maze of paths in it. Red, yellow, and blue tape fluttered in the wind, and I wondered who had gone to so much trouble.

Sometimes it was just as good to be lucky as it was thorough. Katie's desk was the first one on the right as I walked in.

Unfortunately, she wasn't sitting at it.

I approached the woman in the office just beside her and said, "Sorry to bother you, but do you happen to know where Katie is? We were supposed to have a late lunch."

"She's probably out in the shed," the woman said. "Knowing Katie, she's lost all track of time. There's an office back there, and she's been working on dispatch orders all day."

"Thanks," I said, just as I heard Harry Duncan coming down the hall.

"May I use your phone for a second?" I asked as I ducked back inside. "My cell's not on me." I patted my pockets and realized that it might be true. My phone was missing, and I had an idea where it had gone. When I used it in my Jeep, sometimes I left it on the dash without realizing it. I wasn't all that crazy about people using their phones when they were driving, so I tried to limit it myself, but there were times when I just had to make a call.

"Sure," she said. I picked it up, got a dial tone, and called the donut shop, all the while hearing Harry come closer and closer.

He was nearly to the office where I was hiding when someone called him from behind. That was my chance. I hung up the phone, told the woman the line was busy, and then peeked around the corner. For the moment, Harry was occupied, so I hurried out the door before he had a chance to catch me. If he had, he'd probably throw me off the property himself.

I hurried out into the fenced yard, hoping that Harry would be busy for quite a while. Looking around, I found the shed's office easily enough, and there was Katie, working alone.

"What are you doing here?" she asked heatedly.

"I came about your gun permit," I said. "If you don't mind, I'd like to see your weapon."

"Not that it's any of your business, but the police already tested it," she said. "It's a .38, so it's not a match to the murder weapon."

"That doesn't mean you don't have others."

She looked aggravated by my questioning. "Why would I kill him?"

"Are you kidding me? He threw you away like yesterday's trash." The words were intentionally inflammatory. I needed to break through her defenses and get to the truth. Katie began to cry, though, and I instantly felt bad about the way I'd treated her.

And then I saw her hand go into her pocket, and I wondered if she still had the gun after all.

Something even more surprising happened instead.

A diamond brooch fell out of her pocket and landed on the floor.

I'd never seen it before, but I still recognized it, since it was exactly as it had been described to me.

Katie had the missing brooch, and I had to wonder if she'd taken it from Desmond's body the night she'd gunned him down.

"Where did you get that?" I asked as she swept it up in her hand and jammed it back into her pocket.

"Don't get so excited, it's not real," she said.

"I'm not stupid. I can tell from here that it's worth more than my Jeep and your car put together."

Katie didn't believe that. "You're crazy. He could never afford something that nice, and if he could, I can't imagine that he'd give it to me."

"You're wrong," another voice said from behind me, and I knew that I was trapped. At that moment, just ten seconds too late, it all came together, and I knew who the real killer was.

With Chet in the doorway, there was no way I was getting out of there unless I could figure out a way to get past him.

And then I turned and saw the gun in his hand, and my odds got that much worse.

Katie reacted before I could. She stood and faced him. "Chet, what do you think you are doing?"

He glanced over at her, but the gun stayed trained on me. "Don't worry, she's not going to bother you anymore."

"What? I don't understand."

"He killed Desmond," I explained.

"No, that's impossible," Katie said, her voice breaking a little. Had she suspected it herself all along?

"I did it for you," Chet said, and I saw that he was silently weeping. "I wanted you to love me, but you couldn't, not with Desmond jerking you around all the time. You'd never give me a chance as long as he was around."

I couldn't help myself as I said, "You stole from him to make it look like a robbery, but what were you thinking, giving Katie the brooch you took?"

"He was going to give it to her," Chet said. "I couldn't let him do that."

"He was going to do nothing of the sort," I said, searching for some way to distract Chet long enough to get away. "He stole it from his aunt, and I'm sure he planned to sell it for whatever he could get out of it."

"Chet?" A voice I recognized as Harry Duncan's came from outside the shed.

He pointed the gun at me, and I noticed that Katie was in the line of fire, as well, though I doubted that she was his target. "Not a word, not even a sound."

"In here," he called out. What was he planning to do? Shoot all three of us? Well, at least Katie was probably safe. I wanted to cry out and warn Harry, but if I did that, I knew that I'd be the first one to die.

"Get out here," Harry said impatiently.

Chet frowned, and then wiped away his tears. He said softly, "I'm locking the door, but I'll be back."

After Chet stepped out, I heard a lock slide into place.

I moved to Katie. "Give me your cell phone."

"It's in my purse in the office, and this place isn't wired," she said with a whimper. "Where's your phone?"

"It's in my Jeep." I looked around, but couldn't see any other way out. I tried to find some kind of weapon, but there was no way I'd be able to catch Chet off guard, and no place to hide.

"Is there another door, by any chance?"

Katie shook her head, but then stopped. "It's not a door, but there is a window in back. We can't get out, though. It's too high off the ground."

"I don't know about you, but I'm willing to risk it," I said.

I hurried in back, found the window, threw it open, and looked out. It was at the back of the property, a good fifteen-foot drop.

Katie joined me and said, "See? I told you."

"A broken leg is a lot better than waiting around to get shot," I said. If I took too much time to think about it, I knew that I'd never do it. Climbing out, I did my best to hold on to the ledge. I planned to drop down, cutting the true distance of my fall.

My left shoe got hung up on the window-sill, though, and I went tumbling out.

As I hit, I did my best to roll with the impact, but my left ankle was sprained, or worse, as Katie had predicted, broken. I tried to stand, found I could do it without too much pain, and realized that it wasn't as bad as I first thought. I looked up at the window and saw Katie's face framed there.

"Come on," I urged her.

She called down to me, "He won't hurt me. He loves me. You heard him."

"Are you really willing to take that chance?"

She just nodded. As much as I hated leaving her there, I had no choice.

I hurriedly limped to the side of the building and peeked around. Chet and Harry were in deep conversation about something, and I almost shouted at them.

Then I realized that if I did that, I'd be signing Harry's death warrant. I'd seen his gun in the safe, so I knew that he wasn't armed. Even if Harry had the weapon he'd bought from Allen on him, it wouldn't do him any good, since the barrel was jammed full of grease.

No, I had to get away so I could call the police.

That left the cornfield, and the maze of dried, brown stalks.

I wasn't going to respect the pieces of tape blocking pathways, though. Not caring about the damage I was doing, I forced my way through the cornstalks, fighting for a chance to save my own life.

No matter what happened, it was better than sitting in that room waiting to die.

My progress was slow, and I made the mistake of checking my ankle once. It was swelling up, and fast. If I didn't get out of there soon, I might not ever make it out at all.

I was buried deep in the stalks when I heard a chilling sound not far behind me.

Chet had found me!

"Suzanne, don't make this any harder

than it has to be. I can hear you."

I tried to be quiet, but there was no way I could manage it unless I followed the maze's paths. I could see glimpses and flashes of Chet as I hurried down the nearest pathway, and I did my best to move away from him. He didn't have to be quiet, though.

"I see you," he said as I came into a clearing, and he shot at me through the corn.

His aim was bad. That was the only thing that saved me. I looked at my red jacket and realized that I'd be an easy target with it on.

But it gave me an idea.

I moved deeper into the maze, taking my jacket off as I hurried, but not abandoning it. There had to be something there, something I could use to fight back.

But all I could see was corn. At least in my jeans and T-shirt, both faded, I'd be harder to spot.

I turned another corner, thinking I might be able to escape, when I saw that it was a dead end.

It wasn't empty, though. There was a mailbox on a wooden stake, and another iron stake made of rebar holding a map of the maze I'd come through so far. I opened the mailbox, but instead of a weapon, I found a great many small squares of paper with the same partial grid laid out on them, along with some of those short pencils that golfers used.

It wasn't much, but it was the best I could do.

I took my jacket, hung it over the mailbox, and then onto a nearby cornstalk beside it, trying to make it look as much like my rough outline as I could. It was tough, but I finally managed to pull the metal rebar with the map on it out of the ground. I discarded the map, and knew that the only way I'd be able to use it as a weapon would be as a spear. That meant that I had to get close enough to Chet to touch him.

It wasn't exactly ideal, but I really had no choice.

I backtracked until I found a small blind alley nearby where I could hide, and then I took a real chance. It was time for all or nothing.

"My ankle's broken," I whimpered. "I can't go on."

"I'm coming," Chet said. I was counting on him spotting my jacket and not going by the sound of my voice. I could almost touch my jacket from where I hid, though I'd taken three turns to get to my hiding place.

If the maze had been made out of bales of hay or something else that was solid, I wouldn't have stood a chance, but if I got lucky, I might just get out of this alive.

I heard footsteps crashing close to me, and I realized that Chet had taken the wrong turn. Instead of going toward my coat, he was heading straight for my hiding place. I braced myself for his attack, expecting him to come around the last corner any second.

Then I heard him say, "Must have taken a wrong turn. I'll be there soon."

He stopped, turned around, and from where I lay on the ground, I could see him on the right path now, heading for my decoy.

I got into a crouch, ready to strike.

As he turned the last corner, Chet was as close to me as he'd ever be. I waited until his back was turned, and then drove the stake toward his back.

Something must have happened to tip him off, though. He turned at the last instant, and my weapon hit his side instead.

At least it was on his right, and with the impact, the gun went flying into the corn.

"I'll break you in half for that," Chet roared as he came at me, the stake still sticking in his side.

If he caught me now, I knew that I'd be dead. Chet didn't need a gun to finish me off. I was sure he could do it with his bare hands.

There was no running away now. My ankle was nearly shot. With every last ounce of energy I had, I launched myself at him, doing my best to drive the stake the rest of the way through him. I hit him solidly, and we both fell backward. I'd done my best, but I knew that it was over. I kept waiting for Chet to roll over and crush me, but he didn't move.

Pulling myself up, I looked closer at him, and saw that blood was streaming from his head. The mailbox was rocked off its perch, and I could see a clump of his hair on the edge of it.

At that moment, I didn't care if he was dead, or just unconscious. I had to get out of there, and I had to do it now.

I had no idea how I managed to walk out of the cornfield, limping all the way. Thankfully, the farmer who owned the field was plowing another nearby plot. It took me a minute to convince him that there was a dangerous killer on the loose, but when I finally did, he called the police as we hurried back to his house on the tractor so he could get his gun.

It turned out that he didn't need it, though.

Chet was still unconscious when the police came nine minutes later. He wasn't dead, just knocked out, and the second I heard the news, I let myself collapse, realizing just how close I'd come to being his next victim.

Malasadas (Sort Of)

I read about these treats online and couldn't wait to try them myself, so since I don't think I'll be going to Hawaii, where they're normally found, anytime soon I thought I'd try to make them myself. After studying four or five recipes, I've found a way to make them my own!

Ingredients

Mixed
- 1/4 cup warm water
- 1/2 package dry yeast (1/8 ounce) I shake the packet horizontally, then cut it in half, but you'd probably be fine using the whole pack
- 1 teaspoon sugar, white granulated

- 3 eggs, beaten
- 1/2 cup sugar, white granulated
- 1/4 cup butter, melted

- 1/2 cup evaporated milk
- 1/4 cup water

Sifted
- 4–5 cups all-purpose flour
- 1/2 teaspoon salt

Directions

Dissolve the yeast and sugar in the warm water and set aside. Beat the eggs, then add the sugar, melted butter, evaporated milk, and water, mixing until thoroughly blended. In another bowl, sift the flour and salt together. After five minutes, add the yeast to the wet mix, stirring lightly, and then slowly add the dry ingredients, incorporating along the way. Mix thoroughly, and then cover the dough and let it rise in a warm place until doubled, about an hour. This dough will not be firm or workable by hand, but don't worry, you won't be rolling it out. When it's doubled, drop balls made from a small ice cream scoop or a teaspoon into hot oil. Fry in hot Canola oil (360 to 370 degrees F) 2–3 minutes, turning halfway through. Drain on paper towels, and then dust with confectioner's sugar or ice and decorate.

Yield: Makes about a dozen balls

CHAPTER 18

Before I'd let them take me to the hospital, I had to know what had happened to Harry and Katie.

I was greatly relieved to learn that they were both alive, and as she'd predicted, Chet had let her live, a privilege he wouldn't have extended to me if I'd hung around.

Jake was at the hospital when they finished wrapping my ankle. I was in a room waiting to be discharged when he came barreling in.

As he wrapped me up in his arms, I said, "Take it easy. It's okay, it's just a sprain."

"It could have been much worse," he said, "and we both know it."

"I'll be on crutches for a while," I said as I pointed to my ankle. "It looks like Emma and her mother are going to have to keep the donut shop open until I'm back on my feet again."

"None of that matters right now," he said.

"What counts is that you're all right." Jake hugged me again, and then said, "Suzanne, you are a trouble magnet."

"Hey, it attracted you to me, so it can't be all bad," I said. I touched his hand, and then said, "Chet's dead, isn't he? I killed him." There was a deadness inside me from what I'd been forced to do that I doubted would ever go away, but I'd done what I'd had to in order to survive.

Jake smiled at me. "Well, he's got one whale of a headache, and twelve stitches in his head, but the doctors say he'll be fine."

"Did you find the money? Katie has the brooch, but I never got a chance to ask him about the cash he stole from Desmond."

"It was in his locker at the construction company, at least most of it, anyway."

The money made me think of my new friend. I hoped that learning about Desmond's killer wouldn't drive her back to her old state of uncertainty and timidity. "Did you call Jean? She has a right to hear it from one of us."

"It's been taken care of." He looked deeply into my eyes and added, "How are you doing, really? Don't lie to me, Suzanne."

"Jake, I'm so sorry."

"You don't have anything to apologize

for," he said, wiping the unexpected tears from my cheeks with his gentle hands.

"I shouldn't have gone there alone today," I said.

"You thought you would be safe. The truth is, I never should have stayed in Asheville," he said. "The second I found out you were working on this case, I should have come back to April Springs to help you."

"Most of the time I had plenty of rein-forcements," I said. "Nobody could possibly know that they'd both be tied up today."

"About that," Jake said. "George tried to call you, and when he couldn't reach you, he contacted me. That's how I got here so quickly. I had almost arrived in April Springs when the Talbot's Landing police called me."

"His brother died, didn't he?"

Jake nodded. "George said it was just as well, he was pretty bad off in the end."

"I need to call him," I said.

"It can wait until you get out of here," Jake said.

I didn't say a word; I just held my hand out for his phone. He frowned, and then handed it to me. "It's on speed dial."

"I know his number by heart," I said.

George picked up, and the first thing I

said was, "I'm so sorry."

"Thanks, Suzanne, but I'm the one who should be apologizing. I should have been there by your side."

"I already got that from Jake, and I'll tell you the same thing that I told him. I handled it. You were where you needed to be. Can we do anything?"

"No, everything's been arranged. I'll be home in a few days, and you can tell me all about it over a cup of coffee and a donut."

"It's a deal. Would you like us to come to the service? We can be there by morning. Just say the word."

"I appreciate it more than I can say, but I need to do this alone so I can say good-bye once and for all."

"I understand. Call us if you need us."

After we hung up, Jake was staring oddly at me.

"What's wrong?"

He shook his head. "I don't believe it. You were nearly killed today, and all you can think about is your friend."

"He's in pain," I said. "He needs friends right now."

Jake brushed a bit of hair out of my eyes. "Suzanne, I know that this has been a long time coming, but there's something I need to say to you."

He was about to continue when Momma burst into the room and practically launched herself at me. "Suzanne, I was so worried about you."

"I may not be able to handle the stairs at home for a while. Do you mind if I bunk on the couch downstairs while I'm healing?"

"There's no need," she said. "You can have the master bedroom."

So, it had come to that. She'd accepted the chief of police's proposal after all. I knew there was a chance that she would, but I never thought she'd move out of our place so quickly.

"I guess congratulations are in order, then," I said.

"For what?" she asked, looking clearly puzzled.

"Well, if I get your bedroom, I'm assuming it's because you said yes to the chief."

Momma shook her head. "No, I decided this wasn't a good time for us."

I tried to get up, but Jake touched my shoulder lightly, and I settled back down. "If you're doing this because of what happened to me today, I'm going to be extremely upset."

"It has nothing to do with you," Momma said.

"Prove it," I replied. "What happened?"

"I told him no before I heard about your accident today."

I wasn't exactly sure I'd call what had happened to me an accident, but I was going to let it slide. "Was he crushed?"

"On the contrary, I believe he was a little relieved."

"How is that possible? I have my share of problems with the man, but he loves you, there's no doubt in my mind about that."

"I know that, but until I'm ready to return it in kind, the only humane thing for me to do was refuse his proposal."

I tried to take all of that in. "So, does that mean that you two aren't going to date anymore?"

Momma laughed. "Who said that? As a matter of fact, we have another date tomorrow night."

"What's wrong with tonight?" I asked with a grin.

"That's reserved for us," she said, and then turned to Jake. "You're welcome to join us, as well."

"I appreciate the offer, but I owe Asheville one more lecture, and I should probably finish what I started."

"Another time, then," Momma said. "I'll go see what's holding up your discharge."

After she was gone, I turned back to Jake.

379

"You were about to tell me something, and from the look on your face, I had a feeling that it was important."

Jake looked at me and smiled. "All I was going to say was that I love you."

"Pardon me? I didn't quite catch that," I said as my heart danced in my chest.

He took my head in his hands, kissed me gently, and then repeated, "I love you."

As far as I was concerned, I could have died right there. I'd heard the words I'd begun to doubt I would ever hear from him, and suddenly, all of my problems, even my ankle, didn't matter anymore.

He loved me.

That was what really counted.

He loved me.

Bacon Donut Burger

This treat should come with a warning from the surgeon general, it's so full of fat and calories. When they started serving them at the North Carolina State Fair recently, I was tempted to try one, but my doctor tackled me just in time! Don't blame me if you try this one at home!

Ingredients
- 1 Krispy Kreme donut (I'm in the South, it's almost a food group down here)
- 1 1/2 pound hamburger patty, cooked on the grill
- 2 slices cheddar cheese
- 2 slices bacon

Directions
Fry your bacon first, then grill the burger, putting the cheese on top at the last minute. Remove from heat and add the bacon to the top, then pat the skillet you fried the

bacon in, leaving about a tablespoon of grease. Cut the donut in half on the horizontal, and fry in the grease until browned and a little toasted. Take the hamburger stack and place it between the donut buns, and if you still have the nerve, take a bite!

Yield: 1 burger

The employees of Thorndike Press hope you have enjoyed this Large Print book. All our Thorndike, Wheeler, and Kennebec Large Print titles are designed for easy reading, and all our books are made to last. Other Thorndike Press Large Print books are available at your library, through selected bookstores, or directly from us.

For information about titles, please call:
  (800) 223-1244

or visit our Web site at:
  http://gale.cengage.com/thorndike

To share your comments, please write:
  Publisher
  Thorndike Press
  10 Water St., Suite 310
  Waterville, ME 04901